Dead Spread

Bethany Browning

Also by Bethany Browning

WAR OF THE WILLS

Watch Now on Amazon!

On the brink of financial ruin, Will Hadeon III gets a lifeline in the form of an inheritance from the grandfather he never knew. The only problem? He must outlast his scheming, vindictive father in a war of wills to claim what's rightfully his.

SASQUATCH, BABY!

After being cruelly banished from her posh Napa Valley friend group, Tabitha Eggs retreats to her dream house in Del Norte County, California to drink herself to death. But when a curious Sasquatch saves her from a suicide attempt, they form a haunting and everlasting bond. Will it be enough to convince her to live?

Coming Soon

QUEEN OF TENTACLES

Book Two in the House of Cards Mystery Series

When Mariner's Cove fortune teller Baba Caracatiță turns up dead, only one person in town has a motive—rival tarot card reader Carrie Dettwiler. Exhausted and looking to make a fresh start after the last murder she was accused of, Carrie wants to stay out of the way. But forces beyond her control, including her girlfriend Stormy's bizarre behavior, draw her into a world of deceit and misdirection.

Coming Soon

TROUBLE'S AFOOT

A Hollywood icon goes missing, and the only clue is a foot in one of her shoes that washes up on a Malibu beach. The problem? The foot doesn't match her DNA. Professional organizer Everly Aprés is called in to help sort through the missing woman's mess, and unwittingly becomes the lead investigator on a case that has the entertainment industry holding its breath.

Read her short stories and horror novellas, get extras for this book, and more at bethanybrowning.com.

Help an indie author! If you like this book, kindly leave a review on Goodreads or Amazon.

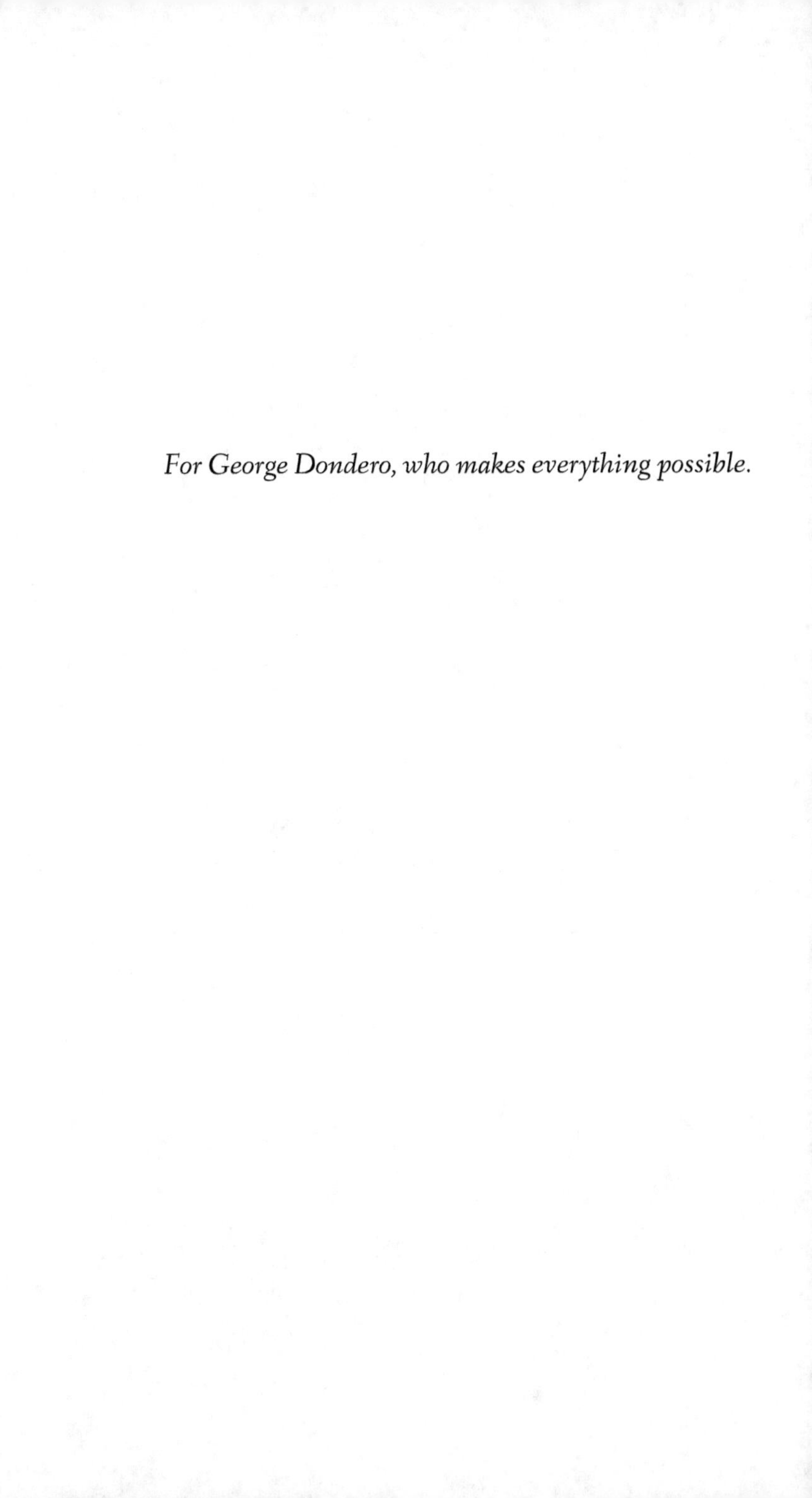

For George Dondero, who makes everything possible.

Chapter One

If you've never spent a morning untangling your pet raven's gnarly claws from the impossibly curly hair of a local clickbait journalist, have you really lived?

"Get. Him. Out. Carrie," the *Prosperity Post's* sensationalist scribe, Daisy Chatterly, shrieked. "Now."

"Hold still," I said. "Waggery wants out of this as much as you do. In his defense, your hair does resemble a nest."

"Quok," Waggery agreed. He flapped his wings, which pulled him backward, yanking Daisy's head with him.

"Why is he wet?" Daisy demanded, wiping a droplet off her cheek. "Did he pee on me? It went into my *mouth*. If I get infested with bird worms, I'll sue you."

I finagled Waggery's claw out of Daisy's ringlets. He flapped into a nearby branch and gave himself a vigorous shake. Water droplets rained down on us both.

"I can see the headline now," I said. "*Urine Trouble: Morbid Corvid Extorted When Pissed Reporter Sues Over Ooze.*"

"My lawyer's going to love this," she muttered under her breath as she continued to inspect herself.

"He didn't pee and there's no such thing as bird worms,

unless you mean the ones early birds catch. He's wet because it's our normal Tuesday spell time," I said with a shrug.

"Spell time?" she asked in a tone that made it sound like she'd caught me in an impromptu confession. "So, you're admitting you practice the demonic arts? Can I get a quote from you for my exposé?" She clicked a pen.

"It's nothing out of the ordinary," I said. "Every Tuesday, Waggery bathes in the blood of Prosperity's virgins and bolts out the window to I.D. his next victim. I'm sorry to say it, but you're next, Daisy. Prepare to be ensorcelled."

I crossed my eyes, stuck out my tongue, and wiggled my fingers at her.

Judging by the look on her face, she was not prepared to be ensorcelled or anything else. Not by me, anyway.

Cute enough to be Homecoming queen and compact enough to always be the top of the pyramid, Daisy was the physical embodiment of high school popularity. I loved getting her riled up, and I'd been perfecting my technique since she launched a vigorous anti-witch bullying campaign that haunted me for four excruciating years.

"I knew it," she hissed as she checked her gingham sundress for blood splatters. She looked up at me, her azure eyes the size of saucers. "What are you going to do to me?"

"I'm joking, Daisy. It's Waggery's bath day. He likes to dry himself off up there." I pointed to where he had landed. "It's a sunny spot."

I couldn't help but smile. Waggery looked adorable perched in Aunt Inez's mimosa tree, a black void with shiny eyes surrounded by delicate wisps of silky pink flowers. He puffed his feathers a final time and uttered a sweet purring sound.

"I'm glad you're happy," she said, blowing a few straggling ringlets out of her face. "That beast could have sliced me to ribbons."

"Seriously, are you okay?"

I only asked because I was raised to be polite, not because I cared one whit if she'd gotten a wee scratch or nick. Served her right. Daisy was forever skulking around my house. I've caught Daisy peering through the windows in the hopes she would catch me in the throes of spellcraft, conjuring spirits, communing with the dark lord, or whatever else she thought the readers of the *Prosperity Post* might pay to read about.

But, since I never did any of those things, she was forced to rely on her imagination.

Most recently, she'd published a Pulitzer-worthy piece entitled *Witch Hunt: Tarot Card Priestess's Craven Raven Spells Hell for Waterfowl.*

That headline ran alongside a photo of me fetching Waggery from an impromptu visit to his girlfriend, a duck we called Ligeia, who lived at Prosperity's duck pond, a shimmering attraction in the center of our town plaza. In my cotton dress, Mary Janes, and the second-hand denim jacket I wore to keep Waggery's quarter-inch claws from puncturing my shoulder, I looked more Polly Pocket than Sanderson Sister. The only thing that spelled hell as far as I could see was that the photo appeared to have been taken from inside the bushes. Daisy'd been crouching in the oleander, waiting for us to appear.

"This is definitely making the paper." She whipped out a notepad and made a big show of scribbling something.

"How about I write the headline for you?" I offered. "*No Deal: Hack Spies, Lies When She Tries to Dig Dirt on Beloved Tarot Reader.*"

"Clever," she said with a hint of a snarl on her lips.

"Stanford English degree, remember?" I said with mock smugness. Everyone in the town of Prosperity knew I was in debt up to my eyeballs for that highly prestigious, completely worthless degree. But it was a worthwhile dunk on Daisy, who was insecure about the fact that the only reason she wrote for the *Prosperity Post* was because her parents owned it.

Waggery wafted down from his branch and landed on my shoulder. "Mwah," he said, giving me a kiss.

"Now, if you'll excuse us," I said. "Waggery and I have a reading scheduled with Miriam Cringe."

"I've got my eye on you," Daisy said. "Soon, my readers will know all about the black magic you're performing at House of Cards Tarot and how it's a danger to our community."

"Yeah, yeah, I get it." I turned on my heels toward the cottage. "You'll get me. And my little bird, too."

§

"Never let them think you're psychic."

These were some of the first words of wisdom my Aunt Inez shared with ten-year-old me when she began teaching me how to read tarot.

"As a tarot card reader," she said, while nimbly shuffling her deck, the same one I began using after she died, "your job, your vocation, is to tease out messages in a near-infinite combination of images, numbers, colors, and symbols found in your client's spread. These messages reveal opportunities, offer encouragement, and suggest safe courses of action when danger is near. But you? You never predict the future. For yourself, or anyone else."

"I don't?" I asked. This was news to me. Part of the appeal of learning tarot—aside from basking in the glow of Aunt Inez's glorious attention—was to foresee what was going to happen to me. What would I be when I grew up? Would I be famous? Rich? Would I find my soulmate? Without these answers, wasn't tarot nothing more than a parlor game with no winner?

"No, Carrie," she said, placing the shuffled deck between us

and looking at me very seriously. "We use tarot cards to help our clients write the story of their lives."

"But what if they want to know how their story ends?" I asked, pretty sure I'd outsmarted her this time.

"It's a dangerous game," she said, her dark eyes twinkling, "drawing conclusions for someone else."

She told me the story of two patients who were diagnosed with the same terrible illness. One was told he had six months to live. The other was told he could live a long and prosperous life, to a hundred or more. "What do you think happened?" And before I could venture a guess, she said, "Exactly what was predicted came true for both. You can offer a roadmap with many twists and turns, but the client must determine their own fate. Let your clients write their own stories."

I'm not psychic. And I don't practice witchcraft. I'm a tarot card reader—one of the best, trained by the G.O.A.T.

"Sometimes," Aunt Inez said, peering at me over her star-shaped reading glasses, "it's best to not know what comes next."

§

"Open up, Carrie Dettwiler." My first client of the day, Miriam Cringe, was pounding on my front door.

'Tis some visitor rapping at my chamber door," I whispered to Waggery as I flounced past his perch.

"Nevermore," Waggery croaked in excitement. He danced back and forth and bobbed up and down.

I unlatched the hook, opened the door, and welcomed Miriam into my reading room. "Always a pleasure," I said, with my hand on my heart.

It wasn't always a pleasure.

"Did the spirits fail to mention that I was on my way?" She shouldered past me toward the reading table and staked her claim in her usual seat, her dark, curly hair bouncing as she settled in.

She sniffed deeply, cleared her throat, and swallowed whatever it was that came up.

"I don't talk to spirits," I told her for the millionth time. "And you're early."

"What's happening there?" she asked, gesturing to the gaping hole where my doorknob used to be.

"Waggery's new thing," I said. "Disassembling doorknobs." I pointed toward the jumble of metal on my kitchen counter. Waggery, hearing his name, blinked and cocked his head. "I'm using that sad little hook to keep it closed now."

"I don't know why you allow that feathered fiend to live in your house." Miriam looked at Waggery with what Inez would have called "the hairy eyeball." She sat down at the reading table, pulled a claw hammer out of her tote, and set it on the table between us. "It's like living with a flying monkey."

Waggery giggled. Miriam wrinkled her nose in disgust.

Most of the things I inherited from Aunt Inez—her mortgage-free home, her beloved Waggery, and her vast tarot card knowledge—were things I cherished. But Miriam Cringe wasn't one of them. Insults shot out of her like a Tommy gun. Negativity gushed from her mouth like an unplugged hydrant. Offensive taunts launched out of her gaping maw with the force of a— never mind. You get the picture.

Unfortunately, she was my most reliable client, arriving every Tuesday like clockwork, exactly like she did when Aunt Inez read her cards. And let's face it, I was in no financial position to turn anyone away.

"Why don't you tuck the wham-stick back into your bag," I suggested. "And we'll begin."

There was a joke bouncing around my brain about Miriam

and a bag of hammers, but I knew better than to make it. I took my normal seat across the table from her and stifled a giggle.

"I refuse to disarm myself while that doom chicken is in the room," she said, clearly not seeing the humor. "He's leering."

I glanced at Waggery to see if he was, in fact, leering. He yawned.

"He's harmless." And that was true.

Mostly.

I tapped the cards a few times to wake them up. I turned them over, relishing the weight of them in my palms. The cool feel of the cards never failed to bring me back to myself, to center me when the world threw chaos my way. My cards were my touchstone to sanity, like a deep, cleansing breath. Some people had crystals, crosses, or charms; I had cards.

"A quick three-card or a full Celtic cross today?" I asked.

"Three for me," she said, and I did my best to hide my disappointment. The three-card spread is universally useful and easy to understand. The Celtic cross was a highly detailed reading, and it cost more.

"We've got to hurry," she said, tapping her watch-free wrist. "I'm going to ambush your buddy Mayor Brix in his office. I need to beat some sense into him about that duck pond, and he keeps saying he's too busy to meet. Reason's gone out the window."

Miriam was singing a tune I'd heard among a lot of the locals. Mayor Brix had spearheaded a wildly successful downtown reinvention campaign that put Prosperity on the radar of day-trippers, second homers, and social media mavens who clogged up traffic and thronged around our town plaza and its perfectly picturesque duck pond. Our once-sleepy hamlet was becoming a playground for the elite, and small, family-owned businesses that catered to the residents were being forced out.

But Miriam's specific beef with the mayor was about the

duck pond. Miriam, obsessed with water hazards after her husband drowned at Lake Liminal last year, wanted it filled in and transformed into a community garden. They'd been battling over it for months.

"What's your question?" I asked, eager to change this controversial subject.

"Wouldn't you like to know?"

"I would." I sighed louder than I should have. Miriam was, in a word, paranoid, and she was fearful I would use her questions against her with the mayor.

"I keep everything confidential," I assured her.

"Get to the cards," she said. "My question has nothing to do with you."

"Waddle it be? Calling fowl on the duck pond?" I smiled at my own joke. She did not.

I continued. "I'm going to read your three-card spread left to right, past to future. In your past position, you've got the Three of Cups, reversed. You're frustrated with a group project or committee."

Miriam stroked her hammer with increasing intensity.

"You've decided to take matters into your own hands," I said, fixating on her hammer. "Is that accurate?"

"Always," she said. "If you want something done right you've got to do it yourself."

"Totally agree," I said, taking the opening. "You have no idea how many group projects at Stanford I did all by myself—"

"Read the cards," she said, tapping the middle card, the one that showed the present. "I'm not paying for your walks down alumni lane."

"In the center, you've got the Five of Cups reversed, which is an interesting juxtaposition next to the three, also reversed," I said. "You might suffer a setback and blame yourself for the outcome."

"I don't blame myself for anything," she said. "Ever."

True. Miriam never said she was sorry.

"The three spilled goblets suggest that you've lost support," I said, silently wondering who supported her in this doomed mission to begin with. "But look at these two behind the cloaked figure. They're still standing. Your wing men still support you. Does any of this fit the bill?"

Her mouth was a thin straight line, her eyes blank. She wasn't going to give me anything to work with, and she certainly wasn't going to encourage my duck puns.

"Let's see what your future card reveals," I said, speeding the process along.

I turned over the final card, farthest to the right, in the spread.

It was Death: A skeleton clad in armor flashing a toothy grimace and parading through a field of corpses atop a white horse.

Miriam snatched her hammer and clutched it close to her chest.

"Don't worry," I said, in as serious and soothing a tone as I could muster. "The Death card is completely misunderstood. Something in your life is ending. Don't forget, there are two other cards in this spread. And they're telling me that this ending will benefit you. You may feel bad about something that happened—"

She narrowed her eyes.

"—or not," I continued. "This ending might be exactly what you need to transition to the next phase. This card is an invitation for a major life shift."

She shoved her hammer into her bag and stood up.

"Who knows?" I asked. "Maybe this means you'll stop worrying and learn to love the duck pond."

Waggery jumped onto the table in front of her. "Twenty dollars, please," he said, in a pitch-perfect imitation of my voice.

"Call off your familiar before I crush his skull," Miriam said.

"Put the money on the table and he'll leave you alone," I said, exhausted from the exchange.

She pulled the bill out of her wallet and before she could set it down, Waggery plucked it out of her hand and flew it to his treasure pile, a small collection that included coins, ticket stubs, bottle caps, paperclips, twist ties, bobby pins, and three discharged bullets.

"That murder pigeon had better stay out of my way," Miriam called over her shoulder as she huffed her way through my hobbled front door. "Everyone had better stay out of my way."

Chapter Two

Most mornings after a reading, I'd putter around in Aunt Inez's garden pulling weeds, picking tomatoes, or simply basking in one of Prosperity's brilliant blue-sky days. But I was feeling feisty after my run-in with Daisy, so I'd gathered some sticks to fashion into the shape of a person.

"She wants a witch," I said to Waggery. "Let's give her the Blair version."

Before I could finish labeling it "Daisy" and dangling it from the mimosa tree with some twine I found in Waggery's treasure pile, my phone rang.

"Carrie, it's Preston Brix." One of the mayor's tactics for seizing control of a situation was being the first one to talk. I didn't even have a chance to say hello.

"How can I be of assistance to you today, your honor?" I asked. I enjoyed teasing my friends almost as much as I enjoyed haranguing my enemies. Almost.

"I lost something of value, and I wonder if you've seen it."

"According to Miriam Cringe, you've lost all sense of reason," I said, picking up my stick doll and admiring it. "Or was it dignity? Perhaps she said marbles. I don't remember exactly. Are any of these things the lost item to which you are referring?"

Poking fun at Mayor Preston Brix was practically my second job. He was desperate to give the impression that he was a big-time politico. But I knew him long before he'd even considered running for mayor, back when he wasn't much more than a beach bum in Puka shells and the thickest, slickest gelled hair you've ever seen, begging my Aunt Inez for predictions about his love life.

"Preston Brix is the kind of man who'll steal your wallet and help you look for it," my Aunt Inez said. *"If he can stay out of trouble, he's destined for politics."*

It was my Aunt Inez's readings that showed a young, impressionable dude that he had potential for great things—or at least things. Under her tutelage, he evolved into an Emperor card from something much less powerful, like a Page of Swords. And, over time and with more attention and power, he fully embodied this role. When he was the upright version of the Emperor, Mayor Preston Brix was authoritative and visionary. But when he was reversed? He was prone to abuses of power, like, well, an emperor.

"As much as I revel in your wit, Ms. Dettwiler, I need your help," he said in a voice I didn't recognize. Was he being... serious with me? "I lost an irreplaceable piece of jewelry, and Officer Bucket suggested I retrace my steps before filing a police report. I suspect it was stolen."

Right on cue, Waggery fiddled with something in his treasure pile.

"Hold on a minute, my liege." I walked over to Waggery's mess. "Whatcha got there?" I spotted something shiny underneath a ticket stub for a movie I'd never seen. "Oh, no." I picked up an ornate ring.

"Oh, no. Oh, no," Waggery said in my voice.

"It's not polite to mock people, Waggery." I was holding an emerald the size and shape of a postage stamp. The weight of it surprised me. My first thought was that I could handily pay off my credit card debt and student loans with such a treasure. My second thought was that I'd had no idea the mayor had such excellent taste. Or taste.

"Oh, no," Waggery said, marching back and forth over my feet.

"Don't worry, buddy," I said. "Ravens gonna raven."

I grabbed a plum from the fruit bowl on the counter and dropped it onto the floor to keep Waggery occupied. He dragged it around like prey for before stabbing into it.

"Welp, it was definitely stolen. Looks like Waggery lifted it from your pocket during your reading last night. You know he can't resist a shiny object."

He breathed a sigh of relief. "I would appreciate it if you could bring that right over. To my office."

"Sure thing, milord," I said, taking a bow that no one else could see. "Are you going to propose to me with this? Are my dreams of becoming the First Lady of Prosperity coming true? Will you make me your F.L.O.P.?

"Oh, and Carrie?" There wasn't a joke I could make that the mayor couldn't ignore.

"Yes, Mayor Haircut?"

"Can you grab me a coffee on your way over? From the Daily Grind?"

"They still won't sell you a latte, eh? That Corporate Cuppa has them steamed."

"Everyone's so mad about that," he said with an exasperated sigh. "But you can't stop progress."

"I think those were Thoreau's final words," I said. "Or maybe it was Genghis Khan? Why don't you go there? Get yourself a Corporate Cuppa joe?" I asked, knowing the answer. Corporate Cuppa coffee tasted like rocket fuel.

"Help me out, Carrie," he said, in a tone bordering on a whine. "Bring me the ring. Get me the coffee." He hung up.

I stroked Waggery's head, careful not to ruffle his feathers, literally and figuratively. "It's like Aunt Inez used to say. *'When you borrow money, you always pay for it.'* Right, Wags?"

I put the ring in my pocket and motioned for Waggery to jump onto my shoulder. "Let's take bets on whether or he deducts the price of this coffee from what we owe him."

"Nevermore," he said.

"That's what I was thinking, too."

* * *

The mayor's office was a quick jaunt from my cottage, north of the duck pond. It was a path Waggery and I had worn well. We both required daily walks for exercise and mental health, and we enjoyed running into our friends like Flynt Burns, Head of Tourism, whom I could see scurrying around in the distance. I spotted my Uncle Grist (not my real uncle—he was Inez's boyfriend before she died), tipping his top hat to a gaggle of giggling tourists. One of his many jobs was dressing in period costume as town founder Agustus Hoggarty and leading historical tours around Prosperity. Waggery's girlfriend Ligeia waddled contentedly next to the pond.

"How's the tarot business, Carrie?" Grist shouted across the plaza, the same question he asked every day.

"Making a fortune, Uncle Grist." The same answer I provided every day.

"Everyone's raven about you," he said, with a peppy wave.

I swept into Daily Grind like a gust of wind, braced for an argument with the owners Walker and Lister, over whether I could bring Waggery in. He'd been banned after our last visit for flinging a stack of plastic lids all over the shop.

The good news was that neither Walker nor Lister were there. The bad news was that, after I'd purchased the mayor's coffee and was attempting to make a quick getaway, Waggery had found something else in the coffee shop that he wanted to play with.

"Whoa. Oh, no. No. Nope. No."

Waggery had landed on the shoulder of a woman I'd never seen before, and he was smothering her with kisses. "Mwah," he said, in his human voice. "Mwah. Mwah."

"Waggery, no." I scolded. "Leave her alone."

Waggery's victim had gray eyes, and her arms were covered in tattoos. She wore jeans, Chucks, and a black T-shirt that read *Think Ink* in white lettering. The logo was a brain.

"I'm so sorry," I said. "Waggery, come here."

"Not a problem," she said, in a way that I could tell she was attempting to appear tough. "Birds of a feather or something like that." She pushed her hair out of her eyes, revealing that she had a small raven tattooed on the inside of her wrist.

"He's never done that before," I said.

"Assaulted a stranger?"

"I guess he has done that," I admitted. "What I meant is that he's never smooched a stranger."

"Is that what he was doing?" She loosened up a bit. "He didn't hurt me. *Only this and nothing more.*"

Literary jokes. Pretty eyes. Stylish haircut. Dimples. It had been a while since I'd been attracted to anyone. And vice versa, for that matter.

"I love the smell of Poe in the morning," I said in a singsongy voice that sounded unnatural.

Waggery flew to my shoulder. "Mwah," he said, giving me a kiss, probably to soothe my embarrassment.

"I love you, too, Waggery."

"Waggery?" she said. "That's cute. It means 'mischief.'"

You're cute, I stopped short of saying. "No one's ever gotten that right," I said out loud. "People call him Haggerty, Wimbledon, Waldorf..."

"Word nerd," she said with a shrug.

"That's funny," I said. "I'm a bird nerd, hehe."

The silence consumed me. I could hear her blink.

"I would love to chat, but—" I said, recovering badly. I showed her the coffee. "Someone's waiting for their hot cup of coffee. Next time you're in town, come to House of Cards Tarot. Three blocks that way."

After that blunder, I was eager to make an exit.

She called after me. "Hey."

I stopped. "Yeah?"

"How did you know I wasn't from here?"

"Psychic," I said, tapping my temple.

"Right," she said, with a little salute. "Tarot card reader."

"Kidding. I'm not psychic," I said.

"Wait. What—"

"It's an inside joke," I said, wishing I hadn't said anything. "But I know everyone in Prosperity. And if you lived here, I'd know you."

* * *

I was mortified by what I'd said to the intriguing stranger, but I tried to focus on the positive. Maybe she'd come by for a reading. I practically skipped to the mayor's office.

What the mayor called the "town hall" was a compact stone building that once served as a wine cellar for Hoggarty Heaven wines, way back when the Hoggarty estate stretched through what was now a bustling downtown. There was a small, makeshift reception area—never manned, just for show—and a large wooden door behind it that was the entrance to the mayor's office.

My footsteps echoed in the cavernous room. Waggery let loose a range of raven-y noises that sounded like a fax machine, clearly enjoying the sound of his own voice reverberating off the hard, cold masonry.

The mayor's door was closed. I knocked. No answer.

I jiggled the doorknob. Locked.

I knocked a few times. I put my ear up to the door. "Your highness?"

I knocked a little louder.

No response.

Waggery thought this was a game, and he banged the door with his beak. He poked at the lock. It was like the one on my front door, and the look in his eye told me that was eager to demolish it.

I could no longer manage his flapping and squirming while simultaneously trying not to slosh hot coffee all over myself. I was annoyed that the mayor had told me to come here, only to abandon me with an agitated bird on my shoulder and a cup of lava-hot liquid in my hand. I considered dropping the ring into the coffee cup and leaving it there to teach the mayor a lesson, but that seemed a step too far, even for me.

What to do with the mayor's coffee turned out to be the least of my problems. By the time I'd walked to the reception desk to set down the cup, Waggery had dismantled the antique doorknob. Its pieces were now scattered about the floor, and he was happily sorting through them, trying to figure out how to get the shinier bits back to his treasure pile.

"No," I said. "Stop it. No." I gently pushed him away from his project with my foot.

He didn't like that.

"Stop it, no," he shouted, in an uncanny imitation of my voice. When he let out a scream that sounded exactly like a woman being stabbed, I instantly regretted teaching him how to do that to scare trick or treaters last Halloween.

"Don't be a brat, Waggery," I hissed. "Shhh."

I fully expected an annoyed mayor to stick his coiffed head out and demand we leave.

But nothing happened.

Had he seen Miriam coming and ducked out the "hidden" door on the side of the building he thought none of us knew about?

"Dear leader?" I said, quietly, in case he was engaged in some important business.

He wasn't. I pushed the door open a little wider, and that's when I saw my friend, Mayor Preston Brix, lying on the floor, face down in a puddle of what I could only assume was his own blood.

Predictably, I didn't see this coming.

§

"I want you to have this."

Aunt Inez had handed me her tarot deck. It was wrapped in a deep purple silk cloth.

"I can't." I held back my tears. "You're going to be using them for a long time."

"Carrie," she said. "I need you to face what's happening.

I placed her deck back on the table next to her. "I already have a deck, thank you very much."

"About that," she began. "There's something I need to tell you about your deck."

I pulled my beloved deck, wrapped in its own silk cloth, from my backpack. I'd been using it for more than a decade. It was perfectly broken in, pliable and a joy to shuffle. And it was filled with memories of my time with Inez. Memories I would cherish always.

"What?" I asked. "What about my deck?"

"Well," she began. "You bought it yourself."

"That's right," I said, straightening. "I earned money by selling the persimmons from the tree and I took the bus to Raven's Wing in Oakland and bought myself this deck."

"And I was so proud of you." She easily fell into her role as provider of unconditional love. "You decide to do things and you do them. But—"

"But what?" I asked. "Spill it."

"It's bad luck to buy your own deck."

"You're telling me this now?" I asked. "I've had this deck since I was in middle school."

"You were so pleased with yourself, and I wanted to encourage your spirit of exploration, adventure and independence," she said. "I didn't have the heart to tell you."

"You're telling me that my deck is cursed?"

"Not at all." She patted my hand. "But let's hedge our bets and get you a deck that's covered in good luck." She handed me her deck again. "This is your legacy. It's your path. Take this deck and make magic with it."

"But no predictions," I said. "Or spells, or incantations..."

"I'm so pleased you've been paying attention," she said, a wry smile on her lips. "Now, what story are you going to tell?"

§

Chapter Three

By the time I summoned my senses enough to call for help, I couldn't feel my face. I'd seen death before when I held Aunt Inez's hand as she peacefully transitioned to her next adventure. I believed in the spiritual plane, but I couldn't summon its inhabitants. She told me not to worry, that she was ready, and her selflessness made it possible for me to share her experience—and the odd physical sensation of feeling the warmth leave her body—with a small whisper of hope.

But this? There's no way to prepare for finding a dead body on a normal Tuesday morning.

I knew enough from watching television not to touch him or anything in his office. I scrambled to the reception desk and dialed 911. Within seconds, I could hear sirens in the distance.

But Waggery wasn't having it. And there was no way for me to communicate to him that this was a crime scene and that he couldn't flap around, scattering his feathers all over the place.

I heard Officer Bucket's squad car pull into the horseshoe drive in front of the building. Waggery was screaming like a woman again. I had to resort to my least favorite way of managing him, which was to scoop him under my arm like a football to keep his wings secure. But he's a powerful bird, and he'd wriggled out of my control before. So far, he'd stopped short of pecking or biting me, but I wasn't willing to risk it under these circumstances.

"When your raven is ravening," my Aunt Inez would say when Waggery threw a hissy fit, *"it's best to take flight."*

Even though I had a vague idea that leaving the scene of a crime was a no-no, I'd known Officer Bucket since I was a child, and I knew that if I could get Waggery home in a few minutes, I could return quickly to make myself useful to him and his investigation. He'd met Waggery. I was sure he'd understand my predicament.

The quickest way out of the building was the "closet" around the corner, a small anteroom marked *No Exit* that was absolutely an exit. The mayor used it to avoid ever-increasing mobs of torch-wielding locals, but it was designed during Prohibition to allow quick escapes for the smugglers who worked for Agustus Hoggarty. Only a few people knew about it, and the only reason I did is because my Uncle Grist was Prosperity's premiere historian.

I conveyed Waggery into the closet as fast as I could. I worried he would, at best, distract the police and, at worst, contaminate the crime scene. We stepped into the room, only to see the briefest flash of light let in from the outside and the silhouette of a person stepping out onto the plaza.

"Hello?"

The door slammed before I could see who was there.

With no light, this room was a tomb. I took four swift steps across the floor, and Waggery and I made our exit through the same door.

* * *

Looking back, it's obvious that I should've searched high and low on the plaza for whomever was skulking in the town hall anteroom. But Waggery was in a full-blown tantrum, and I was in a state of complete shock. I didn't have the physical strength or emotional fortitude to contain him much longer without inviting a violent reaction from him that could potentially hurt us both.

I released him, and he took off toward the duck pond. I took a beat to see if anyone looked suspicious, but my priority was to keep my eye on my raven, for his safety and my sanity.

The shock of finding the mayor in a pool of blood was setting in. For a split second I allowed myself to think it was a dark prank, that he would walk out behind me and say "boo." But it wasn't. And he didn't. I stood there in the blinding sun, torn between running back inside and trying to shake him awake and keeping my eye on Waggery, who could easily escape if he wanted to. My heart told me to watch Waggery closely because it would break if I lost him, too.

Under normal circumstances I would allow him to hang out at the duck pond with Ligeia. A four-pound bird with the mental capacity of a kindergartner wasn't easy to subdue before he was good and ready anyway. But on this day, I did what I hated to do: I gave chase. I needed to corral him at home, ensure his safety, and hurry back to talk with Officer Bucket as soon as I possibly could.

He had landed on a tree branch over some shrubbery where Ligeia liked to hang out and was squawking her name. I can't say for sure that this duck knew her name, but she certainly knew that Waggery sometimes showed up with snacks, and she chattered and wiggled her tail in excitement.

Waggery saw me approaching, which is the worst thing to happen when I'm trying to retrieve him. He loved games even more when he knew I wasn't playing. I chased him from branch to branch more than halfway around the length of the pond, his cackling causing more and more laughter and attracting more of the attention he craved.

He darted into a hedge.

"Not now, Waggery—" As I began to scold, the bushes rustled forcefully, and I was concerned that he was tangled up or had been apprehended by one of the stray cats that prowled the duck pond for easy prey.

"Looking for this?" It was Hank Hoggarty, covered in dirt, wearing a *High on the Hoggarty* ball cap. He emerged from the landscaping that covered another secret stairway to his family's network of underground Prohibition tunnels. Waggery was on his forearm.

"You scared me to death." I put my hand on my heart, which I could feel pounding under my breastbone. "I thought Waggery was being attacked."

"What's happening here?" he asked, gesturing toward the flashing lights and first responders that hurried all about the plaza. His hands were filthy, and he had about three-days' growth on his rust-colored beard, giving him a Prince Harry-on-vacation vibe. If the timing were different, I probably would have hit him with some kind of dirty Harry joke, but now was not the time.

"The mayor was found dead in his office," I said, feeling the tears coming. I didn't know how to tell him I'd been the one who found him.

His jaw tightened. "Choked to death on his own ego?"

"Hank."

"He wasn't good for Prosperity," he said.

Waggery growled.

Hank Hoggarty was my oldest friend, and he was best summed up by the Devil card: he wasn't a bad guy, but he was prone to mischief and the pursuit of pleasure. He was also easily tempted by vices, anger, and obsession. I once commented that he might have been better off if he hadn't been born with a silver spoon in his mouth. He said it's not a silver spoon, it's a golden shovel—and he can't stop himself from digging.

"I'm not going to have this conversation with you again," I said. "Not now."

The heir to the Hoggarty fortune, Hank fled town the second the check cleared, and partied his inheritance away. He'd returned to Prosperity, broke and broken, determined to live on his family's estate, Hoggarty Heaven. But what he found instead was that the only thing he still owned was an old hardware shop downtown that, due to the mayor's new Prosperity Prospers initiative, was only permitted to be a restaurant. In Hank's absence, Hoggarty Heaven had fallen into disrepair, so the mayor created the Historical Society to oversee its repair and upkeep.

My Uncle Grist, who grew up working for the Hoggarty Family on the estate, was appointed caretaker. Grist lived in the carriage house that Hank had hoped to claim.

To say Hank was bitter about all of this was an understatement.

"I won't miss him." He spit on the ground.

"Careful, Hank," I said. "That's meaner than usual, even for you."

"Sorry," he said, in a voice that didn't sound sorry. "I've got a lot on my mind."

"Only thing on your mind is that ugly High on the Hoggarty hat you're wearing," I said. "You should have left it in the tunnels." I made a bad joke to lighten his mood. "What were you doing down there?"

"Thanks to your mayor, may he rest in peace, this hat, and the business it advertises, are two of the only things I have left."

"I'm sorry, Hank—" I had trouble looking him in the eye. We both had struggled recently, and our problems usually drew us together. But today, with what had happened, I feared we weren't going to find common ground.

"You should probably mind your own business, Mizz Dettwiler," he said, with an emphasis on "dett." "Like the stack of letters from creditors I'm keeping for you at the Bar & Grill. I wouldn't want anyone to suspect me of covering up a crime for you."

Deflection was Hank's superpower.

"You don't have to be like this," I said. "It's been a hard day. For some of us."

"Your so-called uncle is waving you down." He pointed to Uncle Grist who was in the crowd, watching the scene unfold. I hadn't thought about him yet. He would be crushed.

I signaled to Waggery to hop onto my shoulder. "I need to go to him."

"You do that," Hank said. "Go to your family." He said the word "family" with a sneer.

"Hank, I—"

He turned and walked away. I wondered if he was going back to his restaurant. Or if he had unfinished business in the tunnels.

* * *

The plaza had erupted into chaos. Tourists were gawking. Residents were rubbernecking. I thought the mayor would love how cinematic this all looked. He'd recently outfitted Prosperity's small police force with vintage 1920s squad cars.

"They're a nod to Prosperity's Prohibition heritage," he said. "They're perfect for Instagram."

"They're expensive to maintain," I said. "They're perfectly impractical." But he'd had his heart set on them, and here they were, looking equal parts charming and silly.

I spotted Uncle Grist's top hat, and shouldered my way through the gathering crowd, many of whom were taking selfies with the police cars, unaware that a man had been murdered.

"Carrie, thank goodness you're here," Grist said, rubbing his salt-and-pepper beard, a self-soothing habit he'd picked up after my Aunt Inez died. "Terrible thing. The mayor. I can't believe it."

Grist Featherweight was my Magician. Like the image on the tarot card, he was always dressed in something fancy, as if he were presiding over an important ritual. The chalice on the Magician's table reminded me of Grist's love of wine; the flowers that bloomed around him represented his stewardship of the natural world and beautiful things. But the thing that reminded me most of the Magician was the infinity symbol over the Magician's head—perpetual reinvention. Grist was a master of adapting to new circumstances.

"Officer Bucket is looking for you." He had taken off his hat and was worrying the edges of the brim with his fingers.

"I found him," I said. "The mayor, I mean. I'm the one who called."

"Oh, no," he said. "Why aren't you cooperating with the police?"

"Oh, no," Waggery repeated.

"Not now, buddy," I said, gently patting his beak. "I'm cooperating by not cooperating. After I found the mayor's—" I had trouble choking out the words "—body, Waggery wigged out. I had to get him out of there. I'm trying to get him home. When he's settled, I'll talk to anyone who wants to talk."

"See that you do, Carrie," Uncle Grist said. "He told me there were black feathers in the building and he wondered if you'd been there."

"What did you tell him?"

"I said I'd seen you on the plaza as usual, and that you probably went by to make a payment on your loan."

"You told him I owed the mayor money?" My palms felt sticky, and I couldn't figure out why. Everyone in town knew I was in debt, but it bothered me that Grist had mentioned this to the police. My debt was becoming both literally and figuratively inescapable.

"I didn't mean to insinuate anything," he said. "I wanted to let him know that it's a common occurrence for you to drop by. I'm sure it's fine. But he wants you to speak with him."

While I was bothered that he'd mentioned the debt, I was unconcerned that Grist had accidentally fingered me as a suspect. He was being honest. And I knew that my actions that day could easily be explained.

I saw Daisy's blond ringlets bouncing in the distance as she trailed behind the first responders, taking notes. I could already imagine the headline: *Mayor Slayer on the Loose: Suspected Enchantress Disappears for a Spell.*

I was going to have to hurry to get ahead of this story. The last time Daisy trash-talked me in the press, my business dipped, teenagers egged my house, and Hank wouldn't stop joking about my 'resting witch face.' I'd had to give away free readings at the Prosperity Porch Potlucks to build my client list back.

Waggery fussed on my shoulder. "I need to get Waggery home soon. He's already ambushed one stranger today."

"It's a terrible day," Grist said.

"It is," I agreed. "But let's remember what Inez always said."

"Stop leaving the seat up in the middle of the night?"

"Grist. No," I said, with a laugh that didn't sit right in my throat considering the grim circumstances. "She would say, *'There's always a way forward.'* Let's agree that no matter what, you and I will always move forward."

We hugged and held on for a little longer than usual, more aware than ever of how quickly you can lose someone you love.

Chapter Four

"Girl, there's gossip."

The great thing about living in a small town is that you can't walk five feet without running into someone you know. The bad thing about living in a small town is that you can't walk five feet without running into someone you know.

I'd barely stepped onto the sidewalk when Walker and Lister, wearing their perfectly pressed, inexplicably stain-free Daily Grind aprons, caught up to me. If Prosperity's currency was gossip, Walker and Lister were the local bank.

"I'm sorry I brought Waggery in again this morning," I said. "I know you hate him being in your shop, but with everything that happened after, I hope you can forgive me."

These two were like a dog with a bone when something bothered them. I'd learned long ago that the path of least resistance was to apologize for something, anything, to get back into their good graces. I deserved overpriced, locally brewed coffee as much as anyone.

"I don't know what you're talking about," said Lister, twirling the dainty upturned curl of his imperial mustache. "But we spotted you sneaking out the back door of the town hall where the mayor's body was found. A door that we had not seen until today."

"It's not like that," I said. "And how's that gossip?" My thoughts drifted to the figure I'd seen in the anteroom, and I was kicking myself for not giving chase. But what would I have done if I had captured a murder suspect? Read their cards?

Walker and Lister exchanged raised eyebrow looks.

"It's gossip now because we're telling everyone," Walker said, undaunted. "We're spreading it all over town, like you do with those creepy cards of yours."

"I, for one, do not think you have it in you," said Lister. "Walker likes to imagine that everyone's got some dark secret, right babe?"

"Everyone's hiding something," Walker said. "Who knew the mayor was going to end up taking a dirt nap today? He's got a lot of enemies, for sure. Seems likely that people would think it's a satanic sacrifice. That's what Daisy's already telling everyone."

Walker and Lister were my Moon and Sun cards. Walker, whose round, hairless head and serious expression was reminiscent of the lunar image on the tarot card, was fear-based and prone to chasing illusion. Lister was energy, vitality, positive messages—a happy baby riding in on a white horse to bring good tidings. But the flip side was that Lister could be irresponsible.

"A satanic sacrifice seems likely?" I couldn't believe what I was hearing. "In Prosperity? Performed by me? Because Daisy said so?"

"People are also saying the police found something rather... incriminating."

My patience was running out. "What did they find, Walker?"

"The mayor was holding a tarot card in his hand."

I scanned my memory and cringed at what I conjured. The mayor's dead body. The blood. But I didn't see a tarot card. I would've remembered that.

"What card?" was all I could think of to say.

"Like we would know," Walker said. "Officer Bucket took it as evidence. Put it in one of those little baggies like on TV."

A fresh chill snaked up my spine. There was nothing inherently negative about a tarot card. But when found in the hand of a corpse, it might relay a dark message from a murderer.

Or it could incriminate me.

I considered launching into my usual diatribe about how tarot cards aren't black magic, but Waggery was doing that thing he does when it's snack time: squawking and wiggling.

"There was a card in his hand. You were at the office, and you are the only person in town who struts around with a literal harbinger of death on her shoulder," Walker said.

He was enjoying himself a little too much.

"I don't strut," I said. "Let's apply this same logic to you two. Last time I checked, you were trashing the mayor to everyone who came into your shop for allowing that Corporate Cuppa to open."

"I don't like what you're insinuating," Walker said with a wag of his finger. "Plus, we were delivering coffee to Emma Fort-Knightly on the plaza when you dashed out. We all saw it. Doesn't look good." He made a little tsk-tsk sound that infuriated me.

Waggery growled, a low grinding sound that he only made when he felt threatened.

"We shouldn't turn on each other," Lister interrupted. "There still needs to be an investigation. I'm sure Daisy Chatterly will get to the bottom of it. She always does."

I rolled my eyes.

"I saw that, young lady. You'd better hope no one finds

anything else," said Walker. "Or you're going to be flipping your little cards over in the hoosegow."

My hand instinctively went to the opulent ring in my pocket. I realized that if the police—or worse, Daisy—knew I had something this expensive that belonged to the mayor, things might be more complicated than explaining my side of the story. Plus, hadn't the mayor mentioned to Officer Bucket that he thought someone might have stolen it? (*Bling Sting: Tarot Temptress Stole Ring* flashed into my mind.)

"I didn't go into his office," I said. "But I have to run. I remembered something important."

"Your cards aren't going to help you here, Carrie," Walker called after me as I hustled down the street toward my house.

"You're right," I called over my shoulder. "This time I need to be the one asking questions."

* * *

Back in the safety of my sunny kitchen, I fed Waggery a handful of unsalted peanuts in the shell, and a few peeled cucumbers from the garden.

"You probably need a nap," I said. "But I've made a dangerous decision, and you are going to help me."

I had his attention.

"Now that you're all fueled up, you wanna go make some mischief?" I asked.

And I swear his reaction sounded like, "I thought you'd never ask."

The mayor's house was around the corner, but it might as well have been in a different world. My little cottage, so lovingly doted on by my aunt, was exactly that: a little cottage. It was on a shady street nestled next to other little cottages, all with similar stucco walls, tile roofs, and water-wise yards. Lavender bloomed in abundance, filling the air with that specific sweet-menthol scent; everyone had a Meyer lemon tree and a row or two of wine-grape vines. Cats lounged in the middle of the lane like they owned the place, unafraid of speeding traffic because there was none. Like myself, most of my neighbors walked everywhere in town. I didn't have a car, though, so my walking was less "charming quirk" and more "total necessity."

Mayor Preston Brix lived in Hoggarty Heights, Prosperity's only gated community. What they were keeping out, I never understood. Maybe they were trying to keep something in? I couldn't imagine what.

The homes here were imposing and grand, kind of like the people who lived there. The mayor's neighborhood was brimming with wealthy winery owners, dot-com millionaires, and a variety of other rich folks who may or may not have used their Hoggarty Heights residence solely as a wine country getaway. That's the kind of thing that galled the long-time residents. More and more businesses were catering to this crowd with caviar bistros and sparkling wine bars when what the rest of us wanted were more farmer's markets, a taco truck or two, and well-funded public schools.

But Waggery and I didn't have time to unpack the tension inherent in gentrifying communities today. We had a job to do, one that I justified by convincing myself that we weren't committing a crime. Quite the opposite in fact. We were here to return something. We were *un*committing a crime.

I felt confident in that idea until I came around the corner and spotted a police jalopy cruising by. I wasn't ready to face Officer Bucket or any other officer for that matter, not while I was in the middle of mischief, so Waggery and I ducked behind an oleander and waited for the car to pass.

"That was close," I said, as I skulked—or at least attempted to skulk as well as one could in broad daylight—toward the wall that surrounded the mayor's neighborhood. If the police were already making rounds through town, Daisy would be close on their heels. I had to hurry if I was going to keep my name out of her headlines, and myself out of handcuffs.

This is absurd, I thought, as I hoisted myself over the wall and dropped to the ground on the other side. If people didn't think I was a criminal before, they sure would after this performance.

I wasn't proud of it, but I had no choice. I knew that once I was in, Waggery and I could walk through without being bothered—the neighbors were accustomed to seeing us. Now that we were inside, we casually sauntered down the street, a gal and her bird out for a walk on a perfectly normal day. Nothing to see here.

Like Aunt Inez used to say, "Act *like you own the place, and people will think you do.*"

We sidled past the mayor's house into the backyard, where I got distracted by his impeccably landscaped garden and shimmering turquoise pool.

"No time for lounging poolside today, Waggery," I said. "Or ever again."

I held Waggery up to the doorknob, and he seemed grateful for not having to fly for once while he destroyed a lock mechanism.

"Go to work, Champ."

A few quick pokes, a yank or two, one final twist, and we were in.

"Shhhh," said Waggery.

The air was still in the mayor's house, and I was reminded of how it felt as a kid to snoop through Aunt Inez's room when she was out. No one ever said I couldn't go in, but no one ever said I could, either. I was experiencing the same combination of anxiety and curiosity, mixed with the thrill of possibly getting caught. But in this case, there was an added sense of sadness.

I wasn't going to get caught, was I? The mayor was gone.

They say that when a tsunami floods the shore, the real power unleashes when the wave recedes, swallowing everything in its path and dragging it hungrily back into the ocean. Standing here in his home, smelling his cologne hanging in the air like a ghost—the tsunami threatened to pull me with it. I needed to hurry before my emotions drowned me, or the murderer found me here.

Or both.

"What would make the most sense for this?" I wondered aloud, as if Waggery would know. "Where would a man like that keep a ring like this?"

Putting it on the kitchen counter out in the open wasn't wise. I didn't want the police to draw any lines between this ring and the mayor's murder. Ditto the living room coffee and the key bowl by the door.

I hadn't thought this through.

I looked around. Waggery flitted to the floor and hopped through the room, inspecting the corners and peeking under the furniture.

"What would you do, Waggery?" I asked.

He waddled to the bottom of the stairs and flapped his wings.

"Upstairs, you think? Aunt Inez always kept her jewelry in a box in her closet, so maybe you have a point."

I stood at the bottom of the stairs and peered up toward the second floor. I'd never been up there. I didn't want to go there now. I didn't belong here.

I put one foot on the first stair. "Here we go," I said, ignoring my gut feeling.

Waggery growled.

My stomach dropped.

"What is it?" I whispered, the hairs on the back of my neck standing up. "What's got you ruffled?"

I looked over my shoulder toward the front door. Was someone there?

"I love you," Waggery said in a voice that wasn't mine or my aunt's.

The voice was oddly familiar.

Every muscle in my body pressed tighter to my bones.

Waggery screeched.

"What's going on, Waggery?"

A toilet flushed.

"Oh, no," Waggery said. He jumped up and down. "Oh, no. Oh, no."

My legs were made of lead, but I had to move. I felt for the ring in my pocket. No one could see that I had this. Not now. Maybe not ever. I had to make sure we got out of there before we were found out. What if Officer Bucket was upstairs right now using the mayor's loo? What if the murderer was taking a potty break between murderings?

"What's going on?" I said, a whisper, as I backed quietly down the stairs. I turned to leave.

"I could ask you the same thing."

I recognized the voice and froze.

It was the tattooed woman from the Daily Grind whom Waggery had smothered with kisses earlier. She eyed me from the landing, and I was torn between wanting to run and wanting to invite her to sit on the mayor's butter-colored suede sofa to braid my hair while telling me her life's story. I had never met anyone like her. So confident. So *herself*. She stole my breath.

She also scared me to death.

"What are you doing here?" I asked after an uncomfortable

stare-down. Her, glowering. Me, trying not to pass out from my competing desires to impress her and run from her.

"Once again, I can ask the same of you." She took a few steps toward me, never breaking eye contact. Aggressive. Unafraid.

"You... you..." I stuttered. I backed into the wall to put some distance between us. "Are you the murderer?"

I heard Grist's dad-joke voice in my head saying, "Because you sure are killing it."

Not now, Carrie.

I'd always had a thing for dangerous women.

Waggery blew a raspberry.

"My name is Stormy Portwood," she said. "I'm the mayor's daughter."

Chapter Five

"**I**'m shocked to hear this," I said. The tsunami came for me again. My thoughts were blurry, my stomach queasy. Waggery sauntered off toward the kitchen, unbothered.

"Are you as shocked as I am to see a tarot card reader breaking into my father's house after he's been found dead? With her bird?"

I shook myself out of it.

"It might be a toss-up?" I joked. Bad idea.

Her face was blotchy, like she'd been crying. Her gray eyes were swollen.

"How are you feeling? This must be a big shock," I said, trying to soften the tone of our interaction. "I know what it's like to lose someone close to you."

"We weren't close," she said, without a hint of emotion. "But thank you for saying so. No matter whether we were close or not, everything is different." She fidgeted with her watch, pretending to be distracted. Waggery behaves like this when I ask him to do something he doesn't want to do—suddenly, he must groom himself or search for a toy. Anything but face the discomfort of doing what he's told.

"I'm so sorry," I said, taking a step closer to show that I was harmless. "My name is Carrie Dettwiler. Your dad and I—"

"Father," she said.

This was an odd, dramatic situation, but the truth remained that a young woman lost a parent. I was overwhelmed with compassion, and I wanted her to know that I understood what she was going through.

She didn't seem to share my need to connect.

"I'll be calling the police now," she said, inhaling deeply as she took her phone out of her back pocket and trotted down the stairs past me and into the living room. "Wait right there. I'll only be a sec."

"Please don't," I said. "I can explain. The mayor, your dad, and I were friends."

"Father. And I bet you were." She looked me up and down. "Though the denim jacket, cotton dress and Mary Janes aren't normally the kind of look Preston Brix goes for in a gal pal."

"Gal pal?" I said, pulling my jacket closed over my second-hand dress. "I'm hardly his gal pal."

"I don't understand anything that's happening," she interrupted. "I think it's best if we get the local authorities involved."

"Oh, no. What are you doing?"

"I'm calling the police," she said.

"That wasn't me," I said. "Waggery's in the kitchen trash. Waggery. What a mess." I moved to clean it up.

"He sounds exactly like you." She hung up the phone. "That's wild."

"He's got many talents," I said as I scooped up dirty paper towels, empty tomato tins, and wine bottles.

"Your father wasn't much of a recycler," I noted.

Waggery chuckled.

"What's this?" Stormy picked up a ball of paper that Waggery dropped at her feet. He was poking at her sneakers, probably hoping she'd be up for a quick game of fetch.

She handed it to me. I unfurled it and saw that it was an official memo from the mayor's office.

It was addressed to the entire town council, and it seemed to reference a private vote held a few days before. According to this, they had all met in secret to move forward with the expansion plans for the duck pond. Construction was set to begin immediately with fast-tracked permits and no environmental impact study.

"I'm confused," I said. "It looks like the town council voted to expand the duck pond without the usual public comment period. I don't know why they would need to do this, but I bet we could get some answers from Miriam Cringe. Hating on the duck pond is her favorite hobby."

"I don't know who that is, and I don't care about the provincial politics of Prosperity," Stormy said. "I don't even know who you are, aside from a random person with questionable career choices whom I only met this morning, and who is now rifling through things at my father's house with her feathered fiend. I don't know if I can trust you. Or anyone."

"I don't know if I can trust you," I said. "Are you who you say you are? But right now, we have an equal amount of damning evidence on each other. If we want to get to the truth before the cops come around, it makes sense to work together."

"I'm not sure..."

"I love you," Waggery said.

"Not now, Waggery," I said. "If you think that Waggery and I are capable of murder, I will sit down at your father's kitchen table and wait for Officer Bucket—who has a very high opinion of our mayor despite the fact that he makes him drive around in a cartoon car—to find out right now that he has a mysterious, estranged daughter who arrived in town from god-knows-where on the same day he was murdered."

"I'm from Mariner's Cove," she said, rolling her eyes. "I'm not mysterious."

"Says you," I said. "I can't verify that. And Officer Bucket won't like it one bit. We should stick together and get some evidence before we go calling the police."

This was a gamble, and I knew it. But I decided to take a page from Hank Hoggarty's book, one I'd seen him use this morning when I caught him coming out of the tunnels: When feeling cornered, deflect.

Plus, I was reminded of another thing Aunt Inez used to tell me: *"Keep your enemies close, and your potential love interests closer."*

I watched her dither, allowing the silence to convince her I knew what I was talking about. I was serious about us needing to stick together, but I could see she was still debating.

Over her shoulder, outside of the window she was standing in front of, I saw a bounce of blond ringlets.

"Daisy."

"Excuse me?" Stormy asked.

"See that woman?" I pointed out the window. "She's a reporter, and a very bad one. If you want everyone in town to know that the mayor's daughter is here, we should hang out here a little longer. Otherwise, I suggest you come with me."

I heard her swallow.

"Let me be clear," I continued. "Unless you want to see the headline *Mysterious Heir Found in Mayor's Lair* on the web version of the *Prosperity Post*, we need to leave. Now."

"Did you make that up right this minute?"

"This bird nerd's also a word nerd," I said.

She shouldered her way past me toward the back door. "I

want answers, so I'm willing to partner up. But the minute things get weird, I'm calling the police."

"Oh, Stormy." I signaled to Waggery to jump onto my shoulder. "Things are already weird."

It didn't occur to me until much, much later that Stormy had deflected the most important question I'd asked her:

Was she the murderer?

* * *

"Miriam is going to be enraged about this memo," I said as we sneaked out of Mayor Brix's neighborhood. We'd managed to squeak past Daisy, but I didn't feel the need to tempt fate. We kept a brisk pace. I kept looking over my shoulder for that springy hair.

"Why would anyone care about this?" Stormy asked.

Since I kept my clients' readings private, I couldn't divulge too much information to Stormy about what I saw this morning in Miriam's cards, and what it might mean for her state of mind. But I secretly wondered if this shady action by the town council was the reason Miriam was on a rampage.

"I can't say," I said. "She's a client and I have some inside info that I need to keep confidential."

"Miriam is who, exactly?"

"Miriam Cringe. Five feet of toxic language and misplaced rage. She's my regular Tuesday appointment. She's lived here forever, and what I can tell you is that she's on a mission to get the duck pond filled in and turned into a community garden."

"You mean the lovely, photogenic water feature in the center of town? She's opposed to that? She's anti-charm?"

"She thinks it's smelly." I wrinkled my nose in a way that I hoped was cute.

"I don't think this Miriam Cringe and I are going to be friends," she said.

"I don't think so either," I said. "She didn't like your father."

"You don't think?"

"She carries a claw hammer in a library tote," I said. "She's got issues."

"Don't we all?"

She had me there.

* * *

"Melvin, if those delphiniums droop a single inch—a single micro-meter—onto my property, I am going to hit you with a fine so big your great-grandchildren will still be digging out of your debt."

Miriam was shouting at her neighbor, who seemed to wilt at every word. "I mean it. And you know the rules state no purple flowers. Why do you always make me report you?"

After taking a circuitous route that successfully kept us out of sight of local law enforcement and that skulking muckraker Daisy Chatterly, we located Miriam at the Hoggarty Homes condo complex, where she was president of the homeowner's association. She lorded over the residents of Hoggarty Homes with an unrelenting iron fist. I had a feeling the sun called Miriam every morning to ask permission to rise there.

"Miriam?"

She whipped around. "What is it? Oh, you and that gargoyle. He'd better not get into my begonias."

"What would Waggery do in your begonias?" I asked, exasperated already.

She leered at him. "Poke? Peck? Pluck?"

"Yeah, that's not normally his thing," I said. "Listen Miriam, this is Stormy Portwood, a friend of mine from out of town."

She squinted. "He looks like a pirate."

"*She*," I looked at Stormy and she gave a nod to confirm, "is here helping me trying to piece some things together. Did you visit town hall this morning?"

She took a step toward me and leaned in. "Why?"

"Did you see the mayor?"

"I don't like where this is going," she said. "Who are you to come here and accuse me of things?"

"Where are you going?" Stormy asked.

"What do you mean?" Miriam took a step toward Stormy.

Stormy pointed to a burgundy minivan with the hatch open and some rolled up papers inside. "Is that your van?"

"That's none of your business. I don't even know you."

"I think it is my business," I said. "The mayor's dead, and I think you might know what happened. You leaving town?"

The question shot out in a tone more hostile than I had intended. Normally I was better at phrasing things to coax information rather than demand. I was trying to look tough in front of Stormy, but I didn't wear it well.

"How dare you. You. You—"

"I know that you and the mayor were locked in conflict over the duck pond," I said, a hint more softly. "And, Miriam, you do walk around with a hammer in your bag."

"Well, look at you, Psychic Friends Network." She looked me up and down with an expression like she'd smelled hot garbage.

"Not psychic."

"You must not be," she said. "Because you would've known I heard you yelling at him all the way out on the plaza. Your voice carries."

Stormy and I looked at each other with raised eyebrows, silently acknowledging the pun. I dared not laugh.

"The whole town knows you were there," she continued.

"You went there this morning," I said. "You were going to 'surprise' him. 'Beat some sense into him' is how you phrased it."

"So, you don't deny it, eh princess? That you and your good friend Mayor Preston Brix got in an argument this morning?" She emphasized the word "friend."

"That's not—Wait, I do deny it," I said. "Waggery and I were there this morning, but we couldn't get in. The door was locked. And if you heard yelling, that means that you were at least close by. With your hammer."

Miriam was a loud person, and she never hesitated to use her voice to intimidate and frighten. When she stepped toward me and spoke in a soft, modulated tone, so sure of herself, I hyperventilated a little.

"I guess you aren't psychic," she said, seething. "Because if you were, you would know that your precious mayor was stabbed." She mimicked a stabbing motion in the air. I took a step back.

"Oh, no," Stormy said, sucking in her breath.

She grabbed my hand. She was shaking. Her palm was clammy. Her grip was powerful.

"And if you're looking to get the police to look at someone other than you," Miriam continued in her malevolent tone, despite Stormy's visible distress over hearing that her father had been stabbed. "I highly recommend you talk to Prosperity's sweetheart, Emma Fort-Knightly."

"Emma? Why?" I asked.

"Oh, another thing you didn't know?" she said. "I'm going to have to take my business elsewhere if you can't even predict the obvious. You read her cards, too, don't you?"

"Miriam, please," I said, my lips trembling. "What are you saying right now?"

"I'm saying that Ms. Fort-Knightly might know exactly what happened to the mayor."

"Why?" I asked.

"Because she's his girlfriend."

§

"What does it mean when the cards are upside down?" I asked, eyeballing a spread that Aunt Inez had placed on the table in front of me.

"It means someone's going to die," she said without looking up. "Obviously."

"Whoa," I said. "Is it, like, one reversed card equals one dead person, or—."

She continued perusing the cards.

"—because this spread has, like, six dead people if that's the case. Are six total people going to, you know, drop dead?"

She looked up and laughed. "I'm joking, Carrie. If you'd done the studying I'd asked you to do, you'd know that 'upside down' cards are called 'reversals' and they mean a couple of different things."

"Like what?" I asked quickly so that she wouldn't get hung up on the discovery that I hadn't done the reading.

"A reversal is a wake-up call," she said. "Kind of like a little kid hanging upside down on the jungle gym, screaming at her aunt to look at her. A reversed card is an alarm."

"Is a reversal bad?"

"Not always," she said. "Essentially, they mean the opposite of what their upright meaning is. But that comes with lots of 'what ifs' that you'll understand better as you learn more."

"What kind of 'what ifs?'"

"Good question," she said. I beamed. There was nothing more fulfilling than praise from Aunt Inez. "First of all, it's important to know that although the reversed card asks you to consider the opposite interpretation from the upright card, it's not

necessarily an exact opposite reading. Sometimes it's a weaker outcome. Make sense?"

"If I get the Sun card, which is a happy, positive card that means 'yes', but it's reversed, it doesn't mean that it's a sad reading that means 'no'?"

"Correct," she said. "That one would still be 'happy,' as you said, but not as intense. You could interpret it as 'satisfying' rather than 'joyful.' It all depends on the context of the reading, the framing of the question, and all the other cards in the spread. Still a 'yes,' but it has a hint of 'maybe'."

"But it would also work the other way," I said. "If there's a darker card, one with more negative energy, the reverse could lessen the impact or mean the opposite."

"You're getting it," she said. "Quick study."

"I can ignore reversals for now, though, right?"

"Also, yes," she said. "You can read everything as upright while you're still learning. There will be plenty of time for opposites, shadow sides, alternative readings, and darkness. Everyone should bask in the light while they still can."

§

Chapter Six

If my head was spinning, Stormy's must have been about to pop right off her neck and fly around the block.

"That was a lot of information all at once," I said. "You got nuked."

"I hope I can trust you," she said, her voice weaker than I had heard so far. "I don't understand what's happening. I didn't ask for any of this."

"You can trust me," I reassured her. "I have a lot on the line here, too. Let's keep moving. Let's go see Emma."

"You know her?"

It dawned on me how distressed Stormy must be. I didn't know yet why she had come here to see her father, but no matter what that reason was, she was confronted with his brutal murder instead. And since she didn't know him very well, she was reliant on strangers to get answers.

I tried to meet her gaze, to show her understood, but I could see she wasn't ready. She closed her eyes and took a deep breath. I wondered where her mind went, but I wouldn't have dreamed of asking. Despite feeling drawn to her, Stormy Portwood was a stranger to me. Plus, my attraction to her was so strong that I was in deep denial that she may have played a role in this.

I was committed to solving this to keep my name and reputation out of the mouths of the town gossips—not to mention the real possibility of being wrongly accused—but I was also powerfully motivated to prove to myself that she was innocent, too. Perhaps it was because of a metaphysical connection, a "love at first sight" experience. Maybe it's because I had lost both parents and felt protective. I didn't know, but it didn't matter. I was all in.

If Mayor Preston Brix was still alive, I would've given him a piece of my mind. Who did he think he was, leaving his daughter to fend for herself like this? And never mentioning her to anyone?

"I know everyone," I said. "Emma's a friend and a client. And she was on the plaza earlier."

"You saw her this morning?"

"Our town gossips did. Walker and Lister. They own the Daily Grind, the coffee shop where Waggery smooched you. But I will say this: Emma's got a reputation as far as her relationships are concerned. She can be volatile."

"And she was dating my father." Stormy said this in a way that showed me she was trying to put some puzzle pieces together. "You didn't know." A statement. Not a question.

"I didn't." And that was true. I'd read her cards recently, where her question was "Will he or won't he?" But she wouldn't tell me who her latest victim, I mean boyfriend, was, and I didn't ask. Emma had a habit of making more of relationships than they were. But in this case, she pulled a Lovers card next to the Ten of Cups. The combination of a pair of lovers standing in a garden while being blessed by an angel placed next to the image of a happy family rejoicing under a rainbow, indicated that she was in a relationship destined for marriage.

"Oh, Carrie," she had said, her beautiful, heart-shaped face aglow, her strawberry hair reflecting the sunlight as it poured in through the cottage's bay window. "I knew it. I knew he was the one."

A curveball. Her future card was the Wheel of Fortune, reversed. This card is exactly what it sounds like: Spin it and hope for the best—but expect the worst. When it's upright in your spread, good luck is likely. But when it's reversed, it probably means that bad luck is on the horizon. I gently warned her that things may not go as planned.

"As long as he proposes," she said, "I don't care what happens next."

"Famous last words," I remember saying.

I wished I could tell Stormy, but there were still some rules I wasn't willing to break. Yet.

"I don't know anything anymore," Stormy said. She looked at me intently, possibly noticing that I, too, was putting puzzle pieces together. Pieces that I would never be able to share with her.

She appeared to be waiting for me to say something, and when I didn't, she said, "I don't even know you."

* * *

On our way to Emma's, Waggery—who was clearly bored by all this shoulder-sitting while I ping-ponged around town—took off toward the plaza.

"You let him fly off on his own like that?" Stormy watched him sail from branch to branch.

"I don't have much choice. Waggery does what he wants when he wants."

"Aren't you worried he won't come back?"

"All the time," I said. "I worry about predators, injuries,

well-meaning people who might feed him something poisonous."

"That's a lot to be responsible for," she said.

"It's hard having a raven. I never recommend to anyone that they get a pet raven," I said. "When he's not trying to escape me, he's complaining that I'm not around enough. They are happiest in pairs, so I think he views me as a twin. So, yes. I worry when he flies free. But I also learned that neither worry nor hand-wringing brings him home faster. And giving chase makes him think it's a game. Waggery's a clever cookie, though. He stays in this area, and he usually visits Ligeia."

"What's Ligeia?"

"She's a duck."

"What?"

"His girlfriend."

"Wait, what? Your raven has a girlfriend. And she's a duck."

"Yes. My raven has more romance in his life than I do," I said.

"That's nest up," Stormy said. She had a look on her face like she'd purposely broken something in my house and was waiting for me to react.

"Waddle you do?" I said, taking the opportunity to play along. I wasn't accustomed to having these kinds of conversations in Prosperity. "Egg-cept wait for the right one?"

"*Eider* know," she said, clearly trying to impress me with some deep-duck knowledge. "I'm down to find out, though."

"Whoa," I said. My knees wobbled. "That's a deep dive."

We stared at each other as if we were each seeing our own reflections for the first time after getting out of prison. Who was this strange, corny creature gazing at me?

I snapped myself out of it. I couldn't afford to get distracted. Not until we got to the bottom of this.

"That was fun," I said. "But right now, we have a date of our own. With Emma."

* * *

Despite coming across as a man-crazy stalker, Emma Fort-Knightly was one of the smartest and most successful long-time residents of Prosperity.

Her roster of accounting clients included nearly everyone in town, from the old-school watering holes like High on the Hoggarty to the brand new, ultra-posh boutiques and bistros that were popping up (like blisters, Miriam once said) in every corner of town.

She may have worn skirts tight enough to choke a python and she may have thrown herself at every eligible bachelor to ever drive through Prosperity in a souped-up sports car, but if you wanted to save money on your taxes or find corners to cut to keep your books in the black, Emma Fort-Knightly was the expert you called.

In fact, she'd offered to pay me in trade for readings, to help me "find ways around those pesky loans you're paying off" and "create a budget that works for someone in your circumstances," but I always declined. Right or wrong, shortsighted or not, at this stage in my life I preferred to be handed cash, not promises.

I knocked on the door. No answer.

I fidgeted. I looked over my shoulder.

"What's going on?" Stormy asked. "Why are you acting so paranoid?"

"Is it paranoia if someone's after you?" I asked. "I don't know about you, but I'm not ready to explain to Daisy Chatterly why we're scurrying all over town trying to scoop evidence before she does. That bouncing blonde bob of doom could totally monkey up the works. Plus, let's not forget the cops."

Stormy swallowed hard. "Yeah, that wouldn't be good. *Mayor Scare: Snooping Pair Beware Villain with Fair Hair.*

"Ouch," I said. "You'll get it. I've been practicing for a lot longer." I thought it was funny, but I wanted to keep her on her toes. *Carrie on: No Shame in Local Girl's Flirt Game.*

Stormy turned bright red. But before I could say anything, she changed the subject.

"Knock again," she said. "You sure she's here?"

"Her car's parked in the driveway," I said, pointing to her late-model Mercedes.

"Fancy," Stormy said.

"You have no idea."

I knocked again. I heard some commotion in the house.

Now Stormy was fidgeting. She cracked her knuckles. She stood on tiptoes and craned her neck to look down the street. "Maybe call her name? I keep thinking I see ringlets on the horizon."

"I'll try one more time," I said.

I rang the doorbell, and Emma opened the door.

She looked flushed. Her eyes were red from crying. "Oh, Carrie. It's you. Sorry, I was taking out the recycling. I tidy when I get upset."

"This is my friend Stormy," I continued, intentionally keeping her parentage to myself. I wasn't sure, knowing what I knew, how Emma would react to this information—or if she knew the mayor had a daughter at all. "Can we come in?" I took one more visual sweep of the street. "Right now?"

"I didn't know you had a...special friend," Emma said, her eyes twinkling. Even in her grief, Emma loved love. She motioned for us to enter.

"Nice to meet you." Stormy reached her hand out. I watched carefully to see her reaction. I was impressed at how neutral she came across. If I had learned a fraction of the information she'd learned today, there's no way I could have played it this cool.

"Did you see him today?" I asked. "The mayor?"

"Do you girls want some tea?" Emma asked.

"No. Thank you," I answered. "I'm trying to get some answers about what happened to the mayor. I know you do his taxes. Do you know if he was involved in anything that someone would have wanted to keep quiet?"

"That's rich coming from you," she said.

"What do you mean?"

"I mean, he sure spent a lot of time with you. And loaned you money."

"Whoa," I said. "What's this about? You and I both know I had nothing to do with this."

I checked to see how Stormy was registering this information. She was serving a practiced poker face.

"What about the yelling?" she said, her eyes filling with tears. "Everyone heard you and the mayor screaming at each other. Then, silence. And you ran out."

I sighed. "Waggery thought it was a game. You know he can mimic voices."

She dabbed her eyes with a tissue. "You've got to stop taking that bird with you everywhere."

I started to defend Waggery when Stormy interrupted.

"Did you know the mayor well?" Stormy asked. Her toughness continued to surprise me.

Knowing Emma as well as I did, I would've chosen a softer tactic, but I waited for the answer. I had to allow that this was as much Stormy's story—if not more so—than mine.

"If you see someone's tax returns, you know everything about them," she said. "What they value, where they go, and with whom. A tax return is a window into someone's soul. Kind of like Carrie's cards, but with money."

"Spoken like a true accountant," Stormy said, leaning against Emma's marble countertops and crossing her arms.

"Who are you again?" Emma asked. She looked at me. "Who is this again?"

"I'm Stormy Portwood," she said. "And I'm the mayor's daughter."

Emma's jaw dropped. "His what?"

"I'm the mayor's daughter."

"His daughter," Emma said, her face going blank. She slumped into a chair. "Stormy Portwood is his daughter."

Stormy and I looked at each other. Emma stared into space, worrying a crumpled tissue in her hands.

The silence became unbearable. A police jalopy passed by, clearly discernible because of the chugging sound of the old-timey motor, and Stormy stepped away from the window.

"*When you're stuck, it doesn't matter which direction you go, as long as it's forward,*" Aunt Inez used to say. I pressed on.

"Emma, we know you were dating the mayor," I said, gently, unsure of how this revelation would land.

"Who told you?" she asked. "We didn't want anyone to know."

"It was Miriam," I said. "I understand that you want to keep this private. But you can recognize how high the stakes are for me right now. I've got Daisy dictating headlines about me into her notes app. Walker and Lister are telling everyone who orders a macchiato that I worship Satan, and Grist told the cops I owe the mayor money. I'm trying to find out the truth so I can clear my name."

"Ugh, Miriam," she said, scowling. "She caught us together and was practically blackmailing us."

"Blackmailing you? How?" I asked.

She waved off my question. "We were going to get married." Tears streamed down her face, taking her mascara with them, and somehow making her appear more glamorous and more vulnerable at the same time. "All I've ever wanted is to get married. All of this," Emma motioned to her well-appointed home, "is meaningless without someone to share my life with. We had plans. For ourselves. For the future. For Prosperity."

Sitting in her throne-like chair, wearing her designer dress, Emma embodied the Empress card. She reveled in luxury and had very fine, expensive taste. Her walls were a gallery of beautiful art; her garden was meticulously maintained. Everything that surrounded her was feminine but tasteful, no ruffles, frills, or cheap, girlie gewgaws. I always believed that she deserved a partner who could appreciate her ability to manifest beauty and abundance. Her only problem was the reverse Empress aspect of her personality, which caused her to put her love interests' needs before her own and to be overly critical of her own appearance. She was bright, successful, sophisticated—and painfully insecure.

"Why were you keeping your relationship a secret?" Stormy demanded.

"Your father liked his secrets," she said, making direct eye contact with Stormy.

"Touché," said Stormy.

"I'm sorry," she continued, shaking her head as if she were trying to rid herself of unpleasant thoughts. "This is all so much. The mayor wanted to keep our relationship on the down-low until he announced he was running again. Something about weddings getting good press. He was always thinking about the next campaign. I didn't mind that much. I wanted whatever he wanted."

"Had he proposed to you yet?" Stormy asked.

"I thought he was going to do it this weekend, after the Wine Museum opening. He's been so busy with Flynt Burns and your Uncle Grist getting that ready, that I thought for sure once that was behind him, he'd propose, and we could start planning the press release."

"That's the most romantic thing I've ever heard," Stormy said. She rolled her eyes and her lip curled in disgust. "A press release. That sounds like him."

"What do you know about it? Emma snapped. "We were getting married by the duck pond as soon as the renovations were complete. Wine Country Weddings was planning a cover story."

"You knew about that?" I asked.

"I called them myself," she said. "They couldn't wait to schedule our photo shoot—"

"No, not about the magazine cover. About the duck pond expansion."

"I did," she said. "But how do you know about it? It was another one of the mayor's secrets. Surprises, I should say. He liked to think of it as a gift for the town."

Was Emma in on the secret expansion plans because she wanted to get married there? Or did the mayor tell her what he was doing? Emma had always upheld high professional standards, so it didn't feel right that she would be okay with the mayor pulling a fast one. I tried to formulate a question, but I was in shock.

"Do you know why the mayor came to Mariner's Cove last week?" Stormy broke the silence. "Did he tell you?"

This was news to me, too. Although I couldn't think of a reason why the mayor would need to tell me all his travel plans. We were good friends, but we weren't intimate confidants. There were plenty of things we didn't know about each other, I imagined.

"Mariner's Cove?" Emma asked. "He was in Mariner's Cove last week? He told me he was meeting with an investment firm in L.A."

"He could have been anywhere, though," said Stormy. She seemed to take some devious pleasure in needling Emma. "He had a whole daughter he never mentioned to the woman he planned to marry. I wonder why that is. Was he afraid of you?"

"I won't dignify that," she said. "I think I'm going to have to ask you to leave."

"Emma, no one is accusing you of anything," I said. "The mayor—Stormy's father—was stabbed to death this morning and everyone is trying to find the truth. We're simply trying to piece together what happened."

"I lost the love of my life," she said. "My Lovers card, right Carrie? Remember, it was in my last reading?"

I reached out and took her hand. "I remember, Emma."

"I need time to mourn, please," she said, the tears starting again. "If you hear anything, please let me know."

"I will," I said.

"I'm sorry things got tense," Stormy said. "It's been a tough day."

"I understand," Emma said, softening. "You lost a father, and I'm so sorry about that."

"Thank you," she said.

"But wait. Carrie, you mentioned he'd been stabbed?" Emma sat up straight in her chair.

"That's what Miriam told me."

"How did she know that?" Emma asked. "As far as I know, Officer Bucket hasn't shared a cause of death yet."

"Maybe she talked to him earlier?" My head was spinning.

"Officer Bucket said he would call me the minute they could release the information. We had a little fling back in the day. There's no way he told anyone before me. Especially not Miriam, not after she had his jalopy towed from in front of her condo complex that one time."

My breath left my body. Miriam.

"I think we let her get away," I said.

"What do you mean?" Emma asked.

"She left town," Stormy said. "Her van was all packed up."

"Fat chance," Emma said, leaning back and crossing her arms. "I know for a fact she's got a homeowner's association meeting tonight because I delivered the financial statements to her myself yesterday. She never misses a chance to lord over everyone in those meetings. If Miriam left, it's because she's on the lam."

Chapter Seven

As we left Emma's, I scanned the trees for Waggery. No luck. I'd usually seek him out immediately, but I ignored my own instincts, believing it was better if Stormy and I kept to the side streets and out of the curious gaze of town gossips, the police, the actual murderer, or worse, Daisy.

"I'm starving," said Stormy. "All this running around. Can we get a bite to eat?"

"Of course," I said. "I'd like to track down Waggery, but let's snack up and map out a strategy. I can't believe we let Miriam get away."

We stuck to the back streets on our way to High on the Hoggarty, and I was relieved that we didn't encounter anyone on the way. On any other day, I would have thought it was a shame that more people didn't know about Prosperity's hidden corners. The route we took was out of the way of the tourist area, through narrow alleyways in the original cobblestones, under arches festooned with ostentatious sprays of bougainvillea, and past small grottoes with trickling fountains filled with bathing house sparrows and goldfinches. Prosperity's workers, who manned the expensive downtown boutiques, would hide away here for homemade picnic lunches out of the demanding eyes of their moneyed customers.

"I've never seen any of this," Stormy said, her eyes wide. "This place is like living in a postcard."

"Prosperity is filled with secret corners," I said. "And no shortage of charm. But today's not about sightseeing. I'm trying to maintain our cover."

"Roger that," Stormy said. "When we sort this out, I'll come back, and you can take me on the local's tour."

I tried not to skip.

This was serious.

Focus, Carrie.

We arrived unseen at the doorway of High on the Hoggarty and, after I checked to confirm that there were no officers or reporters inside, I motioned for Stormy to go in. "I'm friends with the owner," I told her. "It's not the fanciest place, and we had a fight earlier, but it's still my favorite hangout. We can sit in the back, where it's even darker than the rest of the room."

"What friends?" she asked as she slid into a booth.

"It's not like that. Hank took me to prom our senior year. We were each other's first friends, and he often ran interference for me when Daisy and her gang of girl thugs taunted me. I come here because he gives me free grilled cheese sandwiches."

"What a friend we have in cheeses," she said.

"Cheeses love me," I said.

"You're kind of a big cheese," she said.

How could anyone refuse the charms of this woman?

"Hi, Carrie. What a day, am I right?" It was Hank's one waitress, Ayesha. "Everyone's talking about this business with the mayor. It's crazy to think there's a murderer on the loose. We're all looking over our shoulders. Daisy came by looking for you. I told her you ran in, grabbed a broom, and flew out the front door."

"Oh, no," I said. "Normally I'd appreciate the effort, but Daisy has it in for me this time. If she comes back, tell her I returned the broom, ok?"

"You got it," she said.

"Is Hank here? We had a spat this morning, and I wanted to make up."

"You two fight like siblings," she said. "It's ridiculous."

"Is he here?"

"He took off a little while ago, something about 'making this right'. I thought he went to your house, honestly. He hasn't been back. He did not take a broom."

"If he shows up, tell him I'm here."

"Sure." She leaned in and spoke in a conspiratorial tone. "You want something fancier than a grilled cheese? On the house."

"I can't—" I said.

"I'll get this," Stormy said. "Order what you like."

My cheeks flushed. I wanted to slide under the table. "No, no. Of course not. I'll have a burger. Put it all on my tab and I'll tell Hank I'll get it later."

"I don't mind," Stormy said.

"I do," I said.

"How about I get you both burgers and you can sort this out yourselves," Ayesha offered. She took our menus and left us to our conversation.

"This is so embarrassing," I said. "Everyone in town knows I'm broke."

"Broke? What happened?" Stormy asked. "You don't strike me as someone who'd invest in bitcoin or waste your weekends in front of a slot machine."

"It's a combination of things," I explained. "I took out loans to pay for Stanford."

"Stanford? You must've done well in high school."

"I like how you didn't assume I was smart, but that I 'did well in high school.' I laughed. "There's some truth to that."

"That's not what I meant," she said. "I'm admiring your intellect. My friends are smart, some of them are highly educated, but they lack refinement. It's refreshing."

"I guess it's better than saying 'you clearly cheated or donated a medical lab to get into Stanford,'" I joked.

She smiled and my heart skipped.

"Good point," she said.

"The plan was that I would take out the loans for the tuition, I'd get some amazing job right out of school and my Aunt Inez, who raised me, would help me pay them off with her savings. We had a schedule mapped out and everything—the perfect plan."

"Sounds reasonable," said Stormy.

"You'd think so," I said. "But she got sick. Her medical bills ate up her savings. No health insurance."

"Medicare?"

"She was only sixty."

"Oh, no." Her brow creased. "That's young."

"It was a blow. The illness was long and mysterious. The doctors never told me definitively what was wrong with her. The tests, the medications—we blew through her savings in a few months."

"I'm so sorry," she said.

"She left me her cottage. And I promised I would stay there as long as Waggery lived so that he would be taken care of. He's special, as you can see."

"It's paid off? That's a major bonus."

"It is," I said. "Taxes are steep in Prosperity. Someone's got to pay to fill those potholes, I guess. I get behind, but I always figure it out."

"What about getting a higher paying job? You could use your fancy degree."

"I have an English degree."

"Ouch."

I let out a sigh. "Plus, I need to be home with Waggery. It's like having a second grader."

"One who flies. And speaks in code."

"Exactly," I said. "But I don't want to give the impression that I'm not happy. When I'm not trying to make sure my name isn't associated with gossip about actual murder, I have a lovely, low-key life. What about you? What's life like in Mariner's Cove? I've only been a few times, but it seems rather dramatic. Plunging cliffs, crashing waves, that sort of thing. Skullduggery, secrets, and revenge lurking around every foggy corner."

"We should make some kind of list," she said, ignoring my question.

"Of what?" I asked.

"People who knew my father. Motive, that sort of thing."

"Good idea," I said. I was disappointed that she didn't take the bait—I was dying to know more about her. But I agreed we needed to get organized. "It's got to be Miriam, though, right? I hate to say it, but she's a loose cannon who carries a deadly weapon in a canvas sack."

Ayesha brought the burgers. I asked her for a pen and a cocktail napkin, and she obliged.

I wrote Miriam at the top of the list.

"I get that she's a raving lunatic who carries a hammer in her bag, but what's her real motive? What would make her kill someone?" Stormy asked.

"She's a handful," I agreed. "But her husband died last year, and she used the insurance money to finally buy a condo. She feels like she must make sure everything's perfect in her neighborhood—and by extension her town—or she'll be disrespecting his memory."

"That's a lot of baggage," Stormy said. "But she literally had baggage on her way out of town right after a suspicious interaction with my father. "

"True. It doesn't look good."

"What about motive?"

"She has it in for those ducks," I said.

"Are you suggesting my father was killed over his desire to create a delightful destination for families and visitors, and a memorable wedding venue for his beautiful bride?"

"When you say it like that it sounds extreme. But all the evidence points to her."

"For the sake of the exercise, who else had a conflict with my father?" she asked.

"If I'm being perfectly candid, a lot of people did."

"Not surprised," she said. "I didn't see him much when I was growing up, but when we did spend time together everything was always about him. That he made some enemies here makes sense."

"If we're taking the broad view of who might be mad at the mayor, we've got Miriam, Emma, Hank, Walker and Lister from the coffeeshop, Flynt Burns, and Waggery."

"Waggery?"

"The mayor said rude things about him. But he was with me all day, so he has a rock-solid alibi."

"Who is Clint Ferns?"

"Flynt Burns."

"Whatever. What's his problem?"

"I like Flynt," I said. "He hired Grist to curate and plan the exhibits for the Wine Museum. He's been a great friend to me and my whole family."

"But we're not talking about that, Carrie," she said. "Why did you put him on the list?"

"Proximity, mostly? Flynt is like the mayor in a lot of ways. He's full of whiz-bang marketing ideas, but he relies on steadier, more grounded people like Grist to get the job done. For the most part, though, he and the mayor were in lockstep. Now that I think about it, if Miriam is on a crime spree, he should probably take cover as well."

I wondered if I should warn him.

Instead, I decided to impress Stormy with my tarot knowledge. "Flynt's like the Fool card," I said, between bites. "In tarot. Have you seen it?"

"I haven't," she said.

"The Fool—depicted by a young man flouncing about on the edge of a cliff—encourages leaps of faith and promises fresh starts," I said. "What it doesn't guarantee is follow through. And when it's reversed, it reveals reckless behavior. When you get the Fool in a reading, buckle up because you're in for an unpredictable ride. A fun ride, perhaps. But still a ride."

"Tarot works like a personality test?"

"Not exactly—"

She interrupted me.

"If Lint—"

"Flynt," I corrected her.

"Flynt," she continued, "is the Fool. What's Miriam?"

"That's easy," I said, delighted to get to tell someone new about tarot. "Miriam's a walking, talking Tower card. It shows people being violently flung from a building that's been struck by a bolt of lightning. Its appearance means that an unsettling, hyperspeed change is on the horizon. It's alarming, but I always remind my clients that the change the Tower card portends isn't necessarily negative. Dramatic? Definitely. Terrible? Not always."

Stormy didn't respond to this. I watched her chew her food for what felt like a long time. She was lost in thought.

I couldn't stand the silence. "The only other one who may need to be on the list," I began slowly, testing the waters, "is you."

She sat back and crossed her arms. "Oh, zounds, here we go."

"What I mean is, we should probably walk through your day so that if anyone comes looking for you, we have the story straight. I'm trying to protect you."

"I never should've come here." She balled up her napkin and tossed it onto the table. "This was a mistake."

"We never would have met if you hadn't," I said, hoping to soften her up. "Even though this is a difficult day, I'm glad we met."

"Me too," she said. She leaned toward me ever so slightly. Was this a signal? Was this about to happen? I was so out of practice...

My phone buzzed in my pocket.

"Oh, shoot," I said. "I should get this." I didn't recognize the number.

"Carrie?" the voice sounded familiar.

"Speaking."

"It's Flynt Burns. Grist has been in an accident."

* * *

The last thing I needed to see as Stormy and I raced across the plaza to Hoggarty Hospital was Waggery strutting around the duck pond with a lit cigarette in his mouth.

"Dammit, Waggery," I called. He heard me.

"Oh, no. What are you doing?" he called back, dropping the

cigarette like a teenager busted at a house party. He scurried under a bush.

"I can see you," I said. "Go home right now." I picked up the cigarette, put it out, and threw it in the nearest trashcan.

"Does that work?" Stormy asked.

"I have to put the cigarette completely out, or he'll dig it out of the trash and keep smoking," I said. "It's a nasty habit, but I think he might be hooked."

"No," she said, shaking her head. "Not the cigarette. Does he go home because you tell him to?"

"Sometimes it works, sometimes it doesn't," I said. "I'm hoping he'll go home and wait for me there. I don't have time to fuss with a badly behaved raven right now."

"That seems unlikely," she said. "That he would do that. Fly home because you told him to."

"This whole day is unlikely," I said. "And I have a feeling it's about to get worse."

* * *

When we arrived at the hospital, I texted Flynt to find out Grist's room number. We took the stairs two at a time—I didn't want Stormy to notice that the mural of Prosperity's history that covered the walls of the stairwell had her father's face in it. He and Flynt Burns had both posed as pioneers and they grinned out at viewers from their seat atop a Conestoga Wagon with a sign on it that said *Prosperity or Bust.* Looking at it now seemed grotesque.

We found Flynt easily enough. He was pacing outside room 218, his designer loafers—he called them Italian driving moccasins—making soft padding sounds on the tile floor.

"Where's Grist? What happened?" I peered over Flynt's

shoulder to get a glimpse of Grist through the narrow window in the door. The bed was empty.

"Where is he?"

"Who is this?" Flynt asked, looking back and forth between Stormy and me. "I didn't know you were bringing someone."

Stormy introduced herself.

"What's happening here?" he asked. "Are those tattoos? We could use a tattoo shop in Prosperity to attract the younger crowd. How about you get a tattoo with the Prosperity logo, and I put in on our Instagram?"

"Focus, Flynt," I said. "What's going on with Grist?"

"Do you want to speak in private?" He motioned to an empty corner at the end of the hallway. His watch was the size of a guest soap, and the diamonds twinkled under the fluorescent lights.

"No need," I said. "I want to know what happened to Grist. Out with it."

"I don't know this person, and I don't feel..."

"I'm the mayor's daughter," Stormy interjected.

"The mayor's daughter," he said. "That's you?"

"He told you about me? That's a first."

"No," Flynt said. His eyes shifted back and forth. "Someone else mentioned that the mayor's daughter was in town."

"That's weird," she said. "Who..."

"Let's sort out the mayor's secret family tree another time," I said. "What's happening with Grist?"

"He's having a CT scan and will be back when he's done. I found him."

"Found him where?" I asked.

"In the Wine Museum. I told him he needed to secure that shelf where the hundred-year-old Imperial of Hoggarty Heaven Estate and Winery Cabernet Sauvignon was displayed, but I guess he never got around to it. Fell right on him."

"What's an Imperial?" Stormy asked. "Is that a kind of tarot card?"

"It's a six-liter bottle of wine," I explained. "They weigh about thirty pounds." My heart sank. Grist was probably seriously injured.

"You know what you should do, Carrie? You should create a line of tarot cards that feature wine bottles," Flynt said. I could almost hear the gears turning inside his head. "And you could use the faces of Prosperity residents and business owners for the people. We could sell them in the Visitors Center."

"Now's also not the time for your marketing ideas, as much as I appreciate them," I said. "Is it a head injury or something worse? That bottle was huge."

"I told him to secure it," Flynt said. Beads of sweat glistened on his forehead. "I'm sure I have a work order or voice mail or something that proves it. Somewhere."

"Relax. I'm not going to sue you. I don't think Uncle Grist is going to sue you either."

"What a relief," he said. "I'm upset. It's been a difficult day, what with the mayor—."

"It has," said Stormy. "I'm exhausted."

"You should go home and rest," he said. "I can call you when Grist gets back. When we have more information."

"I don't know," I said. "I don't want him to wake up alone. And I should talk to the doctor."

The truth is that I didn't want to be there, in the same hospital where Aunt Inez died, for another second. But my worry for Grist overwhelmed my need to flee.

"The doctor is on her rounds," said Flynt. "And I'll stay here for Grist. I'll ring you the minute he's ready to see visitors."

"I don't want to tell you what to do, Carrie," Stormy interjected. "But Waggery is still out flying around unattended. And smoking like a 1950s gang member. You should at least make sure he's home safe. It's what I would do."

"You're right," I said, equal parts frustrated and relieved. "The last thing I need is for him to get into trouble. Or run into Miriam."

"Don't want them to get into a flap, eh." said Flynt. "It would be murder."

I had to hand it to Flynt. To be that unaware of where charming ends and annoying begins is a skill most can't claim. He had permanent foot-in-mouth disease.

"Super bad timing for that joke, dude," Stormy said. "Plus, a group of ravens is a conspiracy. Crows are a murder. Waggery is a raven."

I fell head over heels for Stormy Portwood.

I took Stormy's hand in mine.

"Let's go home."

Chapter Eight

The ladies from the Prosperity Historical Society loved exactly three things: One, the history of Prosperity. Two, anything tangentially related to the history of Prosperity. And three, my Uncle Grist.

If a gathering of ravens is called a "conspiracy," a gathering of Prosperity Historical Society members would be called a "groupie." And Grist's groupies clustered around the hospital reception desk, the scent of Aqua Net and White Diamonds announcing their presence before I saw them.

"Oh Carrie, this is terrible," cried Lillian Valli. Lillian was a fixture in my life, always on the spot when someone fell ill. Her lasagnas, chicken salads, and cookies were the only sustenance Grist and I could bring ourselves to eat during Inez's illness. And she made the only broths and soups that Aunt Inez could keep down, especially on her worst days.

Lillian was a godsend. But her feelings toward Grist were obvious: she was the first to show up at Grist's carriage house with a steaming hot green bean casserole after my aunt died. She told him he could keep the dish, and everyone knows what that means.

Despite being transparent in her feelings for Grist, I believed Lillian had nothing but good intentions. Lillian was my Page of Cups, hopeful, excited about the next pleasant thing she was sure would come her way if she was on her best behavior.

"Thanks, Lillian," I said. "I'm still trying to figure out how this could've happened."

"So am I, honey. We all came running down here to comfort him. I brought snickerdoodles." She handed me a pink cardboard box, tied together with her small, signature bouquet of Lilies of the Valley. I remembered the times she brought Inez food alongside a vase filled with these fragrant blooms, and my chest tightened.

"Lillian, you're so thoughtful," I said. "You didn't make these this afternoon, did you?"

"There's a murderer out there, so I decided to stay home and bake," she said. "But when I heard about Grist, nothing could keep me—or any of us—away. We're not going out alone, though. Safety first."

"He'll love it," I said.

"Plus, I need to give him this." She produced Grist's phone from her fanny pack.

"Why do you have his phone?" I asked.

"It must have fallen out of his pocket," she said. "I found it behind the welcome sign in the lobby. I heard it ringing, which was funny because his ring tone is your blackbird, Waverly, saying 'I love you' in your aunt's voice. I nearly jumped out of my skin. I thought she was back from the dead, rest her sweet soul."

I ignored the misinformation in that sentence and took the phone. "I'll take it to him. He's having a CT scan and some tests right now, so I'll leave it next to his bed."

"He's not seeing visitors?" she asked, clearly disappointed.

The other ladies crowded behind her and looked at me with wide eyes, like a mob of meerkats.

"Not yet." I wiggled the phone. "But I'll have him call you as soon as he's able. I'm sure he would love to thank you for bringing this. I hope it wasn't too much of an inconvenience."

"Nothing Grist needs is an inconvenience for me or for any of us. I'm so appreciative of everything he has done for us, and now the museum...He never says no to any request. The last time I saw him was when we were putting the final touches on the displays in the wine museum for Friday's opening. I can't wait for you to see it."

"Are you done?" I asked. "Nothing left to finish up?"

"Only some cleaning and setting up tables for the party, paying the caterers, that sort of thing."

"I can't wait for the opening," I said. "Neither can Grist. He's been working so hard."

"Oh, he sure has, Carrie. I don't know what we'd do without him."

"I feel the same way."

I stood silently watching them file out of the lobby.

Stormy was a shade of gray I'd never seen on a living human.

"What's wrong?" I asked her. "You don't look right."

"I—"

"What is it?"

"I think it's hitting home that my father died," she said. "And seeing all these nice ladies being so thoughtful and caring, it's very touching."

"Let's have a seat to collect ourselves," I said. "We don't need to rush."

We sat down.

"If it makes you feel any better," I said. "I'm also having a tough time. With all of this. The hospital especially."

"It's freaky, isn't it?" she said. "How the smells, the ugly vinyl chairs, the bad lighting—I have a bad feeling."

"I do, too," I said. "But I feel better with you here. Even though we just met."

"Everyone in Prosperity is so... pleasant," she said. "I know that sounds super lame. But I am not used to people looking out for each other. Seeing it here reminds me of what I'm missing."

I hated seeing anyone suffer, but Stormy's vulnerability made me feel like I would do almost anything to defend her. I took her hand in mine. I thought of Inez and the mayor. I thought of Grist. I thought how I should never take for granted how lucky I am to live in this community. It's flawed. But wonderful.

I wished I had my cards so I could pull one to give Stormy some comfort.

"How about, when we get home, I give you a reading," I said. "On the house. It will help clarify why you're here and what you're supposed to accomplish."

"I've never had a reading before," she said. "But I've never done a lot of the things I'm doing today, so sure. Yes. A reading would be great." She wiped her eyes with the inside of her wrist, and I made a mental note to ask her about her raven tattoo later.

"First timer, eh?" I said. "I love a fresh victim. I mean, client."

"You want me to wait here?" Stormy asked. "While you take Grist his phone?"

"I'm keeping the phone," I said. "We're going to go to my house and look through it."

She perked up. "I like how you're thinking. But why?" Stormy asked.

"Lillian said she found the phone at the bottom of the stairs, right?"

"Yeah. That's what she said."

"If Grist was in the exhibit when the bottle fell on him, there's no way he would have dropped it there. Not in that location. Flynt would have taken him down the elevator, not the stairs."

"You don't think that sweet lady—"

"Was lying to me? I hope not. But we might need the phone to find out."

* * *

My mood was all over the place on the six-block walk home from the hospital. On the one hand, I was buoyed by the support of my new love interest from the dramatic seaside destination of Mariner's Cove, who intrigued me with her whip-smart insights and take-no-bull attitude. She was nice to look at, too, and when you're facing a lot of ugliness and deception, having an exquisite, symmetrical face to gaze upon certainly takes the sting out.

On the other hand, the mayor, my friend, and her father, had been malevolently murdered in the middle of the day, in a tourist town with a zero violent crime rate. My stomach churned at the thought.

As we rounded the corner to the cottage, I saw Waggery. He was entertaining himself by rolling a walnut from one of Prosperity's many trees around on the sidewalk, and one of the neighborhood cats was pouncing on it. His antics reminded me of the time when Flynt Burns pulled me aside and said, "You know what you should do? You should video-tape your crow and put him on the internet. People will lose their minds, and you'll make a fortune. We could give you the Prosperity logo for the bottom of the screen to promote the town."

He'd had worse ideas. But when I investigated getting a

decent computer with editing software, I got discouraged because of the expense.

Waggery flew to my forearm and gave me a kiss. "Mwah."

"That's impressive," said Stormy.

"He's a wonderful companion," I said. "Aren't you, Wags?"

He purred.

We went inside, and I fed Waggery some fruit and one of Lillian's snickerdoodles since he was being such a good boy. He settled onto his perch and fell asleep almost instantly.

"He's tuckered," I said. "I can only imagine what he got into when he was out there on his own after all this time."

"Smoking, doing shots with his buddies, maybe some alley dice," Stormy said with a chuckle. "He looks like he was up to no good."

I offered Stormy a seat on the sofa.

"Your place is so homey." She grabbed the throw pillow with the evil eye embroidered on it and held it close. "Especially with that little devil snoring on his perch."

"He snores when he's extra tired," I said. "Aunt Inez was big on creating a welcoming space. Her clients would stay for hours, chatting away until the wee hours of the morning, including your father, way before he was mayor. With me, they tend to get their readings and get on with their lives. I'd love to entertain more, but..." I let that drop. Hearing about people's money woes was tiresome, and I didn't want to scare her off.

"How about a glass of wine?" I offered. "Uncle Grist left some Hoggarty Heaven Chardonnay in the fridge last time he was here."

"I would love some. Look at you. Wine sophisticate. Story-book cottage."

I handed her my tarot deck. "Shuffle these while you sip, and I'll do your reading."

"Shuffle like a regular deck?"

"Exactly," I said.

She shuffled with the skill of a casino dealer. I was so flustered by watching her do, well, anything, that I kept talking to avoid any appearance that I was so dumbstruck.

"How does this work?" She passed the cards through her hands like a pro. "I'm not going to walk out of here with the ability to time-travel or an irresistible desire to howl at the full moon, am I?"

"Those selections cost extra."

"What?"

"Kidding. I don't do spells."

"You don't? Or you can't? You look like the exact opposite of a witch. And this cottage doesn't exactly scream 'full moon incantations.'"

"I love and support my witchy sisters," I said, putting my hand on my heart. "I am all about lovin' the coven. But I don't do spells. Tarot only. What's your question?"

She thought about it. "Will I find what I came for?"

I showed her how to lay the cards down and I considered the three-card spread between us.

"In your past, you've got the Seven of Swords," I said. "See this fella? He's sneaking off and taking something with him. You've either stolen something or are trying to get away with something—or someone did those things to you. You might have a secret."

I stared at her. She was a stone wall.

"Alternatively, someone is keeping a secret from you," I said, taking her silence as a cue to continue. "Either way, you might find yourself resorting to shady behavior to achieve your goal. You're going to need to be smart. Use that brain of yours to sort things out. Does any of that make sense?"

"I never believed in psychics, but this is spot on."

"I'm not psychic," I reminded her. "We're writing a story, not predicting the future."

"I like that," she said. "More, please."

"Here in the present, the Ten of Pentacles—a card that looks like it's raining money—shows that you have or are about to have financial security. It looks generational, like an inheritance or something passed down from someone you're related to."

"Hm. That doesn't sound right," she said with a frown. "Business is good at the shop. I own Think Ink Tattoo in Mariner's Cove."

"That's so impressive. You have your own business. With its own T-shirt."

Stormy did not respond to my breathless praise.

"But I have to work for my money," she continued. "It was me and Mom growing up. We didn't have much."

I had been so focused on Stormy being the mayor's daughter that it felt like a gut punch to realize that he not only abandoned her, but her mother as well. I knew he was shallow and self-serious, that he had political aspirations beyond Prosperity. But I hadn't known he was cruel. Not like this.

"Is your mother still in Mariner's Cove?"

"No," Stormy said.

"What happened?"

"I'm concerned by the word *inheritance*," she said. "Mom already left me everything she had, and that wasn't much."

"Don't get too caught up in my choice of words," I said, wanting to press Stormy about her mother's death, but sensing that she didn't want to discuss it. "Think of how it specifically applies to your life, and if it doesn't make sense, that's normal. It's good to write your reading down and take a photo of your cards. Look back in a few days or even weeks to see how events around your question played out. Remember, it's not a prediction in the magical sense, more of a way of looking at things. Some perspective."

She fished a notepad and pen out of her backpack. She snapped a photo of the spread with her phone.

"But we're not done yet," I said. "Here, in the future position, you've got the Nine of Pentacles. This shows a woman who is financially secure, surrounded by beauty, and in harmony with the natural world. She's standing in a garden with money growing all around her. It's a nice card to get."

"She looks like you," Stormy said. "She's even got a bird."

I was taken aback. I'd never noticed this before.

"She does." I said, picking up the card to give it a closer look. "Although, most days, it feels like the bird has me. I wish I would pull this card. You're going to be successful in your business here, I think. Prosperous in Prosperity."

"Do the cards ever mean anything literal?"

"What do you mean?" I asked.

"Could this beautiful woman on this card mean that there's an actual beautiful woman in my future?"

"If that's what you're looking for," I said, butterflies taking flight around my heart. "You might not need tarot cards for that."

She took a long sip of her wine. We sat in awkward silence.

"This is all so charming," she said. "I'm envious. I live above my tattoo shop."

I was grateful she broke the silence.

"Hank lives above his restaurant, too," I said, in a weird, awkward voice. I was trying too hard to impress her, and I wasn't feeling natural.

"What are you guys fighting about? On today of all days."

"He's an original Hoggarty," I began, relaxing a little bit. "Like the ones whose names are on everything around here. He inherited a fortune in high school when his dad died. He spent money like he was a drunken sailor on leave."

"Sounds amazing," she said.

"Hank and I had some good times. I worked my butt off at Stanford while he jetsetted to tropical locations all over the world. If there was sun, sand, and women, Hank was there."

"My dream come true," she said.

She was so cute when she laughed. Her natural resting expression was serious, intimidating.

"I guess. But when he reappeared, he had nothing but the building where the restaurant is now."

"That would be tough to take," she said. "To go from having it all to having nothing but a dive bar and a chip on your shoulder."

"But that's not all," I said. "Grist lives in the carriage house on Hank's family's estate."

"Why?"

"A couple reasons," I said. "First, Grist grew up there. His dad was the caretaker at Hoggarty Heaven for years. That's how I met Hank. We were two peas in a pod. Next, the Historical Society, those sweet ladies we got the phone from? They essentially own it now. Mayor Brix used his power to seize it as a historical monument when Hank let it fall apart. Grist lives there at the behest of the Historical Society. He's not going anywhere. And Hank is furious."

"So, it's nice?" asked Stormy. "The carriage house?"

"Nice doesn't begin to describe it. It's the dictionary definition of quaint. And Grist takes excellent care of it. When he gets out of the hospital. I'll take you by for tea. He loves serving tea and talking about the history of Prosperity."

"I would like that," she said. "Sounds so...civilized. I hang out with rum-swilling buccaneers."

"That sounds fun, too, matey," I said, hoping she'd invite me to Mariner's Cove.

"But wait," she said. "Hank has a problem with Grist."

"For years," I said. "It's very painful for me. My two favorite people—"

"And Grist is in the hospital."

"What are you getting at?" I could feel my neck tighten.

"Follow along. What did you two fight about this morning?"

"No," I said. I stood up. "No. I won't hear anything bad about Hank." Hank was like a brother to me; I could trash-talk him all I wanted, but if anyone lobbed the slightest criticism his way, I would jump to his defense, even if they were right. Sometimes the more spot-on they were, the angrier I got.

"Carrie, what did you fight about?" Stormy pressed.

"We fought about Grist."

I got up and paced the room.

Waggery sighed deeply and twitched.

"You don't think...?" she began to say something, and I stopped her.

"I don't think," I said. "But I don't know. I've learned today that anything is possible."

"We need to get into his phone," she said. "Right now."

I pulled out the phone.

"Do you know his password?"

My heart was pounding so hard I could feel it in my ears.

I was afraid of what I would find on Grist's phone.

"I can probably figure it out." I took in a deep breath to calm myself. "He's pretty transparent."

I typed in *HOGGARTY*. No luck. Same with *PROSPERITY*.

"That's too long," Stormy said. "Try something shorter."

It became obvious.

INEZ

Nothing.

"Try a symbol."

"Oh. I think I know," I said.

INEZ <3

"Ha. That's it. Can you believe it?" I laughed, happy for the easy win. "He's adorable."

I scrolled through his photos and saw what appeared to be dozens of wine tools, bottles, and memorabilia for the museum. Once I got through all of that, I saw snaps of Waggery eating and playing with his treasure pile, a few of me with expressions that said, "stop taking photos," and an assortment of photos of Aunt Inez I'd never seen before.

"Aw," I said. "There's my Aunt Inez. She's wearing a T-shirt I got her from Stanford. Isn't she sweet?"

"You miss her," she said.

"I do. She was the light of my life. My World card."

"Your World card?"

"I assign cards from the tarot deck to everyone in my life," I explained. "The cards provide us with infinite opportunities to interpret archetypes. I believe everyone's got a card that represents them."

"Kind of like zodiac signs?"

"Exactly." I said, making a mental note to use that reference in the future. "Except you get to pick your own, or in this case, I pick for you in my own, inexact way. In fact, many of the major arcana cards have direct connections to the zodiac. Numerology plays a role, too. The colors of the cards, the symbols in each image—all of it. Studying tarot is a lifelong process."

"Like that lady with the coins holding the bird is you?" she asked.

"Nine of Pentacles, and yes," I said. "Although that's more aspirational. At this point in my life, I'm more like the Hermit."

"What does that mean?"

"I'm spending a lot of time alone, trying to sort out my spiritual and material journey. It's a guy in a robe holding a lantern to light his way."

"That's deep."

I laughed. "I don't know if it's deep as much as it's required." I motioned to the kitchen desk where I tossed all the notices from the collection agencies. "See these?"

"Fan mail?"

"Sort of," I said. "If my biggest fans are my creditors. Sometimes I get behind on payments and I get nasty notes from collection agencies."

"That's crazy. And rude."

"I had to change my phone number last year. And any time I need to use an address for any reason, I use the address at High on the Hoggarty." I'd never told anyone this before, and my face warmed at the admission. My debt was a constant source of shame, and here I was tossing it on the floor in front of her and saying, "look at it."

"Why?"

"Because if they knew my real address, they'd repossess all my things. Hank gives me these notices, and the few times they've shown up, he runs interference for me. He can be scary."

"Damn. What about your car?"

"Oh, hahaha." I laughed in a mocking, hoity-toity tone. "You're adorable. I haven't had a car for years, *dahling*." My face still burned, but I couldn't stop. It was like she'd unplugged a chink in the dam and all my most embarrassing secrets rushed out.

"What happened?" she said. "To look at you, in your cotton frock, manicured garden, and tidy home, I never would have pegged you as a person destined for debtor's prison. I mean, out of the two of us, I'd predict it would be me with the money problems."

"Looks can be deceiving," I said. Did I tell her how hard I worked to look normal? How my poverty and my reputation as a witch made it imperative for me to appear approachable? I felt like I was cracking open, and I was relieved when she changed the subject,

"You're not great with money, but you're skilled at tarot."

"Exactly. I focus on the important things," I laughed. "Tarot. Waggery. Grist. It's an embarrassment of riches."

"What card am I?" She leaned in.

"Are we done talking about me?" I asked. It was meant as a joke, but no one had spent this much time asking about me in ages. I reveled in the attention but felt repulsed by my willing-ness to spill my secrets. She was keeping hers. Why couldn't I hold anything back? "I've only known you a short time," I began. "But if I had to make a call..."

"Be nice." she said, laughing. She pulled her legs up, criss-cross-applesauce and leaned toward me.

"I'm always nice. There are no bad cards," I explained. "Only bad people."

"Wait, what?"

"I'm joking," I said. "No need to worry." I mocked sizing her up. "So, if I had to pick right now, I would say you're the Strength card."

"Because of my huge muscles, naturally." She flexed her arms.

"It's all about personal power," I said. "You came here to claim something, and when things got painful, you stuck it out, trusted a stranger, and set out to make it right. To me, you are strength. It's got an image of a woman taming a lion." I pulled the card from the deck to show her.

"See?" I said. "There's an infinity symbol over her head. She's very cool."

Exactly like Grist's Magician card, I realized. Both cards have the same infinity symbol over the character's head. But I kept this thought to myself.

"That might be the nicest thing anyone has ever said to me," she said. "There's that Prosperity sweetness again. I never realized I needed this so much."

"You have me now," I said, fully ready to take any invitation she extended to me.

She stepped toward me.

I nearly burst out giggling from glee.

"I love you," Waggery, doing a spot-on impression of my aunt's voice, broke the silence. "I love you. I love you."

"Grist's phone is ringing," I said, awkwardly fumbling to answer it. "Hello?"

I heard static, and a voice that sounded like it was inside a tin can. "Grist, yeah, hi. This is LeMarcus Green, the antiques guy. Can you hear me? I'm driving."

"LeMarcus?" It was a name I didn't recognize.

"Sounds good," he continued. "Listen, those things you sent photos of from your museum? Those are fakes. You were right. I looked at all the images and I can say with ninety-nine percent certainty that those things are not the original items I scouted for you and that you purchased."

"LeMarcus, wait—"

"You bet it was," he said through scratchy static. "Sorry to tell you that. But it's a good thing you called me. You'd be sitting on top of a phony museum if you didn't let me take a look. I was planning on coming up for the opening on Friday, but you're going to need to sort this out. I don't know what happened."

"LeMarcus?" I was trying to interject. What was he talking about?

"You got that right," he said, completely oblivious to the fact that he wasn't speaking to Grist. "I'm heading to Mariner's Cove to drop off some stuff for a lady there. I'll call you when I get back tomorrow. You've got a good eye. Talk soon."

LeMarcus hung up.

"What was that about?" Stormy asked. "Do you know LeMarcus?"

"I don't," I said. "He says some of the items in the Wine Museum are fake."

"What does that mean?"

"Not sure," I said, thumbing through the photos on Grist's phone. "It looks like most of these photos were taken at the museum, so it's not like we can get in there to look. But wait, oh yes. Here's one, this thing." I showed Stormy the photo. It was an oblong, shiny, silver metal object.

"What is that thing?" she asked. "How would you know if that was fake even if you saw it? What's fake about it?"

"No idea," I said. "But this appears to have been photographed at his carriage house. That's Grist's sofa. I know because I helped him find the perfect fabric for the period."

"Does it mean anything?" She put the cards down.

"No idea," I repeated. I checked to make sure Waggery was sound asleep so we could sneak out. "But I think you're going to see Grist's carriage house sooner than we planned."

Chapter Nine

Walking up the cypress-lined driveway toward Hoggarty Heaven always filled me with feelings of warm nostalgia. The grand manor house, now a tourist attraction, had a welcoming wraparound porch with rocking chairs, wide doors that were flung open on sunny days to let the fragrant breezes freshen every corner, and a cheerful, burbling fountain in the front. Its inviting design aesthetic set the tone for the entire town, and nearly every building around the town plaza was inspired by it, including my cottage.

The carriage house was around the back, and it was a meticulous replica of the main house at a fraction of the size. The entire property was immaculate. Because of Grist's care and attention you'd be hard-pressed to find a single weed, loose hinge, or cobweb.

And even though I'd never lived there, it was my home. I belonged at Hoggarty Heaven like I belonged in Prosperity, for better or worse.

"It's like a painting," Stormy said as we approached. Dusk had settled over the property and the gas lamps were flickering on around us. The carriage house was lit from within, as if it were inviting weary fairytale children inside to protect them from the dark, scary forest.

I felt in my pocket for the keys and was briefly reminded of the ring that was still there and still a danger to me. I'd forgotten I had it in all the excitement of the day, and my stomach flipped. I decided to worry about it later.

"You're not going to need those," Stormy said, pointing. "The door is half-off its hinges."

"Someone's broken in," I said.

"Sure looks like it."

We carefully maneuvered the door to avoid damaging it any further.

"Your Uncle Grist needs a better housekeeper," Stormy said. "Either that, or this place has been ransacked."

"It looks like someone let a goat loose in here," I said, stepping over a drawer with its contents spilled out all over the floor. "I can assure you; this is not Grist's doing. I've never seen a single item out of place. He would lose his mind if he saw this. He would lose his house if the Historical Society saw this. They are a persnickety bunch with an iron-clad contract."

"What do you think they were looking for?" she asked.

"Maybe the same thing we are," I said. "That thingamajig on Grist's phone. Do you see it anywhere?"

We rifled through the items that were strewn about. I looked under cushions and behind the drapes. Throw pillows, sofa cushions, keepsakes from his travels, and framed photos of Grist, Inez and me littered the floor. But I didn't see anything that looked like the item in the photo.

"Do you think he hid it?"

"I don't know," I said. "But I do know that if Grist has something to hide, he wouldn't put it in a drawer."

"What do you mean?"

I navigated my way through the mess to the tiny side room

Grist used as his study. I stopped in the doorway and was over-whelmed by the damage that I saw. The last time I saw Grist's office this disorderly was immediately after an earthquake.

"Follow me," I said. "And watch your step. Everything in here is an antique."

She met me inside and I motioned for her to join me at the bookcase. I scooted all the books that were now on the floor gently with my foot so we both had room.

"Watch this." I pressed on the back of the built-in shelf, and it popped open to reveal a hidden cabinet inside. "Pretty cool, huh?"

"There is literally nothing in the world cooler than a hidden compartment," she said.

"The Hoggarty family put this in during Prohibition," I explained. "It's where they hid wine."

"A winery hid all of its contraband wine in this small compartment?"

"This one's so small it was probably for personal use, or maybe weapons," I said. "You should see the hidden cellar underneath the main house. Their winery was fully operational during Prohibition, and they kept thousands of bottles, along with barrels and huge tanks. Hank and I used to play hide and seek down there. I don't know how we did it. It's so dark, it's like light goes there to die."

"That sounds like a dream childhood," she said.

"It was, and it's one of the reasons I have such a soft spot for Hank," I said. "We spent hours exploring the grounds at Hoggarty Heaven. We were pirates plundering. We were space travelers lost on a toxic planet. Hank will always be my first friend, and I hope he'll be my last."

"But that doesn't mean your friendship is easy," she said.

"Aunt Inez said that we were in each other's lives to teach each other patience," I said. "I don't know that it's working."

"Tell me about the tunnels." Stormy seemed energized by this last bit, and I was happy to oblige.

"There's a tunnel system that runs from the Hoggarty Heaven hidden wine cellar and through the town. It connects to the old Hoggarty Savings and Loan Building, where the Wine Museum is going now, and High on the Hoggarty, and a few other buildings." I didn't mention that the tunnels also ran to the town hall. I didn't know why, but it seemed best to keep this to myself.

"I get why you'd have a secret tunnel to a bank, but not to a pub...?"

"Prohibition," I said. "High on the Hoggarty was a speakeasy with a hardware store as a street-front cover. The joke was you could get screws in the front and get hammered in the back."

I paused for a minute to let my joke land. Stormy didn't crack a smile. She was pushing all the shelves to see if she could find more hidden compartments.

Nevertheless, I continued. "The Hoggarty family got very, very rich. And Prosperity is the result."

"Nice turn of phrase," she said. "I guess wine is a good way to get rich. I wonder if I should change professions?"

"You know what they say? How do you make a small fortune in the wine industry?"

"How?" she asked.

"Start with a large one. The Hoggarty family was already wealthy, don't forget. Naming the town 'Prosperity' wasn't aspirational. They had to have money to dig tunnels already."

"Good point," she said. "Maybe you're better with money that you think."

I'd never thought of it that way. I shook it off. I'd spent so many years seeing myself one way—as desperately bad with money—that this one conversation wasn't going to undo that.

"But when we get this sorted out," I said. "I'll take you down there. Haven't been since I was a teenager."

"It's a date," she said.

I nearly swooned.

* * *

There was a small stack of papers and a metal lockbox inside the hidden compartment. I leafed through the documents. "These are all receipts for items he curated for the Wine Museum. Looks like they spent over a hundred thousand dollars. I knew it was an expensive undertaking, but I thought they at least got a lot of stuff donated. Wow."

"But didn't LeMarcus say that a bunch of the stuff was fake?" she said. "What was that about?"

"I'm not sure," I said. "I know that Grist knows his stuff when it comes to history. I find it hard to believe that he was duped by fakes."

"Do you think maybe..." She stopped, like she caught herself about to say something she would regret.

"Do I think what?" I asked, the hairs on the back of my neck standing up. I didn't like where this was going.

"Well, Carrie, he's got a bunch of receipts for fake stuff hidden in the wall. At least one of them was from a thrift store."

"What are you trying to say?"

"Do you think Grist is skimming off the museum?"

"Never," I said, in a voice angrier than I intended.

"I understand," she said, backing off. "I thought I'd better say something in case he was in trouble, and we could help."

"I know. I get it," I said. I tried to release the tension in my shoulders, but Stormy's question infuriated me. "All of this has been scary and frustrating. I need you to know that Grist is an excellent person."

"I think you need to know that," she said. "He's all you have left. I understand."

"It's true," I said. "But he's the one who called LeMarcus. If he was guilty of passing off fakes as real antiques, he wouldn't have paid to have them appraised."

I showed her the invoice for the appraisal.

"Oh, wow," she said, looking it over. "You're right. It looks like your Uncle Grist caught someone up to no good."

I was glad she shifted her attitude. All of this was difficult enough without me flying into a rage.

"And he was worried enough to hide the evidence." I scanned through the receipts again, double checking to make sure I saw what I thought I did.

"And his accident?" Stormy asked.

"I should ring Flynt to see if he can take visitors." I pulled out my phone.

"No, Carrie. What if it wasn't an accident at all?"

"I need to sit down," I said, taking the papers with me to the plundered living room.

"Let's go through his phone," she said. "We need to read his texts, his emails, everything. I have a feeling he's in danger."

"The only person who's in danger is the person who ransacked my family's carriage house."

Hank stood in the doorway, backlit from the setting sun.

"What do you think you're doing here, Carrie?"

Chapter Ten

"I could ask you the same thing," I said when I realized who I was speaking to. "You have no business here."

"Flynt sent me to find some things to make Grist's stay more comfortable while he's in the hospital."

If I'd been sipping a drink, I would have spit it out. "You're here to find things to make Grist more comfortable," I said. "You hate Grist."

"Oh, this must be Hank," Stormy said in a mock cheerful tone, like a 1950s housewife. "Carrie's mentioned you. Had lunch at your place earlier. Good burger. Meaty."

"Did you pay for it?" he asked, his lip curling into a snarl. "Or did Carrie leave me a basket of peppers from her garden in trade?"

"Low blow, Hank," I said. "We paid."

"Who's this?" He pointed at Stormy.

"I'm Stormy. The mayor's daughter."

"Whoa," he said.

"Right?" I said. "Bet you didn't see that coming."

I loved seeing Hank surprised. He had been so irascible the

past few months that any other expression of emotion was a welcome change.

"What's that in your hands?" he asked. That didn't last long, He snapped back to his old self quickly.

"Nothing you need to concern yourself with, Hank," I said.

"We'll see about that," he said. "Have you called the police?"

"We're leaving," said Stormy.

"Let me get the facts straight, Carrie. You came to your uncle's house with the mayor's 'daughter' who no one has ever heard of. The house has been ransacked, and you don't call the police? Who's the suspicious one here?"

"Hank, it's not what it looks like," I said, exasperated that he was pulling this attitude with me right now.

"No matter what it looks like, it doesn't look good." He pulled out his phone.

"Don't bother," I said, spotting an antique squad car pulling into the driveway. I broke out in a sweat. Stormy turned pale. "It looks like they're already here."

* * *

"Well, well, well," said Officer Bucket. "If it isn't the terrible twosome. The last time I saw both of you with that look on your faces, I was confiscating wine from you at one of Hank's high school house parties."

"And who is this?" Officer Bucket was looking at Stormy. "I haven't seen you before."

"I'm S-stormy Portwood." She straightened up. She seemed unable to make eye contact.

"Where are you from, Ms. Portwood?"

"I'm from Mariner's Cove, sir."

"Can I see some I.D.?"

She fumbled around in her pockets, as nervous as if she'd been caught shoplifting. She pulled her license out of her wallet and dropped it on the ground. She picked it up and handed it to Officer Bucket. Her hand was shaking.

He looked at the photo and back at her. "Checks out, Ms. Portwood. But it looks like your license is expired. You might want to take care of that at the DMV as soon as possible."

He handed her back her license. "Looks like you have some new neck tattoos," he said, barely concealing a smirk. "Is that a skull and crossbones?"

"Yes, sir."

"Why are you here, Officer Bucket?" I asked.

"You tell me, Ms. Dettwiler. You're the psychic. Mrs. Bucket suggested I get you on the mayor's case, like they do on TV."

"I'm not a psychic," I said. "I read tarot."

Officer Bucket was being such a Knight of Swords: domineering, assertive, not thinking things through.

"What do your tarot cards say about the predicament you are currently in?" he asked absentmindedly while he surveyed the damage in the house.

I chose not to answer.

"Ok, okay," he said. "I like how you have chosen to stay silent, but you aren't under arrest. Not yet anyway. Someone called in an anonymous tip. Says your Uncle Grist might know a thing or two about what happened to the mayor. Gave some compelling evidence."

"That's insane," I said. "You've known Grist for years. You know he's incapable of hurting anyone."

Hank snorted.

"What's that, Mr. Hoggarty?" Officer Bucket asked. "You got something to add?"

"Yes sir, I do. Grist stole my family home from me. I wouldn't put it past him to do something underhanded."

"Now wait a good, god-damned minute," I said. "You and I both know that's not how any of this happened."

"Calm down, Ms. Dettwiler," said Officer Bucket. "Now, Hank. I'm not here to hash out this soap opera. I want to have a look around and be on my way. But from what I can tell, it looks like someone beat me to it. Any of you have anything to do with this door off its hinges and this mess?"

"No, sir," the three of us said in unison.

"Did any of you call this in?"

"I was about to, Officer," said Hank. "Those two were here before I got here."

"Interesting," said Officer Bucket. "And Ms. Portwood?"

"Yes, sir?"

"I'd like to ask you to stay in town, please."

"Yes, sir."

"What's going on?" I whispered to Stormy. "You look like you've seen a ghost."

"I'm nervous around cops."

"Psht," I said. "His first name is Beverly."

I said this casually to calm her down, to appear braver than I was. But my knees were shaking. Officer Beverly Bucket may be an old family friend, but he still had the power to implicate me in a murder if the town gossip made it to his ears before the truth did.

She smiled. "You're joking."

"Plus, I think you could outrun him on foot. He drives a Model T."

Stormy snickered.

I didn't have time to share in the joke.

"Ms. Dettwiler." Officer Bucket was scribbling something

on his pad. He didn't look up while he was speaking. "I've been expecting a call from you. Are you avoiding me?"

"No, sir."

"Uh-huh," he said in that off-putting, detached tone cops use when they think they know something you don't. "I'm going to need you down at the station soon. I've got baggies full of feathers and a group of people from the town plaza telling me they heard you screaming."

"It's not how it looks," I said.

"It never is," he said. "Grist says you owe the mayor money?"

Hank cleared his throat. I could sense that Stormy was tensing up.

"He paid for some of Waggery's vet bills last year, yes," I said. "But I would prefer to discuss this in private."

"That sounds reasonable," Officer Bucket said. "Come in voluntarily. Don't make me hunt you down."

"No sir," I said.

"And one more thing," he said. "He had one of your cards in his hand."

"Oh?" I said, pretending I didn't already know this. "I don't think it was one of mine."

"Good point," he said. "Allow me to rephrase. A card that appears to be of the tarot variety was found underneath the mayor's palm."

That explains why I didn't see it, I thought. It was hidden by his hand.

"Yes, sir?"

"It was called 'The Lovers.' Naked people. Garden of Eden or something."

I immediately thought of Emma. I could feel Stormy's gaze boring into the side of my head.

"I'm familiar with it," I said.

"Any idea what it means?"

I didn't want to discuss this yet, so I decided to flood the zone. No one liked to hear a tarot card reader go off on symbolism when it had nothing to do with them.

"It could mean any number of things, Officer Bucket," I said, adopting a professorial tone. "And I am glad you asked. The Lovers card is a signal that a partnership is feeling blessed. It can refer to a love relationship, certainly. But it can also hint that a friendship is blossoming, a business partnership is flourishing or that you're feeling great about a family member. You were spot-on when you said it was the Garden of Eden. In fact, there is a snake there, tempting the woman. But there's no need for concern—"

"All right," he said. "That's impressive. But I'm thinking more along the lines of why he had it in his possession. You think about that and let me know."

"Wow," Stormy muttered under her breath. "You learn that with an English degree?"

"High school debate," I whispered back.

"That's enough amateur hour," Officer Bucket said. "Why don't you three get in your Mystery Machine and head back to the clubhouse so the real police can get to work?"

We were already walking down the drive when Officer Bucket called out.

"Hey, Hank?"

"Yes, Officer Bucket?" he said.

"Next time you find yourself in a pickle, try not to throw your oldest friend under the bus. It's not a good look on a suspect."

"Is he a suspect, Officer Bucket?" I asked.

"That's an interesting question, Ms. Dettwiler," he said, not looking up from his notepad.

"In what way?" I asked.

"I should think you would know that bad news travels fast in this town. In answer to your question of whether your friend here is a suspect, I have only one answer."

"Which is?"

"He certainly is a suspect. In fact, all of you are."

§

"Why are tarot decks not like playing card decks?" I asked. "It's a shame that I can't also play solitaire with mine."

"It would be awkward to play solitaire with your tarot deck," Inez said. "But you can read tarot with a regular deck."

"You can?"

"Sure," she said, like this was the most obvious thing in the world.

"But there's no Hermit card in a regular deck," I said. "Nor is there a Fool or a Wheel of Fortune, or—"

"Ah, the twenty-two Major Arcana cards are missing, that's true. But they're a bonus, an additional boost, more powerful message. What is the rest of the deck made of?

"I guess it's Page, Knight, Queen and King."

"Like Jack, Queen, King," she said.

"What happened to the Knight and the Page?" I asked. "In the regular deck, I mean."

"Over the centuries, they blended into one card," she said. "The Jack is a combo of the Page and the Knight."

"What about hearts, spades, diamonds and clubs?"

"Cups, swords, pentacles, and wands."

"Whoa," I said. "That's very cool."

"It is," she said. "A playing card deck has fifty-two cards to a tarot deck's seventy-eight. If you remember that cups and hearts are abundance and creativity, swords and spades are action and intellect, pentacles and diamonds are material fortune and

wands and clubs are inspiration and ambition, you can still get a detailed reading. You're missing out on the extra oompf of the Major Arcana, like you mentioned before, but totally do-able. In a pinch."

"What kind of pinch?"

"Impossible to predict," she said, clearly enjoying her play on words. "But in life and in tarot, the most important thing is to be adaptable."

§

Chapter Eleven

Under normal circumstances, it would have been unimaginably romantic to stroll home from Hoggarty Heaven through the downtown plaza. As part of his and Flynt Burns's efforts to make Prosperity a tourist Mecca, the mayor had installed old-fashioned lampposts on every downtown street. The light they cast was soft and twinkly, designed more for atmosphere than for finding your way.

The alleyways between each shop and café, paved over with asphalt in the 1980s, had been restored to their original cobblestone. Tonight, there were no fewer than three couples canoodling at the duck pond, giggling at the adorable antics of the animals that lived there. It was a popular spot for proposals, prom photos, and first dates. That anyone wanted it destroyed was confusing to me, to say the least.

"This town has dialed the adorable up to eleven," said Stormy. "And I thought Mariner's Cove was quaint."

"A lot of this had to do with your father," I said. "Don't get me wrong. Prosperity was always pretty. Anywhere you can be outside in the sunshine three hundred days a year is a nice place. But it was very much a farm town. You had the Hoggarty family in their estate, which you saw, and everyone else who worked for them. When I was growing up, these shops were drug stores, banks, grocery, farm supply, a deli. Now all of that's gone and you have Bistro Cannibale with its forty-dollar entrées, and Boutique Clochard that sells four beige things, all in a size two. It's different."

"I remember it that way," she said.

"You do?"

"After he was elected mayor, Mom and I drove here to beg my father for money. I don't have the happiest memories of being here. But I see how it's changed."

"I'm sorry to hear all that," I said. I tried to imagine a young Stormy and her mother, about whom I knew less than nothing, coming here and asking the mayor for scraps. I was distressed by his sudden death, but his secret history made my blood boil. "I can only imagine what you must think of Prosperity now."

We arrived at the cottage, and I opened the door. Waggery was still sleeping, much to my relief. The last thing I needed was to have to clean up another mess in front of Stormy. But before I could settle in, my phone beeped with a notification.

"Oh no," I said when I read the push from *Prosperity Post*. "I think I know who may have told Flynt about you."

I held up the phone and Stormy came over to look. "*Same-Hex Attraction? Psychic Suspect Spotted Spellcasting with Suspicious Sidekick*," she read out loud.

The article—long on sensationalisms and short on facts—accompanied an unflattering image of the two of us darting through town. We looked like one of those old Sasquatch photos.

"How did she? What is this?" Stormy had taken my phone and was scrolling through the "article," which was a generous word for the kind of writing Daisy produced.

"It's typical," I said. "Does she mention that you're the mayor's daughter?"

"No," she said. "But that doesn't mean that she didn't tell Flunt."

"Flynt."

"Right." She handed me back my phone.

"Well, one thing's true," I said. "Daisy's hot on our trail, so I suggest we keep digging to get ahead of the next story."

"Righty-o, boss," she said. "I'll try. But there's something about this same hex attraction that's got me distracted."

"Focus, Stormy," I said in a mock-serious tone. "There will be plenty of time for witchy business once we clear our names."

We looked at each other awkwardly for what felt like hours.

"Have a seat on the sofa," I said, breaking the silence. "Let's finish the wine. I'll see if I can scare up a snack for us."

"No going back to High on the Hoggarty tonight, I guess." She took a seat.

"I don't think that's a good idea," I agreed. "I don't know what's gotten into Hank. He can be salty, but I've never seen him like this. His behavior is borderline abusive."

I cut up some fruit and found some not-too-stale crackers in the pantry. One benefit of being broke is that I didn't waste much. I rarely had food lingering around long enough to go bad.

"I'm not impressed," she said. "You deserve better."

I tried to hide the smile that was fighting its way to my face. Stormy Portwood thought I deserved better.

"I can't account for it," I said. "He's been in a mood."

"What do you think his real story is?"

"What do you mean?"

"That was obviously BS, that he was there to get Grist's jammies. I mean c'mon."

I had to laugh at the image of Hank carefully folding Grist's flannel jam-jams and packing him a toothbrush.

"You're right. It was a strange assertion. And I agree that it's BS. I wonder if maybe he heard that Grist was in the hospital, so he thought he'd go snooping for something that could help him get his property back?"

"Or, maybe he's in on it."

"In on what?"

"In on whatever landed Grist in the hospital."

"You still don't think it was an accident?" I was equally impressed and disturbed by Stormy's inability to trust anyone.

"Let's retrace what's happened. The mayor, my father, was murdered. You find out that Miriam knows that he's been stabbed before anyone else has that info. Then, you uncover the mayor's secret girlfriend. Grist gets in an accident, and Lillian's story casts doubt about how it happened. You get a call from LeMarcus who tells you the wine museum artifacts are fakes. We scoot over to Grist's house. It's been ransacked, and we find receipts for hundreds of thousands of dollars of wine items that are supposed to be real. Hank shows up—why? The police get a tip, and we get dismissed without being questioned."

"When you put it all together like that, it sounds bad," I said.

"That's because it is bad," she said. "There is some dark maneuvering going on here. We didn't even find that thingama-jig. The item we saw on his phone. Where is it? What is it? Is it even anything at all, or are we headed down a rabbit hole?"

"It's late, too. And I haven't heard what's going on with Grist."

"You should call the hospital," she said. "When you're done, we need to read all of Grist's texts, emails, everything in that phone."

"I'm so tired," I said. "I didn't ask for any of this. I want things to go back to the way they were before."

"I'll help you," she said. "We're in this together, remember? Make the call."

I picked my phone up off the coffee table.

"Open up, Carrie Dettwiler."

Someone was pounding on the door so hard I feared my makeshift hook would rattle right off its screws.

"Open this door right now," a deep, male voice boomed. "It's Officer Bucket, and I need to talk to you right now."

What had changed? I thought we'd left things with a friendly "See ya soon." Had he discovered some other piece of evidence that tied me to the murder?

The banging was loud enough to wake Waggery, who was now screaming like a victim in a horror flick and flapping his wings so hard I was afraid he might hurt himself.

"You'd better get that." Stormy cagily paced around the room. She looked like she was ready to bolt. "Before he busts the door in."

I couldn't imagine why Officer Bucket was so enraged. But I hoped it had nothing to do with the ring I was still hiding.

* * *

"I told him pounding on your door and pretending to be Officer Bucket wasn't funny," Lister said, shaking his head. "It's too soon. A man is dead, and Walker is already making jokes. I don't even know where to begin with him."

"Oh, lighten up." Walker rolled his eyes. "You brought a one-night stand to your cousin's funeral."

"Fourth cousin," Lister said. "It's like they didn't install your sensitivity chip at the factory. If there are ninety-nine exact right things to say and one exact wrong one, you'll say the wrong one, every time."

"I need to sit down for a minute," I said. "You scared me to death."

"Are these your friends, Carrie?" asked Stormy. She looked angry.

I nodded.

"You guys know her uncle is in the hospital?" Stormy continued. "And that it's deeply distressing to have everyone in town gossiping about how you murdered a public figure in his office?"

"Oh heavens, Carrie," said Lister. "I had no idea. What happened to Grist?"

"Not sure. But it's serious," I said.

"Walker, you have terrible judgment," Lister scolded. "If anyone should be locked up, it's you."

"Sorry," Walker said, his tone more annoyed than remorseful.

Stormy introduced herself and I watched them take a beat to size her up. They seemed wary, but curious.

"And where did you come from?" Walker asked, looking Stormy up and down. "I've never seen you in Prosperity before."

"Stormy is from Mariner's Cove," I said, taking a step between them, unsure whether she wanted to reveal her relationship to the mayor, and if she wanted to keep that secret, I wanted to help her.

"I'm mayor Brix's daughter," she said.

Stormy could take care of herself.

"Whoa," Walker said. "You know someone for years and—boom—you find out his life is a Louis Vuitton duffel bag filled with secrets."

"Close your mouths before a fly gets in," I said. "You act like you've never seen the mysterious, hidden daughter of a controversial local public figure before."

"More like 'secret' daughter," Stormy added. "I wasn't locked in a basement somewhere. Semantics matter."

"Wow," said Lister. "We came over here to drop a truth bomb on you. But this... Well, it's the second biggest story of the day."

Walker laughed at something on his phone.

"What is it?" I asked.

"Can't believe I missed this," he said, still giggling. "*Same-Hex Attraction.* Ha! That Daisy sure has a way with words. Does she know who Stormy is?"

"Unclear," I said, losing my patience. "What's the story?"

Whatever it was they had to share, I was sure it would be of little use to my investigation.

"You're not going to believe this," Walker said. "But the mayor was dating Emma Fort-Knightly this whole time."

Lister bit his knuckle and bounced on his tiptoes, like Walker had revealed the world's juiciest secret by accident.

"I saw the headline," I said. "*Pretty Lady Pretty Shady: Buxom Bean Counter was Mayor's Undercover Lover.*"

Walker vigorously scrolled through his phone. "How did I miss that?" he whispered.

"I'm joking, Walker," I said, with an eye roll. "Miriam told us earlier today. And we've spoken to Emma directly about it."

Lister and Walker exchanged shocked glances.

"That's interesting," Lister said, too slowly.

What was he piecing together?

"Miriam knew that Emma and the mayor were an item?" he asked, making a face like he smelled something bad.

"Yes," I confirmed.

"How did she know and the rest of us didn't?" Walker asked. "Doesn't that seem weird to you?"

"I didn't think about it," I said, not wanting to encourage too much speculation.

"Are they even friends?" Lister asked.

"Can you imagine those two hanging out?" Walker interjected. "Ugh. It'd be like Ariel palling around with Ursula. Unnatural."

"Don't be unkind," I said. "Miriam's not evil."

"The headline would be *Handbag Hammer Hag Secret Pals with Popular Local Gal.*" Stormy blushed and looked pleased with herself.

The three of us stared at her in stunned silence. Waggery cleared his throat.

"Oh, come on," she said. "I'm trying to play along."

"Jokes aside," I said, with a little wink to let her know I appreciated this ill-timed attempt at lightening the mood. "Miriam's complicated. And if you must know, I think she caught them together somewhere and that was that."

"Let's go have a chat with Miriam," Lister said. "My spidey sense is telling me she's at the center of this whole thing."

"And what are you going to say to her?" Walker said with an astonished look on his face. "You gonna ask her if she murdered someone? Lister, our housekeeper has been stealing from us for three years and you're too scared to say 'boo' to her. Now you're going to waltz up to Miriam Cringe and yell '*j'accuse*'? I don't think so, dear."

"You know I have a fear of conflict," Walker said, his eyes downcast.

"You're off the hook, Walker. I think she may have left town," I said.

Stormy nodded her head in agreement.

"Oh honey, we dropped off tea and pastries for her homeowner's meeting a little while ago," said Lister. "She was there, bitching about stale crullers. Our crullers are farm fresh and never stale. The nerve."

"We asked if she was going on a trip somewhere and she didn't tell us otherwise," I said. "This afternoon."

"She went on a trip like I orbited the moon," said Walker. "You got hoodwinked. And now you need to figure out why. You. Not me. Lister's right. I couldn't intimidate a dandelion."

"Maybe activate your psychic powers." Lister waggled his fingers in the air like he was casting a spell. "Summon the dark lord, perhaps? Maybe have Revelry do a fly-by and report back?"

"It's Waggery, and I'm not psychic." I decided I would have Stormy tattoo this phrase on my forehead when this was all over.

"That's for sure," Walker said. "Or you would have known that Miriam has been up to no good for years. Emma mentioned to me that Miriam has been after her to cook the homeowner's association books."

"That's illegal," Stormy said.

"Emma would never do that," I said. "She's got an impeccable reputation as an accountant. As a girlfriend? Not so much. I'm surprised she kept doing the books after that."

"Probably wanted to make sure Miriam didn't try anything funny," said Lister. "Emma's got clients who live in that neighborhood, and she probably wants to protect them from hurricane Miriam."

"And you're going to die when you hear this," Lister said. "Emma said she thinks the reason Miriam was trying to skim off the homeowner's association was because Miriam wants to run for mayor."

"You buried the lede on that one," Stormy said. "You came in here with all this other nonsense and we're finding out now that Miriam had designs on my father's job?"

I thought about Miriam's reading this morning. It showed she was growing weary over a group project or committee and that she was going to take matters into her own hands. She also might feel regret or remorse. How did that jibe with a run for mayor?

"When did Emma tell you all of this?" I asked.

"A few minutes ago," said Walker. "We walked past her house as she was putting out her recycling bins. She said she thought Miriam was the most likely suspect. Because of her political aspirations."

"She didn't mention this to us earlier," I said.

"No?" said Walker. "She couldn't wait to tell us. Flagged us down and everything. I thought she needed help with those heavy bins, but she wanted to talk."

"Regular chatty Cathy," Lister said. "It was almost like she was in charge of launching Miriam's campaign herself." He snickered at his own joke.

"That seems so unlikely to me," I said. "Miriam has too many enemies. She wouldn't stand a chance."

"She might now," said Walker. "As I recall, her main competition is dead."

Chapter Twelve

When Walker and Lister realized I had no cocktails to offer them, they suddenly realized how late it was and made a swift exit.

"Whew," Stormy said. "Those two have energy."

"They're fueled by double espressos, pastries, and gossip," I said. "They're mostly harmless. But you should watch what you say around them unless you want the whole town to know within three hours."

"That can come in handy in certain situations," she said.

"How do you mean?"

"I mean," she continued. "That if everyone in town knows that they're the town criers—if you wanted some information to get out quickly—you'd tell them first."

"You're saying that we can use them to get information out to people, like something that shows I am innocent?"

"That kind of thing, sure. But what I am saying now is that Emma probably knows this, too. Why, on the day her fiancé turns up murdered, would she suddenly drop this info about Miriam right into their laps? Right after she supposedly found out?"

"Probably because she's suspicious of Miriam," I said.

"Maybe," she said. "You know her better than I do. But let's consider whether Emma might have some reason to direct the narrative away from her. And maybe she knew the blabber-mouth duo would come straight to you."

"Oh, man," I said. "That's a lot for me to process right now."

"I'm processing a lot, too," she said. "I came to see my father and now he was murdered before I made it to his office. If I can focus, so can you."

"Stormy, I—"

"It's ok," she said. "I'm not mad. I'm saying that both of us are being forced to confront shocking realities. My father had the same level of closeness I have with, say, my dentist. I have complicated emotions about him, but I never thought he deserved to be murdered. I'm trying to sort out who would want him dead. All the while realizing that our relationship will never be resolved. I don't get another chance to have a father."

"I'm so sorry, Stormy." Her raw emotions moved me to tears, and all I wanted to do was help her. And if that meant putting aside my need to see the good in everyone, even for a few days, that's what I needed to do.

"I don't need you to be sorry," she said firmly. "I know that you have a soft heart and that you care. But now is the time to use our heads. I'll deal with my sad emotions later."

"That sounds like a plan," I said. "I can do that for you. For your father. For Grist."

"Great," she said. "Let's keep moving. You wondered if Emma might have some involvement."

"Not exactly," I said. "I wanted to know what she knew since she was his girlfriend. You were the one pointing fingers."

"Fair enough," she said. "But follow me as I pull at this thread. Emma was hastily throwing something in the trash when we arrived."

"I don't know that I'd agree with hastily." Despite Stormy's request that I open my mind to the possibility my friends have ill intent, I was resisting this idea. Old habits die hard.

"Tomorrow is pickup day," I said. "It's not suspicious that she would've taken out her garbage today."

"Let's not argue about word choice," she said. "Let's go through her trash instead."

It was nearly dark out, and I recognized that it was probably a good time to orchestrate a garbage heist. But I was so tired, Waggery was waking up, and I needed to find out what happened to Grist.

"I know you don't want to think Emma is involved," she said. "But if you go there with the idea that you are looking for something to exonerate her, would it be a problem?"

"You mean I'm treating her like a suspect in order to find evidence of no wrongdoing?" I had to laugh at that.

"Exactly."

"That's twisted, but I like how you're thinking," I said, silently musing about how I liked a lot more than the way she was thinking. "But it would be irresponsible for me not to find out what's going on with Grist. No news may not be good news."

"You call, I'll strategize." She paced around the room.

I called the hospital and asked to speak with Grist's doctor.

"Dr. Wong here," she said, all business.

"This is Carrie Dettwiler, Grist Featherweight's niece," I said. "What have you found out? Does he have a concussion?"

"A concussion?" she asked, confused. "No, Carrie. Your uncle has a broken neck."

Stunned, I stuttered, "From, from a… bottle falling on him?"

Stormy was watching me intently. She mouthed, "What's going on?"

I motioned to her to give me a sec.

"A bottle? I don't think so," she said. I heard papers rustling. "His injuries are consistent with someone who fell. And from the location of the bruises on his body, it looks like maybe stairs or a ramp of some sort."

"But Flynt told me—"

"I don't know what Flynt told you," She said. "But we can ask Grist when he wakes up. Right now, he's heavily sedated. Best to sort this out in the morning."

"One more thing, doctor?"

"Yes?"

"Is anyone going to be able to access his room?"

"What do you mean?" she asked. "Visiting hours are over. There's no one with him now."

"Where's Flynt Burns?" I asked. "Did he leave Grist there alone?"

"I don't know what you are asking me," she said, sounding annoyed. "No one is here, and we don't allow access after nine o'clock. You can come by in the morning. I am sure he'll be happy to see you. The nurse can go over his needs at that time."

"I'm worried that he'll be lonely when he wakes up."

"I understand," she said, her voice relaxing a bit. "But he's in good hands. If he wakes up, which is unlikely, we'll be there to take care of him."

I hung up.

"What was all that?" Stormy asked.

"They think he fell down some stairs," I said. "His neck is broken."

"Fell?" Stormy asked. "What about the bottle? His head injury?"

I shrugged.

"You don't think he was pushed? Do you?"

"That's difficult for me to imagine," I said. "But I wonder if the answer is in Emma's trash bins."

Chapter Thirteen

Everyday life in Prosperity was nothing if not predictable, especially on the heels of Mayor Brix's popular Prosperity Works program. One of the campaign's biggest successes was the requirement that residents put their garbage bins by the curb no earlier than seven p.m. the night before their scheduled pickup at five a.m. the following morning and removed their bins no later than eight a.m. Why was this important? No messy bins cluttering up Prosperity's pristine streets during peak tourist hours.

Interestingly, Miriam Cringe was one of the co-sponsors of this new set of regulations. She loved rules. Or she loved enforcing rules, I should say.

Lucky for Stormy and me, all we had to do was saunter on by, casually open Emma's bin, and take whatever we wanted.

"Easy peasy," I said to Stormy after I explained the plan.

"Famous last words," Stormy warned.

After Waggery's disco nap, we had no choice but to take him with us. He was wide awake, off his schedule, and ready to party. I couldn't leave him home alone to scream bloody murder all night or we'd be seeing Officer Bucket again when the neighbors called to complain. It was a risk I wasn't willing to take.

I put him on a leash to make sure he stayed close, and he immediately pecked at it.

"Be patient, Waggery," I said. "It's temporary."

Waggery fidgeted the whole way there, but I didn't try to calm him down. Something about being with Stormy filled me with fresh confidence. I mimicked her boldness, and in doing so, it became my own. I'd always wondered what Aunt Inez meant by *"fake it 'til you make it, and you'll discover you were never faking after all,"* and now I finally got it.

As I'd expected, Emma's bins were in front of her house awaiting morning pickup.

What I had forgotten was one of Mayor Brix's other successful programs: Prosperity Porch Potlucks.

Every week, a different neighborhood hosted a party, and anyone in town could come. This week, it was Emma's neighborhood. I loved these parties.

"Prosperity perfection strikes again," Stormy said, hands on her hips, mulling over how to navigate this roadblock.

If I hadn't also had an ulterior motive, I would have enjoyed the free food, the homemade ice cream, and the little kids doing cartwheels on their front lawns. But I wasn't in the Porch Potluck Party mood. I didn't understand why anyone else was either, until I realized it was mostly kids running around while the adults clustered together, whispering to each other. I understood the need for things to feel normal when there's a brutal murder in your town, so I tried to accept that having the Prosperity Porch Potluck as planned was the right thing to do.

"Let's come back later," I said. "This is too much. We'll get noticed." I scanned the crowd for springy golden hair.

"Bad idea," she said. "I didn't think this through. Even if this carnival of cuteness wasn't in full swing, we wouldn't have been able to pull this off."

"Why not?" I asked.

Waggery yanked at his leash, hard.

"This is a well-lighted street. The bins are big. Someone would have seen us."

"Good point." We hung back a bit down the block in the shadows, deciding what to do. "Are you always this good at crime?"

"Ha." she said, laughing. "I don't like to think of it as crime, exactly, but I have had my share of shenanigans."

"Not shenanigans?" I feigned surprise. "Have you also partaken in monkey business? High jinks? Tomfoolery?"

"Now that you mention it, I may have been party to some folderol," she says, "But not until thirty minutes after I've finished my flapdoodle."

"That sounds almost quaint," I said.

"Oh me? Yeah. I'm quaint as hell," she said.

"Quaint is not the word I would use to describe you," I said.

She leaned in. "How would you..."

She lit up and I thought it was because of me. It wasn't. A group of kids whooshed past us, caught up in a game of flashlight tag.

Waggery flapped and fussed at the light in his eyes. I could tell he wanted to be let loose, but I couldn't risk it.

"Mwah," he said, giving me a kiss.

"Not now, buddy," I said.

"I told you it wouldn't be easy," Stormy said. "Best laid plans, as they say."

"Robert Burns," I said, appreciating the reference. "My guess is that if she had papers to hide, she would have put them in the recycling as opposed to the trash. Let's not bother with the garbage. Do the small blue one."

"That's good thinking," she said. "How California of her to recycle her incriminating documents."

"There's no need to destroy the planet while you're destroying evidence." I shrugged.

Waggery flapped and croaked.

"What's going on with him?" Stormy asked.

"This is not his normal routine, and he's not sure what's happening," I said. "He's not accustomed to being on a leash. He's also not accustomed to being forced to do what I want to do. I usually cater to his every need."

"You're his pet," she said,

"Exactly," I said. "Who trained who here?"

"If you were to let him off the leash what would happen?"

"He'd fly off somewhere, like he did earlier," I said.

"He comes home though, right?"

"If I go home and wait for him, and he shows up quickly. He doesn't like it when I'm not focusing one hundred percent of my attention on him."

"He needs to pipe down if we're going to get this done without getting caught," she said.

Waggery tugged at his leash.

"I think we should go home," I said. "He's not settling down."

"You want me to do this myself?" she asked. "You take home the willful Waggery, and I will—"

And before she could finish outlining her plan, Waggery had picked his way through the leash and flown to a roof four doors down and across the street from Emma's house.

I could feel the sweat in my armpits.

"Trust me," she said. "I have an idea. Follow my lead."

Waggery shouted, "Nevermore."

"I don't know," I said. "If he doesn't stay quiet, he's going to attract a lot of attention. It's what he does."

"You want to get into those bins or not?" she said.

"I think we should grab him and go home," I said, with conviction. I was all for a caper, but out here, surrounded by bogeys and possibly Daisy Chatterly? This felt unnecessarily reckless.

"We aren't going to find anything anyway," I said. "And we'll probably get caught. By flashlight taggers. Or cartwheelers. Or worse. Muckrakers."

"I'm going to be totally honest with you," she said.

"You mean you haven't been?"

"I'm the leader of a crime syndicate," she said, ignoring my question. "I am a ruthless, trained assassin."

"If you thought that would build my confidence in you, you're wrong," I said. "In fact, I am more committed than ever to plan b, which is plan 'bedtime for Waggery.'"

"Stay where you are," she said. "You'll know what to do and when to do it."

"Waggery, woo-hoo." Stormy yelled. "Hey birdie, come back."

"What are you doing?" I stage-whispered. "He's going to think you're playing."

"I'm creating a diversion," she said. "While you had your nose in a book in high school. I was pulling fire alarms so I could sneak out unnoticed. Sometimes the best way to get away with something is to do it right out in the open, during a big commotion. Stay there until you know what to do."

She ran toward the house where Waggery was now gamboling about the roof. He watched her intently. I could see him looking back and forth between us, trying to make sense of what Stormy was doing.

Waggery flew to a roof another full block away. I could tell he was having fun; the feathers around his ruff were puffed up.

People were starting to notice. Quite a few Prosperity residents were familiar with Waggery and me. If they didn't know us personally, they had at least seen us. But many of the newer folks in town didn't know us, and even if they did, the novelty of a talking raven never failed to get people to stop doing what they were doing and pay attention. Waggery was his own circus act.

A small crowd had gathered.

Stormy ran to Emma's front porch and rang the doorbell. Emma appeared, holding a full wineglass, and wearing the least-comfortable looking silk peignoir I'd ever seen. Very on brand. She always felt the Porch Potlucks were beneath her. She preferred to stay home, swathed in silk, while sipping something expensive.

"Ms. Fort-Knightly, it's me, Stormy. I am so sorry to disturb you, but I don't know anyone else who can help me."

The pleading look on Stormy's face surprised me more than anything. What a little actress she was.

"Stormy, I'm surprised to see you." She looked past Stormy into the street, as if she was checking to see if anyone was looking. "What's the matter?"

"It's Waggery. Carrie's bird? Carrie went out to pick up some dinner and left me in charge of him. I wanted to let some cool breezes into the house, you know it's so nice here at night, and to set a romantic mood..."

"That is so sweet," she said. "Do you need to borrow some candles? Bath bomb? I've got one that smells like frangipani, it's divine. Tell me how I can help. Chocolate truffles?"

Stormy was playing Emma like a virtuoso villain. Maybe she wasn't kidding about being the head of a crime syndicate. Maybe those tattoos were Yakuza?

"That's so nice," she said. "And I would definitely love to hear more about the frankincense tub grenade—"

"Frangipani bath bomb," Emma corrected her. "I've also got mulberry."

"Right," Stormy continued. "But Waggery flew out—he escaped—and I followed him here." Stormy was putting on a big show of being stressed out.

"Where is he?" Emma asked, looking around.

"He's over there, on your neighbor's roof. I don't know what to do. I don't know anyone else here and there's this party going on—"

"Of course," Emma said.

Stormy paced back and forth on Emma's porch.

"Carrie will be so angry with me—"

"We can't have that," Emma said. "Between you and me, it's about time that Carrie found someone. She's getting weird."

I frowned.

"Let me see what I can do. Maybe a ladder?"

"Do you have one?" Stormy asked.

"I don't," she said. "I call a handyman for any work around the house. But I know how to get one."

Within five minutes Emma, in nothing but her peignoir, and still holding a goblet of wine, had rounded up everyone at the neighborhood party to help Stormy get Waggery off the roof.

All the neighborhood men gathered around to see Emma in her nightie; all the women stood by to watch their men. And all the children were amazed at the raven on the roof—who was pleased as punch to be the center of attention—screaming "Nevermore" repeatedly.

Stormy made a big show of theatrically dropping the ladder a few times and dragging it over the neighbor's flower beds, tearing up their flowers in the process.

"Oh, no. I am so sorry," she shouted. "Are those pansies? I cannot believe I tore up your pretty pansies."

"They are Impatiens," the neighbor said, looking confused and flustered.

"Gahhhk." Waggery screamed. "Quok. Quok. Quok." He

strutted back and forth like Mick Jagger on the main stage at Glastonbury.

"Impatience?" Stormy said. "I bet you're feeling impatient with me, hardy-har-har."

What a dork, I thought. An adorable dork who is clearly cut out for a life of crime. And wordplay.

"No, it's...Never mind," said the neighbor.

"Stormy, why don't you go get the raven?" Emma said. "Go on, now."

I swiftly snuck into a shadow a little closer to Emma's bins. No one noticed me.

"First, I need to pay this man for his flowers," she said. She patted her pockets. "But I seem to have forgotten my wallet in all the excitement. Can I have your address, kind sir?"

"Quok. Quok." Waggery had found his happy place.

"You're standing in front of my house," he said. "But don't worry about it. Please. Get your bird."

"Oh. He's not my bird." Stormy launched into a convoluted story about how Waggery ended up on the roof, all of it made up on the spot. What a clever liar. She never broke eye contact.

She bought me several minutes with her yarn-spinning.

Once every man, woman, and child had turned their attention to the fiasco unfolding on their street, I sneaked up to Emma's bin and lifted the lid. The multitude of wine bottles clanking threatened to reveal me, so I was forced to be precise in my movements as I made an opening to pull out a stack of documents, stained with wine dregs, which seemed to be purchase orders for the museum.

I quietly shut the lid. I dipped back into the shadows as fast as I could.

"Quok. Quok. Mwah."

Waggery was still putting on his show, and Stormy was

yelling something that sounded like, "once up on midnight dreary."

Despite this absurd commotion, I knew Waggery could see exactly where I was. I waved to him.

I turned and bolted toward the cottage.

I didn't look back.

I didn't stop running until I got to my garden gate.

I pushed open my unlockable front door and let out a huge sigh of relief. I put the items on the coffee table for us to look through together when Stormy returned.

I waited.

What was happening?

Who was I becoming?

"While I pondered, weak and weary," I said, finishing the next line of Poe's *The Raven,* before collapsing on the couch.

* * *

Waggery made it back first. Emma's street was only a block or so as the crow flies, for lack of a better way of putting it.

I gave him a bunch of neck scritches and he cooed and kissed me.

"You're a star, Wagger-ino," I said. "Star of the show. Maybe I should get you your own YouTube channel like Flynt suggested. People love you."

He settled onto his perch, his daily need for fun and adventure fully sated. He was snoozing within minutes.

Stormy didn't even knock; she burst in and collapsed on my sofa.

"I need a drink," she said with a half laugh.

"Were you a theater major?" I asked. "Because that was some supreme scenery chewing out there."

"Sometimes you don't know what you're capable of until pushed into a corner," she said. "And we were in a corner."

She said "we."

"A corner of our own making, I think."

"It's a good corner," she said, still out of breath. "I'm okay with this corner."

"You are?"

"Now, how about that drink? I need to calm my nerves before we start unraveling this mystery."

Chapter Fourteen

"I'm not sure what I am looking at here." Stormy leafed through the documents retrieved from Emma's recycling bin. "It's a game of concentration. I'm matching these up, and it looks like Grist has receipts for every single one of these items. What's Finder's Keepers?"

"It's a thrift store," I said. "He shops there all the time. Could be unrelated."

"I think we have to assume everything is related," she said.

"According to Emma's documents, which are dated a few weeks after Grist's receipts, someone sent everything back."

"But why?" she asked. "It looks like they bought them, sent them back and then, according to LeMarcus, replaced them. Why not keep the originals? It's a museum. Authenticity is the whole reason to visit."

"Why, when Grist was so adamant about everything being perfect, would anyone replace the items he found?"

"Do you think Emma was acting alone?" she asked.

"I don't know," I said. "I have a hard time imagining Emma doing anything unethical. She was opposed to Miriam skimming."

"That might have been because she was opposed to her running for mayor against her boyfriend. Emma was quick to throw Miriam under the bus by telling the tweak twins that whole running-for-mayor thing," Stormy said.

"I don't think she could get away with dishonest practices in a town this small," I said. "I told you before that everyone in Prosperity uses her services. And she makes a good living. You saw her house. She doesn't act like someone who has a cash flow problem."

"You'd be surprised," she said. "A lot of people who live opulent lifestyles do it on credit."

"I live on credit, and I don't have a luxury car or original art," I said. "I must be doing it wrong."

"Better to be in debt and working on it while living within your means rather than setting up a system where you're accruing more debt to pay off other debt," she said. "That's a house of cards."

"Are you mocking me?" I liked it.

"No," she said with a laugh. "But we should probably check to see what Grist knows about all of this."

"I'll check his texts now."

I scrolled through his phone to see if there were any voice mails. There was one from Lillian from last Monday. I played it on speaker.

"Grist, hi sweetie. It's Lillian. We need your man muscle over here to tighten those loose shelves. When you get a chance, can you swing by with a drill? Some of these items are looking wobbly. Thanks, hun."

"That's hilarious," I said to Stormy, giggling. "And uncomfortable."

"The wording is funny but think about it. She's the one who asked Grist to come fix the shelves. You don't think—?"

"Lillian? Absolutely not. But now that you mention it, she did find his phone and she may have lied about where."

"That doesn't raise a red flag?" she said.

"Yes, and no? The idea that Lillian could be involved in this is unthinkable. Her little untruth is probably because she was in the museum at off hours or broke some other procedural rule."

"Let's put a pin in her," Stormy said. "But I still wonder."

"Fair enough," I said. "Let's see who the next message is from."

"Grist. It's Emma. I need those Wine Museum receipts. Bring them by as soon as you can."

"Is it unusual for Emma to ask Grist for receipts?" Stormy asked.

"I don't know," I said. "She does accounting for the town, so if there were receipts for the Wine Museum, it might make sense that she'd need them for some kind of accounting. I guess?" I shuddered. My fingers tingled.

"Okay, we'll file that in the interesting-but-not-necessarily-incriminating pile," Stormy said.

I was glad to move on. "That's it for voicemails. I'm going to check the texts."

He had a few messages from numbers I didn't recognize, mostly tour clients confirming dates and times. There was a funny back and forth between Grist and a high school student who was asking him questions for a history report. Grist was clearly trying to be cool.

CHAD: It's Chad Santos. We met on the plaza.
Can u answer some history questions

GRIST: You bet, bro. Fire away

CHAD: Um, ok. Why did Agustus Hoggarty
settle here

GRIST: Dude, u won't believe it. It's the most far out story.

CHAD: Ok....

GRIST: He was a wealthy pig farmer on his way from Sacramento to San Francisco. His wagon wheel broke, and his pigs ran away. But he saw that he could make some cabbage with wine.

CHAD: Wait, he made the town so he could plant cabbage?

GRIST: Cabbage is dough, my man

CHAD: He made a cabbage sandwich?

GRIST: He made moolah. With his wines and vines, dude

CHAD: Can I come to the plaza and ask you some questions? I don't understand what is happening

GRIST: I'm large and in charge, hanging with the ducks. SYLA

CHAD: ?

GRIST: See ya later, alligator

CHAD: k

I showed the texts to Stormy.

"I can't believe people like this exist," she said. "I'm seriously thinking of relocating here."

My heart jumped to my throat.

"The architecture," she said. "The pond. The tarot cards. This pillow. Your little dress. The raggedy denim jacket that's all torn up on one shoulder from carrying an actual raven around—."

I quivered in my little dress and denim jacket. It had been a long time since anyone had noticed my little dress. Or me.

Waggery snickered.

"Can I give him a treat?" she asked.

"He'd love it," I said, trying to ignore the inconvenient feelings I was having. "There are some grapes from my own vines in the fridge. Or another snickerdoodle. Oh but, hello, what's this?"

It was a text from Emma:

EMMA: he knows

"That's not cryptic at all," Stormy said. "What the actual hell does that mean?"

"This is from yesterday," I said. "He didn't respond, and the time is from before I got the call about his accident. That's not like him at all. If anything, he's an over-responder."

"I can see that," she said. "He knew something was up. That's why he hid the receipts."

"We need to talk to him first thing tomorrow," I said. "We need to get there before Emma. I'm starting to see that she may be up to something. Maybe not murder. But something."

"That's my cue," Stormy said, standing up. "I guess I should go find a hotel."

"I didn't even think about that," I said.

"I didn't either," she said. "I've been so caught up in everything that I didn't think about how late it was getting."

"It's not like you can drive home, either," I said. "You don't want Prosperity's finest dragging you back here by your ear."

"I definitely do not," she said. "So... I wonder if I should go to my father's house. It's empty, obviously."

"Oh, no. That creeps me out. Have you ever stayed there before?"

"I haven't."

"I don't think the day of his murder is the time to start. It seems... I don't know. Wrong? Suspicious, even?"

"Totally agree," she said. "It's also likely that your good friend Officer Biscuit—"

"Officer Bucket."

"Right, Bucket—because that's a more legit name than Biscuit—might have closed it off for evidence gathering or whatever they do."

"Probably," I said. "That Biscuit's a tough cookie."

She ignored the pun, and I was crestfallen.

"Forget I suggested that," she said. "Can you recommend a place?"

"Everything in Prosperity is expensive," I said.

I was trying so hard to play it cool when all I wanted to do was scream at her to stay with me.

"The hotel Prius it is," she said. "Wouldn't be the first time. Probably won't be the last. Fortunately, I've booked the upgraded backseat package. Comes with a three-year-old glove box granola bar. Should be fun."

She stood up.

I panicked.

I've been accused by girlfriends of sending out mixed signals. In situations where I thought I was being accommodating—like helping them find a hotel in a strange city—they thought I was being dismissive. I didn't want to make that mistake with Stormy. I needed to tell her how lost I was until she arrived, and how her strength inspired me to be more, do more. I needed her to know, in no uncertain terms, that I wanted her.

"I know we only met today," I said. "But I think you should stay here."

"I don't want to impose," she said, pulling out her keys. "I'll be fine."

Oh, no. Was she trying to get out of this?

Be brave, Carrie.

"It's not an imposition," I said. "I want you to stay. With everything that's going on, I don't want to be—"

"You don't need an excuse," she said, taking my hand and pulling me close to her. "I wanted to be sure."

She kissed me, and I melted into her.

"Mwah," Waggery whispered woozily.

"I'm sure," I said, kissing her again.

She smelled like sandalwood and sea spray. She tasted like wine.

"I could stay on the couch, I guess," she said, pulling me closer and kissing my neck.

The feel of her hands on my waist released my resolve. I succumbed to her.

She lightly sucked my bottom lip, and I was done for.

"Well," I said, allowing her hands and her tongue to explore a little more. "It's a good place to start."

Chapter Fifteen

O h, sweet, glorious, sunshiny morning. If there's a more magical place than Prosperity when you're falling in love, I've never heard of it. I suppose that's why *Hopeless Romantic* magazine put Prosperity on its "Top Ten Places to Propose" list ten years in a row, and *IDoIDo.com* named it the "Best Place to Honeymoon" last year. How did I, a single gal, know this? Mayor Preston Brix bragged about it all the time. It was part of his and Flynt's ultra-successful Fall in Love with Prosperity campaign.

There's something about the cool, bright mornings, the scent of lavender in the air everywhere, the cobblestones, all of it. I had always known that Prosperity had a romantic vibe. But it had never happened to me.

Not like this.

I surveyed my kitchen and was struck by Aunt Inez's good taste. Her home welcomed people who were in search of answers, and she created a quiet, reflective space for them. Far from the gaudy, ornate style you'd expect in a classic fortune teller's domicile, there wasn't a single curlicue, crystal ball, patterned scarf or velvet cushion in the whole place. Instead, there were tidy cabinets, sparkling windows, and pine-planked floors. Earthenware ceramics, created by local artisans and collected over decades, sat atop shelves and tables, and I filled them with fresh herbs and flowers as often as I could (and refused to sell them, even when people begged. Even when I needed the money.). This home was peaceful, fragrant, and filled with sweet memories.

Stormy shuffled out of my room wearing her Think Ink T-shirt and not much else, her hair fluffed up like a baby chick. I tried not to stare.

Not only was she jaw droppingly beautiful, but I wasn't sure I'd seen all her tattoos and I was trying to sneak a peek. Was that an anchor? Classic. Oh, and a spyglass. Maybe Stormy *was* a pirate?

I handed her a cup of coffee, and I experienced a sad pang of familiarity. The mayor and I had tea right here, two days ago.

In the span of forty-eight hours, my entire life had been upended.

"What a morning," I said.

"I was going to say, 'what a night,' but sure, morning is fine, too."

Stormy had a devilish twinkle in her eye.

"You have a point," I said.

She nibbled my earlobe, and my legs buckled.

"I like today's little dress almost as much as yesterday's," she said, running her hand along the hem. "Pink. Suits you."

I was swept up in imagining how I could get this dress off as quickly as possible. I grabbed her around the waist, but she pulled away.

"I hate to change the mood," she said, sitting down at my kitchen table. "But we need to discuss what the plan is today."

I was disappointed, but she was right.

Focus, Carrie. There will be plenty of time for fooling around later.

"I fed Waggery already. He's quietly amusing himself for now," I said, as I watched him contentedly push his toys around and hop from shelf to shelf. "I usually have clients now and throughout the day, but I only have one person scheduled early this afternoon."

She leaned over and took my hand. "You're funny. But today is not normal and we can't pretend like it is. There's a murderer in town and there are plenty of people who think it might be one of us. One of whom writes unsubstantiated stories. Don't let yourself get distracted, or emotional. Not yet."

"I understand," I said, hearing the seriousness in her tone. "I'm hoping Grist is awake so he can tell us what all of this purloined paperwork is about."

"The Purloined Paperwork," she said.

"Is that why you have a raven on your wrist?" asked. "Poe fan?"

She stopped flipping through the papers. "Well, yes, in a way. Poe is the inventor of the modern detective tale. What's not to love? But this was for my mother. Her name was Lenore."

"Like the woman in *The Raven*. When was the last time you saw her?"

"It's a long, sad story," she said. "One day I hope to share it with you, but as I mentioned earlier, we have a lot of work to do right now."

"You promise you'll tell me one day? I mean, you plan on having a one day...with me?"

"I plan on having a lot of days with you," she said, kissing me lightly. "Let's focus on this, and..."

"Bwak. Sqwok," Waggery shrieked from the bedroom. I heard him dragging something and then a quick hard thud on the wooden floor outside my room.

"Oh, no," he said.

"What the heck?" said Stormy.

"He does this," I said. "Terrible timing. Always making a mess."

We went to see what was wrong. We found Waggery standing over the emerald ring.

He must have pulled it out of my pocket. He was trying to give it to me as a present.

Stormy snatched it off the floor.

"What are you doing with this?" she demanded.

"I, um."

"I, um,'" she said in a mocking tone. "Start talking, Dettwiler."

"I can explain," I said. "Your father was here for dinner and a reading the other night. Waggery has a way of locating shiny objects and stealing them from my clients."

"Waggery randomly found this?"

"Yes. Waggery is attracted to anything that glimmers. Jewelry, bottle caps, tin foil—"

"When were you going to tell me?"

"I wasn't not telling you," I stammered. "I had it. I was going to return it to the mayor and things got crazy. I didn't realize you had a personal connection to this ring. It's not what it looks like."

Clearly, she'd seen this ring before and knew it belonged to her father. How could I explain how it had come into my possession?

"It's not what it looks like? It looks like you, a person who has admitted to having massive debt, stole something valuable that doesn't belong to you. Were you planning on selling it? To pay off your student loans? To get these collections agencies off your back?"

"What? No." I said. How dare she accuse me of stealing. "I was going to return it."

"To whom?"

I tried not to let her impeccable grammar get me off track.

"Your father," I said. "I fully planned on returning it because I knew that if anyone saw that I had the mayor's clearly valuable item, combined with the fact that I owe him a little bit of money—"

"How much is a little bit, Carrie? Twenty dollars?"

"No—"

"Fifty dollars?"

"More, I — You don't understand. We had an arrangement."

"An arrangement? Please, go on." She folded her arms. "I'd love to hear about this arrangement."

"I owed him a few hundred dollars. For a favor." I couldn't believe I was talking about this. The real story and the story we told people were two different things.

"What kind of favor?"

"When it comes up, we tell people that the mayor paid for some vet bills so I could be certified to keep Waggery legally," I said. "Prosperity is full of nosey neighbors and Waggery, as you've seen, can be a menace. We needed to make sure everyone knew he was legally under my care so no one can take him away from me."

"That sounds sort of legit," she said. I could tell that she was waiting for the other shoe to drop. "But what's the whole truth?"

My mouth was dry. This secret wasn't coming as easily as the ones about my debt. "Your father paid the guy at Fish and Game a hefty bribe. I couldn't sleep at night thinking that someone could take Waggery from me after Inez died. Your father saved Waggery from a life at a wildlife rehab center."

"You and my father bribed a public official for personal gain."

"Yes," I said, feeling equal parts relieved that the truth was out and horrified that the truth was out. Hearing someone confirm that you were on the instigating end of a corruption scheme stings more than you might think. "But for the right reasons."

"How, exactly, were you returning this favor?"

"The mayor agreed to tea, dinner, and the occasional reading to pay it off. That was all. And when I had extra cash, I paid him."

"Is that what we're calling it? Tea and a reading?"

"What are you insinuating?"

"I'm not insinuating anything," she said. "I'm implying."

"I'm inferring this," I said. "You think I stole from your father and that I was, I was—"

I couldn't form the words.

"You should have mentioned this to me," she said with a wild look on her face. "Did you know he was going to propose to Emma and you, you—"

"You've got this so wrong," I said. "Nothing was going on with me and your father. Waggery found this ring, and I had plans to return it. I was returning it when I was in his house. You saw me there."

"This all sounds made up," she said. She was putting on her clothes and gathering her things.

"Where are you going? I asked. "Let's calm down and you can help me take the ring back right now. I don't even want it. I can explain everything."

"There's no need to return it to the mayor," she said. "I'll be taking it back."

She put it in her pocket.

"I'm not sure I can let you do that," I said. "Don't you think we need to put it back in his house? It might be evidence."

"Carrie, it's not evidence. Not for this crime, anyway. This ring was my mother's. I came to Prosperity to get it back."

"Can't we talk about this?"

Stormy was making her way toward the front door. "I'm not sure what there is to say. You've been dishonest with me. If I can't trust you, whom can I trust?"

"This is a misunderstanding. Why don't we have some breakfast and talk about it? I need you to help me solve this case."

"At this point," she said quietly, "I am not completely sure that you don't have something to do with 'this case.'"

She shut the door behind her. It bounced open, and I watched her walk down the sidewalk and disappear.

"I love you," Waggery said, from the safety of his perch.

"I love you, too, buddy," I said. "And that's a good thing, because it looks like it's you and me, all alone, again."

Chapter Sixteen

Stunned and confused by Stormy's sudden departure, I busied myself by cleaning up our coffee mugs, making the bed and tidying up my reading space in preparation for my upcoming appointment.

I sat down at the kitchen table, exhausted. "It's not even ten," I said to Waggery, who blinked at me like he understood what I was talking about. "And I'm already worn out."

I shuffled the papers in front of me, but I wasn't motivated to dive into the numbers to figure out what it all meant.

Where did Stormy go, I wondered. Did she go home? Was she still trying to solve her father's murder? Was she somewhere cooling off and would come back soon so we could talk? As the minutes ticked by, I was left with more questions than answers.

I needed to see Grist, but taking Waggery to a hospital ward was out of the question. Not only would the hospital frown on a live bird in their building, but I didn't know how to explain to him why he wouldn't see Grist in his usual post on the plaza, greeting tourists in his period costume. Not to mention the fact that I wasn't in the mood to prevent Waggery from harassing Ligeia.

I rang the hospital and spoke to Grist's nurse.

"He's still pretty groggy," the nurse said. "We've got him on a painkiller cocktail to keep him comfy. His injury is likely quite painful."

"Is it serious?"

"Yes, it's a serious injury in that all neck injuries are serious," he explained. "But the good news is that there's no spinal cord damage. It's a light fracture."

"Is he in a lot of pain?"

"An injury like this doesn't tickle. And he's an older fella so he might have a longer healing process. But ultimately, with proper pain management and physical therapy I would bet that he will be back to taking tour groups on fictitious tours of our town in no time."

"Oh, you know him," I said. "What did you say your name was again?"

"I didn't, but it's Brian. And everyone knows Grist," he said. "Every tenth-grade class in Prosperity takes his tour as a field trip. All we were interested in was getting him to admit that there are tunnels under the town, but his lips were zipped. I can't count the number of times me and my friends had too many beers and went looking for them."

I decided not to tell this nurse the truth about the tunnels. The last thing anyone needed was folks going down there and getting lost or hurt.

"Can you put him on?"

"I can have him call you from his phone when he's up for it," he said.

"I have his phone."

"He can talk for a few minutes on mine. But I will warn you, he'll probably be goofy if he doesn't fall asleep on you completely."

I heard him hand the phone over.

"Grist?"

"Who's this?"

It was so good to hear his voice.

"It's me, Carrie."

"I don't know her," he said.

Oh, boy.

"How're you feeling?" I asked.

"Oh," he said, sighing. "Woozy."

"I bet. Get better and I'll come see you as soon as I can."

"You do that," he said.

"Talk soon."

"Hey," he said before I hung up. "Carrie? Don't... What is this?"

"What is it? Grist?"

"What does this mean? What is happening?"

"I don't know, Grist," I said.

"I'm sorry," It was the nurse. "Like I said, he's groggy. Might be seeing flying elves again. Come by later when he's less impaired. There's a group of those ladies from the history whatever coming by. You should come when they do."

"But how will I—"

The line went dead.

* * *

"I miss Grist," I told Waggery. He chattered at me in a way that made me think we were having a back-and-forth conversation. He was an animal that could speak actual words, and even though I knew he was only repeating sounds I had spent hours teaching him, I liked to think he understood more than he let on.

"Maybe you can figure out what all of this means," I said to him. "Let's look at this paperwork. I think something's up, don't you?"

He brought me a pen and flew back to his perch.

I matched up each of the receipts from Grist's hiding spot with the return slips I found in Emma's trash.

Riddling racks, grape presses, grape baskets, bottle cleaners, branding irons, cellar lamps. Any of these items would have been found in older wineries. In Prosperity, or any of the surrounding wine country towns, one could probably find an assortment of similar things collecting dust in a back room. That's not what made his Wine Museum special. What Grist set out to do was to find each specific item that was used in the Hoggarty Heaven Winery the year they made the famous Hoggarty Heaven Blend that took home the Gold Medal in the 1976 French World Cup of Wine.

"They should have called with the World Glass of Wine," I remembered him joking.

"I pinot point in changing it," I said.

"I suppose all of the prior winners would be crushed."

"They wouldn't stop wining."

"But what do vino?"

Aunt Inez loved it when we did that.

I did, too.

Grist was adamant that the tools and equipment in his museum were one-hundred percent authentic, down to the maker, year, and materials used to craft them.

"No one is going to want to look at a bunch of tools on the wall," he said. "People want context. I'm going to build an exact replica of that winery so that people can see exactly what it took for Prosperity's hometown heroes to win that award."

I'll never forget how he beamed with pride when he talked about how authentic the museum would be. "It's going to set the standard for preservation of our local memories," he said. "It's crucial that we remember everything. Exactly as it was. We must be uncompromising."

This was right after my aunt died. I understood his need to hold on to memories.

Nearly everything he had sourced and paid for had a corresponding return slip, even down to something called a "bung driver."

"This is so weird," I said to Waggery. "Why would they return all these items? Maybe they had too many? Maybe Grist ordered multiples? It makes no sense. The museum opens this Friday."

I looked at Grist's text from Emma again.

Emma: he knows

Aside from the obvious spookiness of those words, I was surprised that the text was dated after the items had been returned. Is this what "he" knew? Was "he" the mayor? Did he catch Emma and Grist doing something untoward, unethical, or illegal? I couldn't envision a single scenario where Grist had done something that would harm Prosperity. But the way these clues were unfolding, I had to accept that it was at least possible that Grist knew something. Something that could get a man killed.

I was going to have to go talk to him about this today, whether he was drugged up or not.

I wished Stormy was here. I picked up my phone and remembered that I don't have her number. If we were going to sort this out, she would have to come back here—and I didn't have a good feeling about that.

There was a knock at my door.

I'd forgotten my appointment.

Since this was a new client, I put Waggery on his perch in my bedroom and closed the door, crossing my fingers that he would keep himself occupied without too much fuss.

"Hello, I'm Carrie," I said, extending my hand.

"I'm Misty," she said, taking my hand with the strength and conviction of a dead fish. "Misty Möerning. With an umlaut."

"Great to meet you," I said. "My doctor said I need more umlauts in my life."

Her expression remained blank.

"I'm joking," I said. What a stuffy little Queen of Swords. "Come on in."

I motioned for her to have a seat.

"What brings you in today?"

"I want to know what my boyfriend is up to."

"That's a common inquiry," I said. "Do you care to offer more details so I can help you come up with a question?"

"He said he doesn't see a future. So, I'm here to find out if he's right."

"I don't even need to read your cards to tell you he might be doing you a favor," I said.

"What do you mean?"

"If he's telling you that he doesn't see a future, you might want to take him at his word."

"I don't believe him." She smacked her gum.

"Right," I said. I'd seen this before. Misty was a big girl, and she could make her own decisions.

I shuffled and told her how to split the deck. "Did you want a full Celtic cross or a three-card reading?"

"What's the difference?"

"Celtic cross is more detailed, and it costs more. Three-card is primarily your past, present and future, and costs less."

"Let's do the full one," she said. "It comes with lottery numbers?"

"Not exactly," I said. "That's not what this is."

"But you're psychic?" She looked around the room. "If you

were good at psychic-ing you'd have gotten your own lottery numbers, and clearly you haven't done that."

"Not psychic," I said, stunned by Misty's imperviousness to my cottage's charms. "But I am a well-trained tarot card reader. Do you want to share your specific question with me or keep it private?"

"I thought I already did," she said.

I couldn't remember the last time I met someone so joyless.

"Do my boyfriend and I have a future?" She asked again.

"Great." I spread out the cards in a straight line in front of her. I flipped them back and forth. I needed to show off or prove myself for some reason. "Pick one card out at a time, and I'll tell you where to place them."

My heart fluttered at the idea of doing a full Celtic Cross reading. Except for events like bachelorette parties and corporate retreats, the bulk of my clientele preferred a quick three-card spread. I think it's because they came by frequently—some weekly—and didn't feel the need for deep dives. Getting a full Celtic Cross each time would be like getting all over color instead of getting your roots touched up at the hair salon, or at least that's what I liked to tell myself.

"So, this reading, the Celtic cross it's called—"

"Yeah, you mentioned that." She looked at her nails.

"Right. It's an exciting way to get a reading because it's so detailed. It was made popular by Arthur Waite in the early part of the last century, and it's only been widely used since the 1970s. But there's evidence that it's based on a more ancient spread used by pagans and by traveling Roma—"

"I don't need to hear the past," she said. "I need to know the future."

I gave up. I loved to share my knowledge about tarot when I could, but the sad fact was that most people were like Misty— they only cared how it applied to them.

"Your wish is my command," I said.

"Ha, genie. I get wishes too?"

"Not exactly."

Immediately, I noticed a few things about her spread.

The Six of Swords card in the central position—a man rowing a boat with a woman in it away from the viewer— showed that she was on her way out, possibly from this relationship. But if I were to take the fist holding a wand literally, the Ace of Wands that crossed this first card suggested that Misty may be hanging on too tightly. Or it could be taken at face value to represent an opportunity to be seized.

I explained what I was seeing, and I could tell that she was getting more interested.

She leaned in. "What about this one, with the guy handing out crumbs to beggars?"

"This is the Six of Pentacles in the fourth position," I said. "It shows a recent event. Have you given him money?"

"I have."

"That's what this is."

"This is cool." She looked at me and almost smiled.

"I am glad you're enjoying it. Follow me on social media and you can get updates, suggestions, see what I'm up to—."

"Nah."

I continued, convinced that if I put some pizazz into the reading she'd come around. "Up here, in position five, you've got the Fool. This is a potential outcome, and I'm seeing a new adventure for you. The rest of the spread supports that. Here's the Two of Pentacles—a clear indication that you may be juggling things. That, coupled with the Eight of Pentacles, here in the position that describes your attitude," I pointed to the seventh position, "shows that you'll be hard at work soon."

"What's Satan doing in my reading? Am I going to hell?" She asked this in the same tone one would use when asking to pass the salt or what time it was, as if it didn't matter either way.

"The Devil card is who you're dealing with. Someone two-faced, possibly with a dark secret. Does that track?"

"He has dark secrets."

"It's interesting, because the Devil card is the opposite of the Lovers card."

I flipped through the deck to show her The Lovers card. Tarot decks were filled with complementary and opposite cards. The Devil/Lovers duo was one of my favorites to show because they truly were two sides of the same coin, metaphorically speaking.

But I couldn't find The Lovers.

Flustered, I told her, "It's set up like this except the colors are brighter and instead of a leering devil, there's a pretty angel. Whoever this is has you stuck."

Where was my card? Between me and Aunt Inez, this deck had been in the family for decades, and a card has never gone missing before.

"That's bad," Misty said, in reference to her own stuck-ness.

"Not necessarily," I said. I'd have to sort this missing card out later. I leaned forward in my seat for emphasis. "Your future card is the Ace of Pentacles, a hand grabbing money out of nothing. I think if you can move past this relationship, you're going to have an opportunity to be successful."

"I've always wanted my own business." She gazed off toward the ceiling and twirled her hair.

"Stop giving money to his business and start your own," I said. "That's what I'm seeing."

"Yeah."

"It shows that you're looking for love in a hopeless place."

I thought of Stormy, and my stomach dropped.

"I kind of figured," she said. "He only comes around when he wants, well, you know."

"Booty call?"

"Exactly," she said. "But lately it's been money, too. I give it to him because I'm a good person."

She sounded so drab that I wouldn't have been surprised if she fell asleep right on the table. But it didn't matter. It appeared that her so-called boyfriend was taking from her and had no plans to return the generosity she had shown him.

"Are you telling me to break up with him?"

"I don't give advice," I said. "I rely on what the cards show me. And it says here that this isn't going to go the distance. Whether you break up with him or not, this relationship is, literally, not in the cards."

"Ohhh, is that what that means?"

"It is," I said.

"That's cool. But bummer. I thought maybe if I did everything he asked, he would come around."

"Classic error," I said. "I had this girlfriend once who always—."

"No," she interrupted. "I don't need to hear your tragic relationship stories. I've got problems of my own."

I looked again at the spread. "It's mostly about this money you gave," I said, puzzled. "It's kind of like you gave it even though he may not have needed or even wanted it. You don't have to tell me any details, but the cards have made it clear that success is around the corner for you if you can let this go."

"It's weird. He comes from money, but he never seems to have any. And he's always disappearing at weird times and coming back all dirty. And it's not like his work is dirty. He's always cleaning, so it makes no sense to me whatsoever."

"I do. Do you mind if I ask—who is your boyfriend?"

"Hank. Hank Hoggarty. He owns that crappy bar and grill

right down the street."

"I know the one."

The Devil. Hank has always been my Devil card, and here he was in a reading about a girl he was supposedly dating.

I had always made a point to tell my clients that there were no "good" or "bad" tarot cards, but to see Hank here, clearly up to something shady, gave me the shivers.

"One more thing," I said.

"Yes?"

"Why did you come see me today?"

"I thought he might be cheating on me with you."

"What? Why? No. Hank and I are old friends and I'm—"

"But when I saw you, I was all, no way." She looked me up and down. "I decided it would be cool to get a reading about the future since he said we have no future. I've walked by here a hundred times and thought it would be interesting to come in. It was. Sort of."

I let her hurtful comments slide.

"Why would you think he was cheating with me?"

"Because I saw your name on a list in his office. Circled in red."

"Who else was on the list?"

"I don't know." She got up. "How much do I owe you?"

"It's on the house if you can remember who else was on the list."

She closed her purse. "Well, in that case it was you, some dude named Brix, and some guy whose name began with a G. Like Grime or Green".

"Grist?"

"Yeah. That's it. The other two were struck through already though, so..."

"I was the only one left."

"And circled in red," she said. "Must be urgent."

Chapter Seventeen

"What's this about a list?" I demanded from Hank after Misty left and I could get myself over to High on the Hoggarty.

"What list?" He put down the glass he was drying.

"You never mentioned you had a girlfriend. With an umlaut."

"Are you stroking out right now?" he asked. "You're not making any sense."

"Your girlfriend, Misty? The one I knew nothing about. She came to me for a reading because she saw my name on a list circled in red. Not to mention the fact that she was worried about you doing something shady. What was she talking about?"

"I thought you kept your clients' readings confidential," he said. "Where was all this sharing when I was trying to find out if Emma was seeing anyone?"

"Don't change the subject," I huffed. "What in the heck is going on here?"

"Watch your language," he said. "'Heck' is a strong word for this fine establishment. You'll offend the ladies."

He motioned to a group of women at the end of the bar who

were several glasses into a liquid lunch. They waved at me and burst into giggles.

"Hank." I banged my fists on the bar.

"Whoa. Why don't we have a seat and discuss all of this like normal people? It seems like you have a lot on your mind right now."

He guided me to the same booth that Stormy and I had sat in the day before, and my heart heaved. I had almost forgotten how she stomped out. Almost.

"First things first," he said. "About Misty. She's not my girlfriend."

"She sure talked like she was."

"Misty would like to be my girlfriend, but that is not my plan," he said. "We've been hooking up for a few months."

"Hooking up? Gross. Grow up, Hank."

"You're hooking up with that hottie I saw you with yesterday."

"That's different," I said. "I didn't ask her for money."

"You should ask her for money. You're so broke you can't even pay attention."

"Not now, Hank."

"Is that what Misty told you? That I asked her for money?"

"Yes."

"That's a no-go. She was the one who came up with the hat idea. I told her if she thought it was so great, she could pay for it. And she did. It's working better than expected. I've been handing them out all over town—"

"Why didn't you pay for those ugly hats yourself? Don't you have a marketing budget?"

He guffawed. "I wish. All my discretionary funds keep getting eaten up by the mayor's extensive permit requirements. I wonder who'll take that over for him. I hear Flynt Burns is interested in running for mayor now. My nightmare—."

"He'll have to get in line," I said.

"What?"

"Nothing. Never mind. Why was my name on a list, circled in red?"

He leaned back. "Now that could be any number of things. Could be a list of people I want to hate but are like sisters to me."

"Hank."

"Could be a list of people I've asked for help getting my ancestral home back but have refused to intervene."

"Stop it."

"But it's probably a list of locals who owe me money. Or it could be that she saw that your mail gets sent here, and your name is often in red because you're in the debt danger zone. Who knows what Misty thought? She's got a different way of looking at things. Satisfied?"

"No, but it looks like you're not in the mood to give me straight answers about anything. Like why you were at Grist's the other night."

"Why were you there?" he asked. "Why were you there with the mayor's daughter? I have to say, Carrie, that your actions over the past twenty-four hours have been odd."

"Why did Misty say you have some secret?" I asked.

"Is that what she said? Huh." He bit his lower lip, but his expression remained unchanged.

"What's your big secret, Hank? Where do you disappear to?"

"Who knows what Misty thinks she saw or heard? I don't disappear. She gets mad when I'm not available to her all day long."

"She said you think you two don't have a future."

"Not sure where she's getting that. Probably an offhand joke I made. But she's not wrong. She's sort of a drag. Especially now. Going behind my back to snoop. Misty's a wild card. And she has a habit of meddling. Now that you're on her radar, you'll probably be hearing from her too, about all kinds of things."

"What about the list?"

"What list? I have no idea—. Oh, wait."

"Yes?"

"She offered to make some calls for me. As a joke, I told her to write down the mayor's number and to keep calling until someone answered. To keep her busy."

"She didn't know? About the mayor?"

"No. She's not from around here. And she's not into current events."

"That's dark, Hank."

"I'm not proud of it, now that I hear what it sounds like. But she wanted to do something. I added Grist's name to it after I found out he was in the hospital."

"Come on, Hank." I was stunned by his heartlessness. Hank had never shied away from a prank, but this felt grim.

"I know, I know. When he didn't answer, I told her to call you. But she went to see you instead."

"You can be a real jerk sometimes, you know that?"

My eyes filled with tears. Hearing that Hank could be so cruel was breaking my heart.

"I've got a dark side, Carrie. You know that."

I pulled myself together. I didn't have the luxury of getting emotional. I needed answers. I soldiered on. "You said Flynt sent you to Grist's house. You don't like either of them."

"Correction. It's my house, Carrie."

"Fine." I said, conceding the point so we wouldn't get into another fight. "Why, though?"

"I knew that Grist was laid up, and I wanted to go in. I haven't been in there in years. Honestly, I only wanted to see it.

I didn't know I was going to find Nancy Drew, Nancy Two, and a ransacked mess."

"Why would she say—"

He let out a tired sigh. "At this point, Carrie, I don't care what you or anyone else thinks."

"Hank." I reached across the table. He pulled away. I noticed his hands were dirty again.

"Maybe one day we can get past this," he said. "But right now, I need to go attend to that." He pointed to a fracas that was unfolding at the cash register. It was Miriam. She was giving Ayesha a rough time.

"Perfect timing," I said. "I need to talk to her."

"No, I said I wanted the aioli on the side, not poured all over," Miriam said. "It looks like goblin slobber, for heaven's sake. Every time I get an order to go, I have to demand a refund."

"Maybe that's a feature, not a bug," Hank interjected. "It seems to me that you're always looking for something to complain about, Mrs. Cringe."

"How dare you imply I am anything less than honest," she huffed. "I will have you know—"

"You lied to me, Miriam," I said, cutting her off. The color drained from her face. "You let me believe you were leaving town. But Walker and Lister said they saw you at your home-owner's association meeting."

"I'll leave you two ladies to it," Hank said before ducking into the back. "Enjoy your sandwich, Miriam."

"That will be impossible now," she said.

"Why don't we talk outside?"

"First of all, I didn't lie to you, smarty pants," she said. "You and your girlfriend said I was leaving town; I did nothing to change your minds."

"But why? Honestly, Miriam, I'm not trying to blame you.

I'm trying to clear my name. This thing is more complicated than you can even imagine."

"You don't think I know that? This thing was complicated before the mayor turned up dead."

"I know you want to run for mayor," I stammered, hoping to put her on the spot.

"Oh, good job," she said. "Way to find out something that was public record anyway."

"But I—."

"Keep digging, girl genius. This is only the beginning."

§

"People think I'm a witch," I said.

"Other people's opinions of you are none of your business," Aunt Inez said. "I love you. Grist loves you. And Waggery loves you. These are the most important things."

"Mwah," Waggery said. "Mwah. Mwah."

"See? He's giving you kisses," Aunt Inez said. "He adores you."

"I think you're misunderstanding me," I said. "I kind of like it?"

"Oh-ho-ho!" Aunt Inez said. "That's something else entirely."

"I need some spells," I said. "Can you teach me?'

"I'm not a witch," she said. "And neither are you. Since that's the case, what difference does it make if your spells are real?"

"I need Daisy Chatterly to leave me alone," I said, sulking. "I need a 'shut your stupid face' spell. She can think I'm a witch all she wants. But I would prefer for her to do it silently."

"I don't have one of those," she said. "But I bet if you make this face—" she contorted her placid, round face into a grotesque shape. "And make this motion—" she pinched her fingers and

released them, like she was sprinkling something with salt. "And make a sound like 'puh,' she'll back off."

"That's amazing," I said. I practiced in front of the mirror. "Puh, puh, puh."

"That's all you need to know about witchcraft," she said. "It works because you believe. Or, I should say, it works because they believe."

"Quok."

"What's that, Waggery?" Aunt Inez asked. She liked me to believe they had complete conversations, and I played along because it was more fun to imagine my aunt and her raven gossiping like two old biddies than to tell her that birds can't talk.

"Yes. Good point. I'll tell her."

"What's he say?" I asked.

"Waggery wants you to know that the most important thing to remember with spell craft is that what you wish on someone else, is what you'll get in return, but three times more powerful."

"That's okay," I said. "I can do three times as much shut up as Daisy. I hardly speak at school as it is."

"Be sure that you can," she said, her face darkening. "Because you never know when it's going to be payback time."

§

Chapter Eighteen

I followed Miriam outside.

The bright sunlight was an assault after sitting in the den-like confines of High on the Hoggarty. And being forced to talk to Miriam after she lied to me was the icing on the cake of an already stellar day.

She was picking through the bag with her lunch in it. She scowled.

"They screw up my order every time," she said. "That Hank. He turned out like we all thought he would."

"That's unkind, Miriam," I said. Hank and I weren't on good terms, but I knew better than anyone how he was hurting. "He made some mistakes, but we all do."

"Oh, boo-hoo," she said. "My husband died, but you didn't see me moping around and making everyone miserable."

That's debatable, I thought.

"No, I took the life insurance money and bought a condo with it," she said. "And I keep the place shipshape to honor his memory. I don't serve middle-aged ladies fried chicken club sandwiches swimming in enough sauce to drown a person."

"Come on, Miriam," I said. "Work with me here. I'm trying to sort out what happened to the mayor."

"What happened to hotsy-totsy?"

"Wait, who? What?"

This was exhausting.

"Your little girlfriend. Where is she?"

"Like you said, it's none of your business. But since I'm not keeping secrets, I'll tell you we had a falling out this morning."

She feigned shock. "You mean your one-night-stand didn't work out?"

"Miriam, please." I could feel a headache coming on. "Where were you going yesterday?"

"If you must know, I was going to see my attorney."

"Why wouldn't you tell me that? That seems like a normal thing for an HOA president to do during the course of the day. Especially on the day of a board meeting."

"I didn't feel like I needed to explain to you that I was on my way to see an attorney after everything that had happened that morning. It's none of anyone's business."

"So why are you telling me now?"

"Because you've been blabbing all over town how you think I had something to do with it," she said.

"Let's be clear," I said, stepping toward her to reinforce my point. "I never accused you of murdering the mayor."

"See that you don't, or I'll sue you, too. I may have been suing him, but I didn't want him dead. You'll remember that I also needed him to approve the Spring Garden Show. Our relationship was complicated, but not violent."

"You were suing the mayor?" This was news to me. "You were suing him and running for his position?"

"That is also none of your business. I'm a free citizen, and I'm allowed to sue anyone I want and run for any office I want."

My head was pounding. "Okay, Miriam. If you hear anything that might be helpful, will you please let me know?"

"Let *you* know? Never."

"Of course. Enjoy your sandwich."

"It's probably soup by now. That's why I like the aioli on. The. *Side*."

She stomped off toward her house and before she was out of sight, I remembered something.

"Hey. Miriam."

"What now?" she shouted.

"How did you know he'd been stabbed?"

"What?" She leaned toward me with her hand up to her ear, indicating that she couldn't understand me.

"Stabbed." I said, making stabbing motions in the air. "How did you know?"

"You're psychic," she shouted. "You figure it out."

I watched as Miriam charged down the street toward her condo, and my head felt as if it was filling with screams.

* * *

Turns out it was my ears that were filling with screams. I'd left Waggery alone, and even though I hadn't been gone for more than a few minutes, he was letting me know that he strongly objected to this decision.

I moved swiftly down the block. But as I approached the cottage, I saw the door was open.

"I need a new doorknob, stat," I muttered to myself as I stood, stunned, in front of my porch. What struck me as strange was that Waggery hadn't flown out. Why would he stay inside screaming when the door was open?

Had Stormy returned?

I dashed inside.

"Shh, birdie. Hush. You're freaking me out."

Someone was in my house.

Waggery was shouting from his perch and flapping his wings. He was upset by the intruder, but not so threatened that he attacked.

I was relieved to see that Daisy was unharmed. One thing she'd been right about during their earlier altercation was that Waggery could do permanent damage if he chose to.

"Oh, Carrie, thank goodness you're here. Wingman completely flipped out when I came in. But the door was open, so..."

"It's Waggery," I said. "You know that Daisy. And why did you break into my house?'

"I did no such thing," she insisted. "I heard you say something after I knocked, so I gave the door a tiny push and, *et voila*. It opened, like most doors do for *moi*."

"Are you here for a reading, Daisy?" I asked. "You're in luck. I'm available right now. Have a seat."

"Oh no, honey," she said. "I don't do—" she looked around in disgust "—all of that. I have some questions. For the *Post*."

"I refuse to comment on anything," I said. "And I mean anything."

She was undeterred. "Ms. Dettwiler, what did you know, and when did you know it?"

"I'm sorry, what?"

"When you found the mayor?" She put the word "found" in air-quotes. "Was it because your psychic ability tipped you off? Or were there other dark forces at work?"

"I have no idea what you're talking about. I have no comment."

She made a big show of scribbling something in her notebook.

"So, you're not denying that you didn't not have anything to do with the mayor's untimely passing?"

"What's with the triple negative?" I asked. "Are you trying to trick me into saying I murdered my friend?"

"If he was your friend, why did you murder him in a satanic sacrifice?"

"Where do you come up with this stuff?"

"Oh, so you admit it," she said.

"I did not admit—"

"Did you think the mayor's death would give you ever-lasting life? Grant a wish? Find you a mate?"

"I'm a tarot card reader," I said. "I sit at that table, the one right over there, and look at pictures for a living. Nothing satanic about it. It's not even religious."

"What was the significance of the black feathers?" she asked. "Were they an offering to your evil god to deliver the mayor's soul to the fiery depths of hell?"

I thought of the Emperor card and how Aunt Inez had explained the volatility of its orange background. I shivered. "Daisy. No." I pointed to Waggery. "He's a bird. With feathers. They pop off sometimes."

"I can quote you as saying that Walgreens was also involved in the slaying?"

"I'm going to need to ask you to leave," I said. Waggery was still screaming intermittently, probably sensing my stress, and I could feel my pulse in my temples.

"I'm a news reporter," she said, with a stomp of her foot. "It would be irresponsible for me not to speculate on how this happened."

"That's literally the opposite of what you should be doing, Daisy," I said. "You should be gathering facts. Not manipulating people into giving you quotes that support wild conspiracies."

"Quok," Waggery agreed.

"You're infringing upon my free speech by refusing to talk to me," she said, with a straight face.

"My Aunt Inez used to say, '*Everyone has the right to speak, but no one has the right to be listened to.*'"

"What are you saying to me right now?" she asked.

"I'm inviting you to leave, please."

Waggery blew a raspberry.

"If I leave, I can't get you on the record as saying you didn't drink the mayor's blood," she said. "I like the sound of *Blood Lust: Mayor Murdered in Satanic Spree. Did Home-Grown Crone Work Alone?*"

"Daisy. Out."

She ignored me and instead started rifling through things in my kitchen.

"I mean it," I said. "You have no right, not as a so-called journalist, or as a person, to be looking through my things."

She turned to look at me, her face bone white.

"You look like you've seen a ghost," I joked. "So we're clear —aside from not being a witch, my house is also not haunted."

She held up the bundle of sticks I'd made earlier in one hand and the small label that read *Daisy* that I hadn't yet attached.

"Voodoo," she croaked.

"Boo," Waggery yelled.

"It's a joke, Daisy," I said. "I made that this morning before all this happened. A prank."

"I'm not laughing," she said, pocketing the doll. "I am going to name her exhibit A when I file my report with Officer Bucket."

"Get out of my house."

My voice trembled involuntarily. If Daisy didn't think I was worried before, she knew I was worried now.

"Puh," I said, trying to recover. "Puh! Puh!"

"Stop cursing me!"

"Puh! Puh!" I had committed to this course of action, juvenile as it was, and I was going to see it through.

"This is not over, Carrie," she said as I corralled her toward the door. "I've got a deadline and I will get my scoop."

As the door closed behind her, I heard her say, "Hag."

To which I responded: "Hack."

I showed her.

* * *

I'd only known Stormy for twenty-four hours but being at home, alone with Waggery, felt lonelier than it ever had before. After the electric energy generated by Daisy's quasi-journalistic onslaught dissipated, the air in the cottage was heavier somehow, sadder.

Where was Stormy?

Waggery was antsy, having missed his morning outing, so I rolled his ball for him a few times on the floor.

I fed him some grapes.

"I love you," he said, this time in Grist's voice.

I was rudderless.

I wished I had someone to help me sort all of this out. Hank was unreachable. Emma may or may not have known about some financial double dealings with the museum—and she either was responsible for it or thought Grist was. Miriam was suing the mayor for some unknown reason and carried a hammer in her bag, but somehow knew the mayor had been stabbed before anyone else did. She was also planning on running against him in the upcoming election, so that seemed like a strong motive. Flynt Burns was kindly tending to Grist but didn't know the true nature of his accident. Lillian was possibly lying about what she knew. Quite a few people in town seemed to think that my visit with the mayor resulted in his death.

You think you know a place. Then something like this happens and you realize that every single person is hiding something, including yourself.

Why didn't I tell Stormy about the ring? And what did she mean by she came back to get it from the mayor? Did she loan it to him? Did he steal it? Why did he have it at all?

If he stole it, would that have prompted her to murder him? Did she kill her father and then, unable to locate the ring she came for, go on a sleuthing expedition with me to find it, using me as cover?

I wondered if that was why she came undone in front of Officer Bucket.

Maybe she was the leader of a criminal enterprise. Or at least a high-ranking member.

Had I been seduced by a sexy murderess? Did she use me to introduce her to people in town so that she could unfurl a dastardly plan?

I needed some guidance.

"When life is hard, check your cards," Aunt Inez always said.

I got my deck, gave it a quick shuffle, and pulled one card.

It was the Chariot card. The image is a man standing in a traveling chariot being pulled by two Sphynxes. This was a card of energy, motion, bravery.

"She's on the move," I said. "She's on a mission. Determined. No stopping her now."

I put the card back in the deck and stared out of the window.

"Or maybe that's me. Or maybe it's what I should be doing —moving, running—rather than sitting here and letting my sadness overtake me."

I went back to the stack of papers on my kitchen table, and

rifled through them, looking for something, anything that would tell me what to do next. The Wine Museum was Grist's passion. I hadn't had anything to do with it, other than offering support and cheerleading his efforts. Reading over lists and prices for glass bung closures and riddling racks was as confounding to me as my first lessons with tarot cards. I was trying to solve a mystery in a foreign language.

What was clear to me, despite my rudimentary understanding of anything financial, is that several hundred thousand dollars-worth of art, equipment, and tools had been purchased for the Wine Museum and returned.

I may not have ever learned how to balance a checkbook or to set up auto-payments on my online bank account, but I knew how to return things I couldn't afford.

If all the items Grist had receipts for now have corresponding return slips, what was in the museum, who bought it, and why? According to Lillian, the museum was ready to open.

"It's a puzzle," I said to Waggery.

"Puzzle." he said in return, his signal that he wanted his actual puzzle—a tray with a maze that he could solve for food— to play with. He was being so calm and cute; how could I say no?

I put a grape in his maze, placed the maze on the floor, and watched him go to work. "We're doing the same thing, in a way," I said. "But I have a feeling you'll solve yours faster and have a better reward. I don't think there will be a sweet treat for me at the end of all of this."

But I didn't have too much time to feel sorry for myself. My phone rang.

"Carrie Dettwiler? This is Brian. Grist's nurse?"

"What's happening, Brian?"

"Grist is awake. Those sweet ladies from the historical

society were here. He's in high spirits. I think it's a good time to visit."

"I'll be right there." I grabbed Grist's phone in case he needed it—I certainly had some questions about what I had found.

I left Waggery on the floor playing with his puzzle, silently praying that it would keep him occupied while I was gone. The last thing I needed was for Waggery to get me into any more trouble.

I was on the move. Like the card said.

Chapter Nineteen

Despite Brian's assurances that Grist was probably going to be fine, what I saw alarmed me. He seemed to have shrunk overnight. His skin was the color of the pebbles mined from the Hoggarty Hill Quarry, the ones that lined the pathway around the duck pond. This wasn't the rosy-cheeked, robust Grist Featherweight I relied on for laughs, emotional support, and the occasional fix-it job in the house.

He was awake, but he seemed weak.

"Grist?" I began. "I would have come sooner, but they said you were drugged up and resting."

He had a strange look on his face.

"Plus, I've had a weird twenty-four hours. Some people think I had something to do with the mayor's death, can you believe it? Someone ransacked your house. I found some receipts in the hidey-hole in your office. What was that about? I kicked Daisy out of my house. She's trying to get me to confess that the mayor's murder was a satanic sacrifice."

He appeared to be struggling to speak. Was this normal for this kind of injury?

"Brian?" I called. "Could you come here?"

He appeared.

"Is it normal that he would have trouble speaking? Is it his medication?"

"Let me see," he said. "Mr. Featherweight are you having trouble speaking?"

Grist looked at him.

"I think that's a yes," I said. "It's not like he can nod with that brace on."

Brian gave me some side eye. "I'm going to get the doctor. I don't like the look of this."

I sat on the edge of Grist's bed. "I think you're in some distress, but we're going to get it sorted."

His flailing arm hit me on my side. I jumped, startled.

Grist moved his mouth, but no words came out.

"What is it? What is happening? Brian."

Brian and the doctor rushed into the room. "Carrie, can you give us a minute? Step out to the hallway so we can see what's going on?"

I backed toward the door.

"Carrie, please." Brian closed the door. "We need some space."

Bewildered, shaken, and deeply concerned about what was happening with Grist, I paced the hallway in front of his room.

His phone buzzed in my pocket. He had a text. It was from Lillian, and it read:

LILLIAN: So nice to see you this morning. Call when you can, in private. XO

I started to type back to get more information when Brian emerged from the room. The doctor breezed right past me, not making eye contact.

"His tongue swelled up," Brian said.

"What does that mean?"

"We're not sure. The doctor has ordered some tests and we're trying to reduce the swelling."

"But what could have—"

"We're not sure yet," he said.

"Surely, you've seen this in school or something, right? What can cause a tongue to swell up?"

"Ms. Dettwiler, I am not going to diagnose your uncle standing here in the hallway. That is the doctor's job. Possibly poison."

"Poison? You can't be serious."

"And this is why we don't diagnose in the hallway," he said, shuttling me toward the stairwell. "We will do our best for your uncle. Right now, you should go home or take a walk outside. It's a beautiful day. We'll call you when we have an answer."

"Who would poison him?"

He let out a long sigh. "I'm sorry I said anything. I'm reading *The Count of Monte Cristo* and I'm obsessed with poison. And revenge. The only people who have been in to see him are those sweet old ladies from the Historical Society and they wouldn't hurt a fly."

"I guess you've never read *Arsenic and Old Lace?*"

"What?"

"Never mind."

Chapter Twenty

I couldn't do anything for Grist, and I couldn't do anything for myself, so I decided to go home and take Waggery out for a walk. It was a beautiful Prosperity day, and the town looked as rich and colorful as it did when it was featured on the cover of *Cottage Country* magazine.

Waggery whooshed off toward the duck pond and I followed, if for no other reason than to protect Ligeia from his over-assertiveness.

My gut was telling me I needed to talk to Lillian. I called her and she agreed to meet me.

"Carrie, what a terrible few days you've had," she said, giving me a quick hug and handing me a small box. "It's cheese straws," she said. "You loved those when you were little. I was thinking of you and thought they would help."

"Thank you, Lillian,"

"How's Grist?" she asked. "We were all dying to see him this morning. Oh, I should have chosen a better word. You know what I mean."

"I do," I said. "Grist values your friendship."

I wasn't sure if Grist had romantic feelings toward Lillian or not, but I did know that he liked her. I wanted to acknowledge that he would appreciate her concern without encouraging her in case that isn't what he wanted.

"I don't know what the Historical Society would do without him," she said. "He handles everything. Everything. He's a competent man."

"That's kind of you to say," I said. "But Lillian, I have something to confess."

"Oh no, Carrie? Is it true? Is everything Daisy is saying true?"

"I don't know what you're—"

"Everyone in town thinks you had something to do with it," she said. "Except me. I know you didn't."

"I'm sure not everyone—"

"I would never believe it. Never in a million years. Not Grist's Carrie. You don't have a violent bone in your body and the mayor was your friend. I refuse to believe it."

"Thank you, Lillian. On that note, I am trying to piece together some information that may or may not be related to the mayor's murder."

"Go on."

"Do you know anything about the purchase of the items for the Hoggarty Heaven Winery display at the museum?"

"Like what?"

"Did you see the items being unpackaged and placed?"

"What do you mean?" Her doe-like eyes blinked.

"When the items arrived, did you see them?"

"Not exactly," she said. "I helped unwrap a few things. But Grist did most of the heavy lifting. There were some large items."

"What was the problem with the shelf?"

"Oh that? Flynt had installed a shelf to display those large format bottles of the Hoggarty wine that won that French Wine

Cup. But I noticed it was wobbly. I asked Grist to fix it and he did."

"Do you think one of the bottles could have fallen on him?"

She looked puzzled. "I suppose anything is possible. Do you think that's what happened to him? Is that why he's in the hospital? Because that seems—not quite right."

"I didn't think so either. Do you know anything about Flynt Burns returning the items that Grist ordered?"

"Returning? No. I can't imagine why he would do that. We didn't have much time and Grist had taken such special care to get the specific items needed to make the displays as perfect as possible."

As the day progressed, I realized that the more information I uncovered, the more questions I had. I needed to broach the subject of the phone with Lillian, but I didn't want to hurt her feelings.

"Here's something a little more delicate," I said. "Why didn't you tell me the truth about where you found Grist's phone?"

"What do you mean?" She looked at me pleadingly with those deep blue eyes, and I felt like I was kicking a kitten.

"You said you found the phone in the stairwell. But that's not possible. Based on the way the exhibit is configured, it would have been easier for Flynt to get Grist out of the building by using the elevator. I doubt he would have been able to walk down the stairs."

"I don't know about any of that," she said. She sat up straight and clenched her purse in her lap. "But when I say I found the phone behind the sign in the lobby, I found it behind the sign in the lobby."

I wasn't inclined to press her. Her mind was already clearly blown by the drama of the recent events, not to mention her crush being in the hospital. But something occurred to me, so I posed it as a thought, not a question.

"That must have been a huge mess to clean up," I said. "That huge bottle hitting the marble tile. It would have been like a wine bomb dropping."

Lillian appeared to be shutting down. "Oh, I don't know about any of that." The volume of her voice trailed off at the end.

"Thanks, Lillian. I appreciate your help," I said. "I also appreciate you standing up for me when people attach my name to the mayor's murder."

"Of course," she said. "Oh, what is it you wanted to confess?"

"I have Grist's phone. I read your text to him a little while ago. What did you mean by 'in private?'"

"You shouldn't read people's messages, Carrie. Shame on you."

"I'm being implicated in a murder, Lillian," I said. "Frankly, all bets are off at this point."

"Speaking of private messages..." Walker, followed by Lister, with Daisy Chatterly looking positively parched for information behind them, sauntered up to where we were sitting. "Why did the mayor die with a tarot card in his hand? Was it a macabre message left by a murderer bent on revenge?"

"Are you three working together now?" I asked. "This is my nightmare."

"What do you have to say about that tarot card?" Daisy demanded, shoving a micro-recorder in my face.

"What I have to say for myself is that you three are making things worse," I said. "For everyone."

"Is that true, Daisy?" Lister asked. "I thought you said Carrie confirmed the card was hers?"

Daisy shifted on her feet. She shook her blonde ringlets defiantly.

"It was Miriam who told me about the tarot card. I never liked you, Carrie."

If I hadn't been so shocked to hear someone in this town finally speaking the truth, this revelation might have hurt my feelings. But I was going to have to circle back to that later. Daisy had also revealed something important.

"Miriam? How would she know about that?"

It dawned on me. The person in the stairwell, the one who ran out before I got to the bottom of the stairs—that was Miriam.

"It wasn't me," I said. "Everyone heard Waggery yelling. He's a mimic."

"That's an interesting alibi," Walker said, barely able to control his smirk. "She's stark *raven* mad."

"I think she's *winging it,*" Daisy chimed in. "*Main Suspect Blames Murder Bird in Crow-by-Crow replay.*"

"She's definitely a *flight risk,*" said Walker, amused by his own cleverness.

"Guys, this is serious," said Lister. "This is nothing to *crow* about. Sorry, Carrie. I couldn't help myself. It sounds so ridiculous."

I continued, undeterred. "What's ridiculous is listening to Miriam Cringe. Maybe you should go to her condo and see why she was hiding in the stairwell of the mayor's office."

For once, they were all speechless.

"Here's your story, Daisy. Go hound Miriam about what else she knows about the mayor's death," I said. "She knows things she should not know, if you understand what I am saying to you three. Ask her what she was doing there before me. You might have a headline that goes something like, *So Cringe: Duck Foe in the Know. Will her Alibi Fly?*"

They exchanged wide-eyed looks.

"Carrie, we're trying to get to the bottom of this," said Lister. "My compatriots can be excitable. But please know that we are trying to get to the truth, not cast baseless aspersions."

"Against Miriam, you mean. None of you seem to mind tossing all kinds of aspersions my way. Now, if you don't mind—"

"Emma said you owed the mayor money," Daisy blurted out.

"What?" Walker's eyes were the size of quarters. "Now that's a twist."

"Stop it. You three need to shoo." Lillian interjected. "She has been through enough. Shoo. And keep your gossip to yourselves. Carrie had nothing to do with this. Shoo. Go on."

I watched as they made their way across the plaza huddled together, sharing secrets like a clique of middle schoolers.

"They're like flies, always buzzing around," she said. "I've had enough."

"I have one more question for you, Lillian," I said. "Who was with you—"

My phone rang.

I answered it.

"Carrie Dettwiler?"

It was Officer Bucket.

"Yes, sir?"

"When you have a minute, I'm going to need you to come to the station. I need to talk to you about tarot—"

"I'll be there as soon as I can."

Chapter Twenty-One

The last time I'd been in the waiting room of the Prosperity police station, Hank and I had been caught with a half-full bottle of Hoggarty Heaven Rosé and pockets full of jawbreakers we'd pilfered from the Prosperity Grab n' Go. We were thirteen. Aunt Inez, Grist, and Officer Bucket hatched a plan to scare us straight, and it worked for the most part. We didn't see Officer Bucket again until we were high schoolers high schooling all over town and someone had to stop us from ruining ourselves. But we never had to go to the station again.

I fought the urge to slip out the way I had come in. Officer Bucket was making me sit and think about what I had done to deserve this, like he did when I was a kid. But I was an adult. Time to put on my big girl panties and face the music, whatever the tune. Or something like that.

Waggery and I ate the cheese straws Lillian gave me and realized how hungry I was when they were gone. I threw the box in the recycling and sat down to wait.

I tried to piece together my thoughts, but without knowing

exactly why I was there, I wasn't sure what I needed to have prepared. Did I need a lawyer? Was this related to the mayor's murder? I assumed it had to be, but what if I was wrong? What did I need to avoid saying to prevent implicating myself?

The longer I sat, the more I stewed in my own questions. Now would have been a perfect time for me to do another reading on myself, to get clarity on what my next steps were, but I never could have anticipated I would have ended up here, not yet.

What was Hank hiding? Where was Stormy? Who ransacked Grist's house and why? Was it possible that Officer Bucket suspected me for stealing that ring? Did Stormy turn me in?

I wished I could talk to Grist. He could to put these puzzle pieces together. He loved puzzles.

Waggery fussed and fluttered around, annoyed that I had cut his romantic duck pond visit with Ligeia short. He pulled at my hair and pecked at my pockets. I tried to calm him down, but he seemed determined to make his point.

"I get it, you're not happy," I said. "Stop fussing and I'll take you home as soon as I can for a snack."

He thrust his beak—which was sharp—into my pocket and pulled out a piece of paper. I didn't remember putting anything in my pocket this morning.

I picked it up and noticed that it was neatly folded. I opened it up to find a receipt from Finders Keepers. But I hadn't shopped at Finders Keepers in a long time.

Officer Bucket finally appeared at the end of the hall. He was walking with a young boy who appeared to have been crying. I heard him say, "Everyone makes mistakes, Jeffrey. And you and me? We're square. You've got nothing to be afraid of."

"Yes, sir."

Gone was the Knight of Swords demeanor from before. Here, Officer Bucket was all Justice: fair and ethical. Great to have on your side when you were a good guy in a jam; a nightmare to deal with if you were on the wrong side of the law.

"What have we learned today?" he asked Jeffery.

"That there's no such thing as the finder's keeper's law."

"That's right. You're a bright young man. Finder's keeper's is a what?"

"It's a thrift store, not a law." Jeffery smiled, and Officer Bucket tousled his hair.

I was caught up in the sweetness of this Mayberry moment before I realized what had happened.

I may not be psychic, but Aunt Inez used to say, "*If you think something is a coincidence, think again.*"

It's possible that Jeffery saying out loud the words "finders keepers" after Waggery had pulled a perfectly folded receipt from my pocket was a complete coincidence. But someone had put that receipt in my pocket in the hopes I'd find it and follow up.

Was Grist able to place it there this morning before his episode? Or did Lillian place it there while Daisy, Walker, and Lister were harassing me?

I didn't know the answer to that yet. But I knew what I needed to do.

Officer Bucket was still chatting with Jeffery and a woman whom I assumed was Jeffery's frazzled mom, and he hadn't seen me yet. I silently got up and made my way toward the side entrance and slipped out before anyone else took notice. Waggery, in a move that was completely out of character, remained silent.

I thought he might be enjoying all this sneaking around.

If I didn't look like one before, I absolutely looked like a murderer now. But I didn't have time to worry about the legal implications of running from the law. I had to take my raven home.

After that, I had some secondhand shopping to do.

Chapter Twenty-Two

As a person of modest means, I'd spent my fair share of time in thrift stores. But Finders Keepers wasn't on my radar as much as, say, Re-Threads across town, where I purchased the sartorial success I was currently wearing for less than three total dollars.

That's because Finders Keepers specialized in home goods and high-end antiques, and I was already well-stocked in my cottage. I simply never needed a new sofa, even if stylish castoffs from the designer homes at Hoggarty Heights could be found for a steal.

As far as I knew, Grist had no reason to shop there either, although now that I was standing in the middle of it, I could see that they had a diverse assortment of things you'd find in a winery. Things you might find in a wine museum, in fact.

"Can I help you find something?"

A man in a red beret sat on a wooden bench in front of a display of second-hand wine goblets, and I immediately made the connection that this man was the human embodiment of the Nine of Cups: successful, satisfied and a tiny bit smug.

"I hope so," I said. "I am trying to locate some vintage wine items."

"Oh, well. In that case, I can tell you that you might be out of luck. If you're looking for an armoire, however, we recently received a beautiful piece—"

"Unfortunately, no, mister—"

"Gonzales," he said. "Hector."

"Pleased to meet you. I'm Carrie. What do you mean I might be out of luck finding things for the wine museum?"

"What I mean is that someone came in recently and stocked up on most of my vintage wine accessories. I had a little of everything, you know, as one does when one has a thrift store in proximity to so many wineries."

"Do you remember who it was?"

"I wasn't here," he said.

"Oh?"

"It happened on a Sunday morning, and I never work on Sundays."

"Who was here? Would it be possible for me to talk to them?"

"To Chad? Sure. I have no problem with that. Want me to get his number?"

Chad? Could it possibly be the same kid Grist was texting with?

"One second," I said. I took out Grist's phone and scrolled through his texts. "It's not Chad Santos, is it?"

"It is," he said. "Do you know him?"

"Not directly. But I know how to reach him. Can I contact him?"

"Tell him I give him permission to answer your questions," he said. "He's a history buff. Curious mind for a kid his age."

"Thank you for your time, Mr. Gonzales."

"You're welcome. Sure you don't want to peek at that armoire? It's got fantastic corbels."

"I'm sure the corbels are peerless, but no," I said. "It occurs to me that you might be able to help me with one more thing."

"I'll try."

I pulled up the photo of the unidentified item on Grist's phone.

"Well, I'll be," he said, taking my phone to get a closer look. "I haven't seen one of those in a while. Aren't too many floating around. People who find them tend to keep them."

It took every ounce of restraint for me to stop myself from making a finders keepers joke.

"What is it?" I asked.

"It's a corkscrew."

"How do you get corkscrew out of that?" I took the phone back and twisted the phone sideways to see what he was seeing.

"That's it," he said. "It's disguised to look like a cigar case. Agustus Hoggarty—you know who he is, right?"

"I certainly do."

"Had to ask," he said. "Young people don't always know history. Anyway, he made a few dozen of these during Prohibition. Gave them to his friends and associates to use on bootlegged bottles of wine. Corkscrews weren't illegal back then—only wine. But he thought it best to err on the side of caution. As cautious as one could be as a notorious bootlegger, I suppose. It's probably worth quite a bit. If you could sell one of those, you could treat yourself to a few nice dinners at some of the fancier places in town."

"What does this part do, here at the top?"

"Foil cutter," he explained. "This top part pops off and reveals a small knife inside."

"Handy," I said.

"If you had one, you'd open the top to pull the knife out.

These blades—you've probably seen them on other corkscrews —are only a few inches long, like the blade of a standard pock-etknife. But this version has a nasty, jagged blade. Great for removing foils from wine bottles. And foes."

"Foes?" I asked.

"Rumor has it quite a few people met their end because of one of these."

"What do you mean?"

"I mean," he lowered his voice to a whisper, even though we were the only ones in the room. "Agustus Hoggarty's associates weren't afraid to use them as weapons."

* * *

I stepped outside and immediately texted Chad.

> ME: Chad this is Grist

> CHAD: Hey man. What's up

> ME: Did you sell some vintage wine stuff to a guy recently

> CHAD: Yeah

> ME: Do you know who he was

> CHAD: Nah. Some dude. Bought a bunch of crap

> ME: What did he look like?

> CHAD: Like a dude

> ME: Did he say anything

> CHAD: Not much. He was in a hurry.

> ME: Did he leave a credit card

CHAD: Paid cash. Does Hector know you texted me

ME: Yes, he says it's fine. Any description would help. I'll tell your teacher you helped with some history project for extra credit

CHAD: Thanks, bro. He had on a hat

ME: What kind of hat

CHAD: He wore a hat from that dump downtown and dark glasses super shady

ME: Thx. Bring me the extra credit form and I'll sign it

CHAD: Cool

I wasn't proud of misleading Chad, but how do you explain over a text why you have someone's phone and why you're trying to find out about an incident they probably hadn't given a second thought to? Sometimes one needs to fudge the truth to reveal the truth, even if it means that Chad might end up wandering around the plaza looking for Grist. There are worse things.

Like the fact that my childhood friend Hank—bitter, recalcitrant Hank who still had my undying loyalty—was behind all of this. I knew he was capable of some low-level dirty dealing, like moving forward with un-permitted and possibly unsafe renovations or overcharging bachelorette parties for drinks. Hank's always been a rapscallion, but I always believed he had a heart of gold. I knew him first as a sweet, innocent kid, and that's how I chose to think of him. Most of the time.

It appeared that he knew way more about what's happened in Prosperity the last twenty-four hours than he let on. And, standing outside of Finders Keepers scrolling through a handful of texts from a disinterested teenager, it became clear to me that

Hank was not only responsible for stealing expensive items from the Wine Museum, but that he could be responsible for the mayor's murder.

I put Grist's phone back in my pocket and made my way toward High on the Hoggarty. I was going to ask Hank some questions, and I was fully prepared to not like the answers.

§

"Do all tarot card readers think of their friends and family as versions of tarot cards?" I asked.

Aunt Inez had finished telling me a story about how when she first met Grist, she thought he was a classic Hierophant— bound to a code of conduct that originated outside of himself.

"I thought he was stuffy," she said. "And I used a negative spin on a card that's not negative at all to convince myself that he wasn't the right one for me. Kind of like people do when they have one bad dating experience with a Sagittarius, and they never date a Sagittarius again. Limiting and unnecessary."

"What changed?" I asked. "When did you realize he was your boo?"

She laughed. "Turns out that, for me, Grist was a Temperance card. Soothing. Calming. I had made him into a fusty, rule-obsessed Hierophant because I was looking for a reason to stay away. I had passed a judgment that I wasn't ready to pass yet, whether through my ignorance or my fear of getting involved with someone at my age."

"I think he's a Magician card," I said.

"I know you do," Aunt Inez said. "But he could still be a Hierophant and he would be the right person for me."

"How do you mean?"

"Always approach the cards with an open, neutral mind," she

said. "Don't put your own opinions into it if you can help it, like whether someone who adheres to rules is 'dull.'"

"Why not?" I asked.

"Because we're human, and we see what we want to see," she said. "Whether you're looking for the good or the bad in someone, you're going to find it. Every time."

§

I'd walked into High on the Hoggarty hundreds of times. This was my *Cheers*—the place where everyone knew my name. Living in a small town for most of your life meant that you belonged everywhere you went, but it also meant that everyone knew your baggage. People knew my sad stories, and they knew about my problems now. A vocal, delusional minority thought I was a witch. My life was, as much as it could be, an open book to the people of Prosperity.

Hank's situation was similar to mine. As the last remaining scion of a powerful family, he had more of his history on display than I did. But, unlike me, he could keep some things to himself. In my case, like keeping my sexuality a secret until I was ready to come out. This would be seen as privacy. In Hank's case, the things he kept to himself, like where his money went and his hidden girlfriend, felt more like secrets. And with the mayor dead, Grist in the hospital and a woman to whom I had forged an instant connection now disappeared from my life, I found myself devoid of patience for Hank's secrets.

"Here for a sandwich?"

Normally I would have taken this as, "Hey, I know we're not getting along great, but I still love you and you're welcome here." Today I took it as him deflecting. And I was angry.

"How's business, Hank? Good enough to hand out free sandwiches to anyone who needs them?"

He stopped wiping the bar and looked at me, hard. "You know how my business is, Carrie. Hanging on by a thread because of people like your uncle and Flynt Burns. And that mayor."

"You don't have to worry about the mayor anymore, though. Am I right? Someone took care of that."

He resumed wiping. "It's awful what happened. But my guess is they'll get some other gentrifying douchebag in there to replace him. I bet Flynt is furiously writing out campaign slogans as we speak. And Miriam."

"That would be collateral damage, though?"

"What are you talking about?"

"Why are your hands so dirty? Your fingernails are all messed up. I remember a time when you said that the Hoggarty family doesn't have to get its hands dirty. That your family 'had people for that.'"

"I've been doing some renovations, not that it's any of your business. And I don't have any money to hire 'people' anymore."

"Looks like you've been moving things. Like heavy furniture."

"Maybe," he said. "Like I said. Renovations."

"You wouldn't have been down in the tunnels lately?"

He clenched his jaw. "What do you want?"

"So that's a no? Or is it a deflection?"

"What are you getting at, Dettwiler?"

"I think you know exactly what I am getting at. Your face says as much."

"My face says it's disgusted with you. Why don't you tell me exactly what you're accusing me of?"

I took a deep breath. My hands were shaking. "I think, Hank, that you are sabotaging my Uncle Grist."

He didn't blink. "Go on."

"I believe you're stealing the items from the museum, smuggling them out through the tunnels and returning them to their original sellers and keeping the cash."

He leaned back on the counter behind him. "You think I would do that?"

"I think if you got desperate enough, you would do anything. In fact, I think that Grist caught you and went to the mayor to tell him what you were doing."

"Grist knows his antiques," he said. "He would definitely know if his precious, period-authentic pieces had been replaced."

"He did. In fact, I intercepted a phone call from a man named LeMarcus who confirmed to Grist that many of the items were, in fact, fake."

"You intercepted a call. From LeMarcus. Continue."

"Yes. I think that Grist already knew what you were up to and told the mayor. I think the mayor called you to his office."

"I murdered the mayor and snuck out through the tunnels." He nodded his head as if he were agreeing. "Sounds legit, Detective Dettwiler."

"I hope not, but this is what the evidence looks like. Knowing it was Grist who ratted you out, you found him at the museum and hit him on the head with a wine bottle. Flynt found him and took him to the hospital. You left him for dead. You left the man I call my uncle Grist for dead. So you could move into his house."

My whole body was quaking with rage.

"It's my house, Carrie," he said, and I didn't know if he meant to infuriate me, but that was the result. "So, your assertion is that I was stealing wine equipment from the museum and got caught."

"Yes. And when Stormy and I were in Grist's house, you were there looking for the same thing we were."

I could feel the clues coming together now, and it made my blood boil.

"And what was that?"

"The receipts that would prove that the items in the museum had been replaced with fakes. You ransacked the place looking for them."

"Is that what you were there for? Those receipts?"

"Yes. As it turns out," I said. "And to see that you'd ransacked the place."

"You think I did that."

"Yes."

He started folding bar towels. "Well done, Scooby-Doo. You've unlocked the mystery."

"Please tell me I'm not right," I said. "I never wanted to be wrong more in my whole life."

"You get your wish," he said, with a flourish of his hand like a bad magician. "You are as close to wrong as you've ever been, my friend. Some psychic you turned out to be."

"I'm not psychic."

"The more you speak, the more obvious that becomes," he said. "Listen, how about I tell you what everyone has been saying about you?"

"Like whom?"

"Like Daisy, who is radio blasting all over town that you killed the mayor as part of an eternal youth spell. Like Emma, who told Daisy that you owed the mayor money. Or Officer Bucket, who I spoke to not long ago, right after he says you ran out of the police station."

My throat was dry.

"You spoke to Officer Bucket?"

"I sure did. He didn't suspect me of any of these crimes, by the way. Funny how the guy who used to chase me through the vineyards thinks I'm innocent, but my so-called best friend doesn't."

"What did he say?"

"I told him the most likely scenario was that your perfect Uncle Grist was skimming funds from the museum for his personal use. I told Officer Bucket it was probably to pay for the upkeep of the house he stole from me. So, you may be right about those items being fakes. But it wasn't me who swapped them."

"I, uh—"

"Save it, Dettwiler. If anyone asks me anything about your involvement, I'll do my best not to tell them what I know about your stake in all of this,"

"And what is that, exactly?"

"That you and Stormy—everyone's gabbing about Stormy, by the way—planned this together. That you have been an item for a while, and this was your scheme to murder Mayor Money-bags for the inheritance and pin it on anyone else in town. They say you tried to murder Grist to get him out of the way."

"That's impossible. Stormy and I aren't even speaking anymore—"

"It's no more impossible than what you're accusing me of. Now get out of my sight. I have work to do."

Dazed, I got up to leave.

"And Carrie?"

"Yes?"

"Be careful what you accuse your friends of. At this rate, you won't have any left."

Chapter Twenty-Three

I nearly passed out on the sidewalk. I had been dashing all over town, and the combination of the physical exertion with emotional stress threatened to overwhelm me.

I remembered poor Waggery; he was quite likely starving. Time to go home and regroup.

"Buddy, I'm home," I called out. Tired, but home.

Waggery let out a wail, the kind that let me know he was mad. His perch was knocked over and he'd ripped into the throw pillow with the hand-embroidered evil eye on it that Aunt Inez loved so much. Feathers were everywhere. He needed to be fed, and he let me know he was displeased, to put it mildly.

"You mad at me?" I asked in a more aggressive tone than I usually used with him. "Everyone's mad at me. Get in line."

"Quok."

"I know, I know." I piled all the fruit I could find onto a plate and set it on the counter, as a treat. I normally liked for him to eat in his area to keep the mess to a minimum, but I thought about what Hank said and realized I needed to keep my friends happy.

"Should I scramble you an egg?"

I decided, yes, I should scramble him an egg, and I did so. I put it on his plate before he'd even finished the fruit. He clicked happily, and I was forgiven, for now.

That oughta do it, I thought.

Fortunately, Waggery picked the pillow at the seams rather than poking a hole in the center. It would be easy to fix, at least. He wanted me to know he was frustrated but he didn't want to destroy our relationship. I could respect that.

Aside from the pile on the floor, I was finding feathers all over the house, as if a light breeze—probably caused by Waggery's flapping wings—had blown through. As I was cleaning them up, I thought about something that Aunt Inez used to say about gossip being like a feather pillow you tear open and release into the wind.

"You'll never get all those feathers back," she said. *"And gossip is the same way. Once you've sent it out into the world, you'll never know how many corners it reaches, how many lives it will touch."*

I could see this metaphor in action now. I made a concerted effort in my life and my profession never to gossip, but I failed, and failed frequently. Now there was nothing but gossip floating into every corner of Prosperity and into every corner of my life. It seemed like the more I did to control it all, the more it was out of my reach.

Content with his mid-day meal, and perhaps feeling sheepish about the pillow he destroyed, Waggery flew to my arm to give me kisses.

"Mwah," he said, and I returned the gesture.

"We're a couple of weirdos, aren't we Waggery?" He gave me a look that seemed to say, "speak for yourself."

My mind was numb from the information I'd taken in, and I needed a way to sort it out. I wanted to sit down and read my cards, but Waggery, now fully sated, seemed to want to go for a walk. I didn't have it in me. Not only did I need to rest a minute, but I didn't feel like parading around downtown in front of the people who thought I might be a murderer. Nor did I want to attract the attention of Officer Bucket. I'd been able to avoid a scene with him to this point and I'd like to continue to do so. I couldn't afford a lawyer and if he got ahold of me before I sorted this out, I would need one.

I made a bold choice. I'd done it before, successfully, but only a few times and only when necessary. It felt necessary. I needed to concentrate.

I opened the front door and motioned for Waggery to take flight. "Go on, Kiddo," I said. "Why don't you go on a solo flight for a bit. Don't cause any problems, and I'll come get you on the duck pond in a little while."

He hopped to my feet and looked up at me. Surely you don't mean this, he seemed to say.

"Duck pond," I said. He knew those words. And he took off right after, probably to avoid sticking around long enough for me to change my mind.

I decided not to worry about him. He'll be fine, I reassured myself. He'd gotten out without my permission dozens of times and that worked out. Usually.

I sat down at my reading table and pulled cards, one for each person I had interacted with in the past twenty-four hours. I wasn't planning on doing a classic reading; past readings for myself had shown mixed results. I had a hard time being objective about my own questions. I wanted a visual of all the players so I could discover the connections between them. After talking to Hank, I needed to be sure of my footing before I set fire to any more relationships.

I pulled everyone's card and placed them on the table. The mayor as the Emperor in the center with the rest of us in orbit around him. The visual took my breath away. I surveyed each one and acknowledged everyone's unique traits. Grist as Magician, capable of dazzling all of us. Emma's Empress, who sits on a throne and surrounds herself with opulence. Flynt, a Fool who brings mischief and possibility. Even Daisy, whose avatar, Judgement, trumpets her opinions from the clouds, has a role to play. Each of us—I, the Nine of Pentacles and Stormy's Strength, wrestling victory from the jaws of a lion, and Hank's menacing Devil—brings a unique set of talents and skills to this small town. If it hadn't been for the sadness and fear that threatened to overtake me, I would have been in awe of how all of us found each other in this lovely place and made it something so much greater than the sum of its parts.

Other than the mayor in the center, the cards were in no order. What order could there be? I still wasn't clear on everyone's role. I meditated on each one to see if I could glean some sort of insight, some sort of direction to take. Did I need to circle back with Hank? I studied cards to see if there was a clue.

Nothing. Perhaps Hank and I were done for a while.

Misty's Queen of Swords gave me pause. What could I learn from her? Other than the fact that Hank had more secrets than I even thought? Officer Bucket as Knight of Swords or Justice—was he friend or foe?

I looked at the Tower card. A lightning bolt striking a building, sending its occupants tumbling toward the earth. Shock. Change. Disruption.

Miriam.

In readings I point out that change is coming, but it might ultimately be for the best. The Tower card is one to pay attention to, but never fear.

Something grabbed me about Emma. What was she willing to do to get the mayor to marry her? Could he have changed his mind, causing her to lash out in a fit of anger? Then there was the incriminating evidence in her trash and the text to Grist. She'd been spreading gossip about me—was this to deflect from any evidence that might point to her?

That's when I remembered about my missing Lovers card. The last reading I'd seen it in was hers, last week. Had it been missing since then? Did she take it? Did she give it to the mayor as a flirty gesture of love? Or was it a threat?

Had Emma left The Lovers card in the mayor's hand after she killed him?

Shaking, I dropped my deck onto the floor. As I leaned over to pick them up, I knocked a card to the floor. It landed face down.

Aunt Inez called these cards "jumpers," and she always told me to take them seriously. I picked it up and turned it over.

It was The Tower. Its dark skies and lightning bolt, its bodies falling to the earth—it looked like a warning.

And it was.

Right on cue, there was a knock at the door. I braced myself. I didn't get up.

"Who is it?" I called out.

"Carrie? It's Miriam."

The Tower had arrived.

"Open the door," she said. "I have something to confess."

Chapter Twenty-Four

"Where's Satan's smallest demon?" Miriam dropped her bag on the sofa and collapsed in a heap.

"Make yourself at home, Miriam," I said. "Can I offer you anything?"

"First tell me if your henchman is going to pop up somewhere to surprise me."

"He went to the duck pond. I think."

"That duck pond," she muttered. "Cesspool of filth. Spring of disease."

"Miriam, it's been an excruciating day. Is there something I can help you with?"

She sat up. She cleared her throat. "I lied to you."

"I know. You're not the only one. It's been a parade of lies through Prosperity over the past twenty-four hours. Oh, who am I kidding? It looks like lots of people have been lying for a long time."

"I never lied." Miriam snapped.

"But you said—"

"Right." She took a deep breath. "It's a habit. I'm so accustomed to being on the defensive that things like that just pop out."

"I understand, Miriam. What is it you wanted to tell me?" I spoke slowly and calmly, like you would to an injured animal you were trying to rescue. No sudden moves.

"I lied," she said.

"What did you lie about?"

"This is painful."

"Take your time. There's no rush."

"All I ever wanted was to honor my husband's memory by finally owning a home and caring for it properly. And now I will probably lose everything. Everything."

"Miriam? What have you done?"

"That and get rid of that mosquito farm the mayor calls a duck pond—"

"Focus, Miriam."

"When you and Breezy came by—"

"Stormy," I said.

"Yes. Stormy. When you both came by to accuse me of murder—"

"We didn't accuse you of murder."

"Yes, you did," she said, her voice shaking. "You have no idea what it's like to be accused of something so dark."

I started to tell her how, oh-yes-I-most-certainly-did-people-think-I-slaughtered-the mayor.

But I refrained.

"Anyway," she continued, squaring her shoulders. "The point is that I was going somewhere."

"Were you running errands? Picking up something for the homeowner's association meeting that night?"

I was antsy about Waggery's whereabouts, and I had the feeling that Miriam was about so serve up a big nothing burger that didn't get me any closer to finding the true killer.

"I went to see my lawyer."

"You told me that already."

"I did a bad thing Carrie," she said. "A horrifying thing."

The hair on my arms stood up.

"Miriam? What did you do?"

"I can hardly believe it myself. It all happened so fast. So fast." She started to cry.

"Oh, Miriam. Tell me," I put my hand on her shoulder. It was surprisingly cold. "Tell me what you did so I can help you."

"You think you can help me? You can't." She was sobbing now. "That's why I went to my lawyer. She says I need to turn myself in, and I agree. But I needed to see if I could protect my house, and my beloved homeowner's association, before they send me away."

"Start at the beginning," I said, my throat dry. "You were on your way to the mayor's office right after you left your reading, correct?"

I handed her a tissue. I kept them close by. Many a tissue was needed after a reading in this house.

"Yes. The night before, I had gotten a call from one of my moles on the town council."

"You have moles on the town council?"

"You don't?" Her lower lip quivered.

"Never mind," I said. "Please continue."

"They told me that the mayor had called a secret meeting and they voted, without public comment, on the expansion of the duck pond."

I nodded like I hadn't seen this information on that balled-up memo Waggery pulled from the mayor's trash.

"That must have upset you," I said, still nodding like a psycho.

"You bet your brainy britches it did. That man. That *man*. He knew I had gathered a coalition of concerned residents.

We'd planned to make such a ruckus at the next town council meeting that they would know, beyond any doubt, that not only does Prosperity not need nor want this expansion the mayor was so fond of, but that we don't need that disgusting duck pond at all."

"You were furious. You acted rashly." This was starting to make sense, though I hoped this conversation wasn't going in the direction it seemed to be.

"I was. I did."

"So, you went to his office," I said, a statement, not a question.

"I stormed it like the beach at Normandy."

"What happened? How did this escalate to the point where you—"

"It didn't. Nothing escalated. I raced in there to give the mayor a piece of my mind. I had a whole speech prepared. I was going to let him know this treachery would not stand, that I would use my influence in Prosperity to out him for the under-handed sneak he is. I was ready to put him in his place. I was going to tell him that Miriam Cringe was going to challenge him in the next election."

"What happened next?"

"I flung his door open, hoping to startle him, hoping to throw him off-balance so I could let it fly. The element of surprise has always been one of my strengths."

"And then?"

"Oh. Carrie. It didn't go that way at all." She dabbed her eyes.

"How did it go, Miriam?"

"The mayor. He was—"

"He was what? Violent? Angry? Unhinged?" I was grasping for anything that would make this self-defense.

"He was dead."

"He was dead?"

A feather from the pillow floated in the air between us, and you could have knocked me over with it.

"He was lying on the floor in a pool of his own blood. It was like my daydreams, Carrie. Only real."

"Miriam."

"I don't think it's a huge secret that I often wished the mayor dead." She said this almost proudly.

I had once thought that Miriam's hostile attitude had lost its power to shock me. I was learning that I was wrong about that.

"Please continue." I could feel beads of sweat forming on my upper lip.

"I saw the plans for the expanded duck pond on the credenza behind his desk."

"Miriam, no." The rolled-up papers in her van were the blueprints.

"I grabbed them, locked the door behind me and ran. I was going to destroy them so that this underhanded plan would die with him."

"You're telling me you went to the mayor's office to read him the riot act about a bureaucratic procedure you disagreed with and found him dead. And you stepped over his dead body to get the plans before you fled."

"When you say it like that, it sounds bad," she said, dabbing at her eyes.

"It *is* bad, Miriam," I said. "Your attorney must have told you this was very, very bad."

"She did."

"You didn't even call the police."

"How could I after I had stolen the plans?"

"Good point," I said.

"It gets worse."

"Other than murdering him yourself, I don't see how this could be worse for you."

"I made it worse for you."

"How?"

"I was in the secret closet when you and Waggery arrived. I heard you both."

"You knew it was Waggery. That I wasn't fighting with the mayor."

"I knew. But that didn't stop me from running to the Daily Grind and telling everyone who would listen that I heard you fighting with the mayor. Walker and Lister were there with Emma, and they all went over to the plaza together. I'm pretty sure they spread it all over town."

"I'm pretty sure they did, too," I said. Ugh. Miriam. "But they said they'd heard it themselves." Another lie.

"I'm sorry, Carrie."

"Why would you try to implicate me in the mayor's murder?" I asked. "I thought we were friends. Or at least—" I couldn't find a word that worked. I settled on "colleagues."

"I panicked. I wanted to look normal, so I went to the Daily Grind to get a cup of tea to calm myself. You know how Walker and Lister love to gossip. They asked me about what I was carrying, and I blurted out that I'd heard you fighting with the mayor. This was before anyone even knew he was murdered. So, by the time word got around, my little story had become that you were the last one to see him alive and that you'd had a loud argument."

"You've made life difficult for me, Miriam," I said. "But the truth is you weren't the only one."

"I'm so sorry."

"I have a mess to sort out, but you've made things much more difficult for yourself. I don't know much about the law, but

I would bet that finding a body, ignoring it, and not reporting it, is a big legal mess. In addition to the stealing."

"My lawyer says I have to turn myself in," she said. "I've brought the plans to you for safekeeping."

"You didn't destroy them?"

"How could I? The man is dead. I would never forgive myself if the taxpayers were forced to pay for another set of plans. And it looks like I'll be going to prison and possibly losing my house anyway. By the time I pay my lawyer off, I won't even be able to afford to live here."

"Oh, Miriam. This is a nightmare."

"I've cleaned and tidied my home. I've left all the rule binders and other information about the homeowner's association on my kitchen table. Here are my keys, in case you or anyone else needs to go in. I'll put these designs on your counter. Make sure they get back to the town council?"

"Miriam, I—"

"I think the duck pond expansion will be lovely. You'll enjoy it. There's a gazebo."

"I'm not concerned about that right now," I said.

"Don't worry. I'll tell Officer Bucket the truth about what I heard. Hopefully that will take some of the heat off you for now."

"Good luck, Miriam."

"Maybe you can do a little psychic spell for me with your cards while I'm away. For luck."

"I'm not—," I said, not seeing any point in arguing with her now. "You bet. I'm going to light some candles and say some words. Do some moves. Sprinkle something."

"That would mean so much to me, Carrie." She put her hand on my arm, and my instinct was to snatch it back. But I didn't. "My best friend," she said.

Fear did weird things to people, I thought. I gave her a weak smile.

She made her way to the door, but slowly, hesitantly, like someone who was trying to savor her freedom. Miriam was about to embark on a difficult path, and I felt sorry for her.

She put her hand on the door latch. "Oh, and make sure you pass on my well-wishes to Grist."

"Sure, Miriam."

"Of course," she said. "I know that my credibility is zero right now, and that I will have to carry the shame of what I have done for the rest of my life. But something isn't right in Prosperity, and I think you're the one who is in the best position to figure it out."

"You don't think I murdered the mayor?"

"Of course not. But I also don't think you're using your brain."

"Thanks, Miriam." I'm not proud of it, but I smiled ever so slightly at the idea of Miriam being behind bars and unable to pelt me with insults.

"What I mean is, what's happening in Prosperity is something someone like you wouldn't normally see. It's something that doesn't enter your mind."

"Well, Miriam, I sincerely hope that you and your lawyer can sort this predicament out for you. Try not to step over any dead bodies on the way to the police station."

She closed her eyes and let out a deep sigh. "I deserve that. But what I am trying to say, rather bluntly, is that you need to stop following your heart."

I was growing tired of this conversation. "What should I follow, Miriam?"

"Follow the money."

Chapter Twenty-Five

As much as I sympathized with Miriam, I didn't have the luxury of time to meditate on her choices and why she made them. I recognized that I could never understand being so powerfully motivated to destroy something that I would literally step over a corpse to accommodate my desires. But I also recognized that unpacking my feelings about Miriam was something I would have to deal with later.

For now, I had to fetch Waggery. For his safety, and for the safety of the public. And Ligeia's.

I walked to the duck pond, and was relieved to see him there, splashing around in the water as if he didn't know what kind of bird he was. I often wondered if he knew he was a bird at all or if he thought he was a short human with the ability to fly.

I also wondered what Ligeia thought. She observed him with an intense look, and I wasn't sure if she was gazing at him lovingly or wondering what in the heck was wrong with him. Maybe both?

"You know what you should do?" It was Flynt. He'd sidled up alongside me unnoticed, his driving moccasins silent on every surface, apparently. I'd lost myself watching Waggery play and watching Ligeia watching him. Waggery was quacking like a duck, and some tourists were laughing and taking video.

"You should bring Waggery out here and have him do tricks for money," he said, throwing some litter in the bin. "People would love that. And it would be extra funds for those student loans you're still paying."

"I'm sure he would love it, too, Flynt," I said. "But I have an icky feeling about putting him to work. He's strictly a bird of leisure."

"As are you, in a way." This was Flynt's attempt to make a joke about how poor I am. I was used to it, but I wasn't in the mood.

I changed the subject. "How you holding up?"

"I'm processing," he said. "It's a tough loss for the town, a tough loss."

"It certainly is," I said. "Has there been a lot of commotion around the mayor's death?"

"A lot of commotion," he said. "Daisy Chatterly is all over me. But I keep telling people that we must stay the course. It's a tragic situation for the people of Prosperity, no doubt. But with the Wine Museum opening this week and the expansion of the duck pond approved, we have a lot to look forward to. Press on, I say."

"The duck pond expansion was approved?"

I pretended I didn't know about that to protect Miriam's privacy. It was her story to tell. Plus, I had a feeling that if I let Flynt feel important, he might start talking—and maybe reveal something I needed to know. What that was, I had no idea. But this situation was teaching me that sometimes it's best to listen more than talk.

"Oh, um, yeah. It was," he said. "There was a vote the other night."

"I don't remember the town council being in session. I would've heard about that."

"I guess they decided that it would be best to move forward before the rainy season kicks in and construction timelines are impacted."

"I think that quite a few townspeople might have something to—"

"What's happening with Grist?" Flynt interrupted. "I haven't been to see him today, I'm sorry to say. It's been chaotic."

"Don't worry," I said. "He'll understand."

"Have you heard anything new?"

"Not much," I said. "I went to see him this morning."

"He's going to come through?"

"You know Grist. He's tough as an ox."

"Huh," he said.

"Did you expect him not to?"

"Not exactly. I heard something else."

"Like what?" I was playing dumb.

"That he was having some other trouble. That it might be permanent."

"His nurse told me that with physical therapy and proper care, that he would — Oh no, Waggery."

Waggery had waded into the water farther than I was comfortable with and was doing a dive that I don't think ravens are designed to do.

"What's he doing?" Flynt asked.

"He probably sees something shiny," I said. "People throw coins in all the time. You know what you should do? Put up a sign telling people not to do that. It's bad for the birds. Waggery! Come here."

"You think he would dive for something shiny in water that deep?" he asked.

"I know he would. Yesterday he—" I caught myself. "Never mind. Waggery!"

I finally got his attention, and he flew to me. He sat on the rail between Flynt and me and shook himself off, showering us both with murky, algae-green duck pond water.

"Baptized by bird," I joked. Flynt looked miffed.

"This is a brand-new shirt," he said, pulling it out in front of him so he could survey the damage.

"Quack," said Waggery. A small group of tourists on the other side of the pond laughed and clapped. "Quack."

I didn't even apologize. I didn't have it in me. "Before you go, what is it that you know about Grist? What did you hear that I didn't?"

Flynt was still trying to wipe the green water off. He let out an impatient sigh. "Oh, I don't know, Carrie. Something about him getting sick."

"Getting sick?" I hate to say it, but I was having a bit of fun now. "Should I go see him? What's happened?"

"No. No. He should rest."

"Who told you such a thing? Why would someone say that?"

He walked away from me in a manner that led me to believe he didn't want to make eye contact. "I don't know, Carrie. Maybe it was a rumor. You know what you should do?"

"What, Flynt?" I was all ears.

"Mind your own business. And keep your vampire bat out of our pond. It's for ducks."

Chapter Twenty-Six

If nothing else, the conversation with Flynt reminded me that I needed to check up on Grist. I looked at my phone and realized that I had missed a call from the hospital. I checked my voice mail.

"Carrie, this is Brian. Grist's nurse. I thought you'd want to know he's improving. He's still listless from the medications he is on, now including an antihistamine."

What was happening? I wracked my brain to think of what could have caused Grist to have a reaction. I took a cleansing breath to calm my frustration at the fact that I was the one trying to figure this out. He was in a hospital, for Pete's sake. Surely, the trained medical personnel could look unlock this one mystery for me. I had too much on my plate. And a wet bird on my arm.

Waggery shook the water off again before flying up to the branch of a sycamore tree. The tourists came running toward him.

"Nevermore," he shouted. Maybe Flynt was right. Maybe I should start pimping out Waggery. Now that one of my regular clients was probably headed off to prison, I was going to have to replace that income.

"Do you know that black bird?"

A little girl was standing beside me, and I had no idea how long she'd been there.

"Yes. I do. He's mine. He's a raven and his name's Waggery."

"I love him," she said. "He's so funny." She did a little dance.

"He is funny. And I love him, too."

"My dad says I can offer you fifty dollars for him."

"Fifty dollars. That's a lot of money," I said. "But you tell your dad he's not for sale."

"He won't like that," she said.

"He'll get used to the idea."

"He told me everything has a price," she said. "And that I can get the bird with money."

"I'm sure that's true in some cases but not this one," I said. "Waggery is coming home with me."

"Daddy, she won't sell her black bird." The little girl screamed and ran back to her father.

Waggery let out a perfect imitation of her scream. It was clear that the people at the duck pond thought it came from me.

"Is that how you treat little girls?" The father yelled at me. "You mock them? Who do you think you are?"

I was starting to see Miriam's point about tourists. They think they own the place because they have money to throw at it.

"Not all of us only care about money, sir," I said. "Waggery is my family."

They turned on their heels and stormed off toward The Screamery, the appropriately named ice cream shop on the plaza. Many a tantrum had been cut short by a trip there, so much so that they had a kid-sized sundae on the menu called the Screaming Me-Me.

I thought about what Miriam had said to me as she left. To follow the money. What did she mean by that?

What did anybody ever mean by that?

I called Waggery to me and he landed on my arm, probably worn out and ready to go home for treats and snuggles. I wanted that too, but something told me I wasn't quite done for the day. There was still a murderer on the loose. Many people in town thought it was me, and I couldn't rest until it was sorted.

What did one do when one followed money?

Only one answer came to mind. I had to take these receipts to Emma, confess to her that Stormy and I had stolen items from her trash, and try to get an honest answer about what was going on with her, the mayor, and the "he knows" character from Grist's texts. Why did she steal my Lovers card? And why was she using my debt to the mayor to point the gossip toward me?

I was ready to follow the money.

Chapter Twenty-Seven

Miriam's confession weighed heavily on me. I was especially moved by how her salty personality seemed to sweeten after she told me her secret. I wondered if her sharp edges were the result of a misguided need to keep herself from feeling vulnerable or exposed. Was she always hiding something? Or was she more sensitive than she let on, and in order to move through the world safely, she had to arm herself with blunt talk and a claw hammer?

I remembered Aunt Inez telling me, after the newly crowned Mayor Brix came by to show off his expensive new suit and over-gelled coif: "*A lot of times what you see on the outside is the opposite of how someone feels on the inside.*"

Miriam showed how hard she could be. Was she a marshmallow inside this whole time?

I considered it and decided, nah. Miriam was a meanie.

I arrived on Emma's doorstep for the second time in two days. I was ready to come clean to her about what I was hiding and have a vulnerable conversation. Throughout this dark turn of events, I had only marginally suspected Emma of wrongdoing. But by concocting a ruse with my one-night stand, and clandestinely rifling through her trash for "evidence," I'd inadvertently treated her like she was suspect number one. When the maelstrom that was battering Prosperity passed, I wanted us to still be friends, and that meant coming to her in good faith to find out what she might know.

I didn't want to be known as the type of friend that would step over your dead body to solve my problems.

Emma deserved better.

And so did I.

I knocked on the door and waited. As I stood there, I wondered if I should have gone home first to get the papers I had stolen so I could return them. I knocked again. Her Mercedes was in the driveway, so unless she walked somewhere, she was probably home. And the likelihood of Ms. Fort-Knightly walking anywhere in her sky-high Louboutins seemed unlikely.

I wasn't going to invite scrutiny by looking in the windows or walking around the back, so I decided I would head home, gather the papers, and come back later. Perhaps she was in the shower or taking a nap—heaven knows she'd been through a lot over the past few days. She deserved a break as much as anyone.

I was walking up her garden path, admiring her perfect hedgerows. Were they trimmed in the shape of capital "E"? I'd never noticed that before.

I was telling Waggery how nice it was that Emma paid such attention to detail, when I heard the front door open behind me.

"Carrie? Don't go. I need your help."

It wasn't Emma.

I turned around.

It was Stormy. She was standing in Emma's doorway, crying.

"Before you come in, I need you to understand something." Stormy was blocking the door.

"Stormy, tell me what is happening. Now."

"I love you," Waggery said, his voice a perfect imitation of mine. I gave him a tickle under his beak and put him down. He waddled around on the lawn and fluttered up into a tree.

"I'm going to let you in, in a minute," Stormy said. "But please listen to me. This is important."

"What are you—"

"I didn't know Emma before I met her the other day."

"I don't—"

"Do you believe me?" Her mouth was a hard line, but her gray eyes were pleading.

"I have no reason not to," I said. "Not yet. Why are you here? What's happening? Where's Emma?"

"I came here because I recognized her name," she said.

"That makes no sense. Why wouldn't you recognize her name? You met her yesterday, and we did that whole thing with the ladder and the nightie and the trash cans? What are you talking about?"

"Let me explain," she said.

"I would love nothing more."

"My father sporadically sent me money over the years. Make no mistake, he didn't send my mom child support for me while she was alive. But after her death, he decided he would deign to help me."

"I didn't know. I don't think any of us did—"

"Listen. It was never a lot of money, and, as I said before, it wasn't regular. But the checks would come with a note in the memo that said, "*With love, from your father*," but someone else signed them."

"Who?"

"Emma Fort-Knightly. And the checks were from a company called 'Ravenous Partners.'"

"He didn't send you checks from his personal account?" I asked. "They were from a company?"

"I know. I thought that was weird, too, but I didn't question it much when it was happening because it was not only a rare event, but the amounts weren't much at all. I'd cash them and get on with my day."

"What is this company? I've never heard of Ravenous Partners here in Prosperity. What do you think they do?"

"No clue. But here's the thing. My father came to see me last week. In Mariner's Cove."

"Why?"

"He came by my place, and I made him lunch. A couple of sandwiches or whatever, it wasn't fancy. Anyway, he said he was craving some seafood stew from this place called Down the Hatch, and I volunteered to go get him one. I may not have been fond of my father, but I was trying to be polite. He didn't tell me why he was there, and I thought he might have come to tell me he was dying or something, and I didn't want to be rude."

"Understandable."

"I get back with the stew and he's—gone. Poof, into thin air."

"No note, no nothing?"

"Not a word. I chalked it up to him chickening out. I ate both stews, went out with some friends, and forgot all about it."

"What does this have to do—" I tried to look over her shoulder to see into Emma's house, but she successfully blocked me.

"A few days later, I was looking for this piece of jewelry I wanted to use for a septum piercing, and I discovered that my mother's ring was gone."

"The big emerald one that you accused me of stealing."

"Stay with me," she said, speaking low and fast. "I came to Prosperity to get it, as you know, and all of this happened. I met Emma and didn't put it together that she was the name on the checks. I realized I recognized her name a few hours after I left you. He probably stole my ring to propose to Emma."

"Whoa."

"Naturally, I had questions," she said.

"Naturally."

"What is Ravenous Partners? How are they affiliated? Did she know he was coming with this ring and was it part of a plan? I needed answers."

"So, you came here to get answers? To help find the killer."

"And that's all I did."

"That's great," I said, impressed. "Exceptional sleuthing. What did she say? Does she have any idea who might have murdered your father?"

"I need you to follow me."

"Hang on," I said. Waggery was still within view, pulling walnuts out of the tree and tossing them to the ground. "Stay up there, buddy. No duck pond."

"Quok. Nevermore."

"I'm serious," I said, narrowing my eyes and pointing to show him I meant business. "No flying. Stay right there."

Stormy led me through Emma's foyer and into the living room where I once again marveled at her sophisticated taste. I longed to sink into her oversized sofa and snuggle underneath layers of faux fur throws.

We walked down the hallway, lined with charcoal sketches by one of Prosperity 's favorite artists. I had never noticed them before, not having spent that much time at Emma's and, when I did, being relegated to the front rooms. The sketches were all of her, and I couldn't help notice how the artist captured her sense of style in only a few lines. That was talent.

"Emma's not napping, is she?" I asked. "I don't want to wake her. This can wait."

"She's not napping," said Stormy, and she slowly opened the door to Emma's room.

To look at her, you'd think that she was resting comfortably on her bed, piled high with fluffy pillows, and tucked deeply into her duvet. You'd think that she was taking the most luxurious afternoon snooze of her life.

And that's what I thought, too, if only for the few seconds it took me to realize that Emma wasn't sleeping at all.

Emma was dead.

Chapter Twenty-Eight

I screamed. I couldn't help it. The sound forced itself out of me against my will, like I was filled with poison smoke that had to be expelled. Stormy wrapped her arms around me, and we fell to the floor in a heap. I wanted to be close to the ground, to feel the earth underneath me. Otherwise, I feared I would fall into some infinite void and never come back.

Numbness overtook me. I couldn't feel my lips. I couldn't feel my hands.

"You—you found her—like this?"

Stormy nodded. Her eyes were filled with tears. And terror.

"How—?"

"I'm not sure," Stormy said. "The door was unlocked when I arrived. I saw her car in the driveway, so I figured she was home. I was angry, agitated. When she didn't come to the door, I barged in, partly to show her I wasn't messing around, and partly because that's how I am sometimes. Bull in a China shop. I wanted answers, and I wasn't afraid to get them. I came down the hall and opened her door. I shook the edge of her bed to wake her, and that's when I realized she had a plastic bag over her head. That she was dead."

I took a deep breath because she couldn't. The thought of being asphyxiated in this way was unbearable to me. I took another breath, and it calmed me.

I needed a clear head to figure out what to do next.

"There was a note," said Stormy.

"A note? From whom?"

"It's a suicide note."

"What? No. There's no way she did this to herself. What does it say?"

"It says, *I loved him, and I can't go on without him. The last time I lost someone I loved, I set his world on fire. Now, there's nothing left to burn, and no reason to go on.* What does that mean? 'Set his world on fire?'"

"Emma was accused of setting her last boyfriend's winery on fire. There was never any proof. I was never convinced that she went that far, but here we are. I don't know what to think."

"Here's the thing, though," she said. "I don't think she wrote this."

"What do you mean?"

"I mean, I've gotten dozens of checks over the years with her signature on it, and I would be willing to bet my mother's ring that this is not her handwriting."

"Whose is it?"

"That's what we need to find out," she said.

"I think we're in over our heads here. I think we were in way over our heads yesterday. It's too much. Two deaths in two days? We need to call the police. We need to tell Officer Bucket everything we know."

"That's going to be...challenging," she said. "For me."

"Why?"

"I think we need to figure this out before we involve the police."

"We're in too deep," I said, shaking my head. "So much has

happened since last we spoke. You won't believe what I found out about Miriam."

"I would like to know what you found out," she said, a little too calmly, given the circumstances. "But if you want to have the time to tell me, we need to not get the police involved. Not yet."

"Stormy, there is a dead woman, who used to be my friend and your father's girlfriend, on the other side of this wall. We have to call the police."

"If you do, I won't be able to help you anymore. Not right now."

"And why not?"

"Because there's a warrant out for my arrest."

* * *

I tried to run out of the house, but Stormy stopped me.

"Let me go," I said. "You're skilled at crime because you're a *criminal*. And I'm a cliché. Innocent and devastatingly beautiful young woman falls for a charming con artist. What's wrong with you? What's wrong with me?"

"Don't leave. Not yet," she said. "Let me explain."

"I need to get out of this house," I said. The walls were suffocating me. "Emma is dead in the next room. I can't stay here for another second. I need to call the police."

"Sit down," she said.

"But wait," I said, remembering something from our first encounter. "You were going to call the police on me when I was in your father's house."

"I was bluffing. Sit down in the kitchen and let me explain."

"Don't you ever tell me what to do," I said, summoning some gumption from a place deep inside, a place I didn't know existed.

I was terrified, more frightened than I had ever been in my life, but I was focused on one thing and one thing only: getting out of that house and going to the police.

"Once you understand where I'm coming from, we can make a plan together," she said. "I need your help."

"You're a murderer," I said, shivering at the idea that we had been intimate only a few hours before. "You're a monster. And a bluffer, which is a cute word for liar."

"I'm not," she said, her lower lip quivering. "You're misreading the situation."

"Misreading? You show up here and suddenly two of my friends are dead? How is that misreading?"

"Please," she said. "Please." She took a step toward me. I grabbed her by the arms with both of my hands and shoved her to the floor.

I ran to the door and flung it open. "Waggery. Let's go." He flew out of the tree and landed on my arm.

Chapter Twenty-Nine

There's no walk of shame quite like the walk of shame you take toward the police station after you discover that the first person you've slept with in three years is a certified murderer.

I hotfooted it down Emma's tree-lined lane toward the plaza, glancing over my shoulder every few seconds to ensure that Stormy wasn't following me. It occurred to me that maybe I should have tried to trap her to prevent her from escaping. She was a prime suspect in two murders, and the odds were good that she was going to flee.

But no, I thought. I did the right thing. I didn't know what she was capable of. Her comfort level with things I found unimaginable was disturbing. I was right to flee for my life and head straight to the police with what I knew. It was time to come clean before more Prosperity residents turned up dead.

Why had I not seen it? When I assign a card to someone, I always consider the reversal. Stormy was Strength: courage, determination, boldness. The reverse was a potential for lashing out and impulse control.

Was she at the Daily Grind when Miriam ran in, casually

sipping her coffee and listening to the first news of the murder she'd committed? What kind of diabolical person kills their father over some jewelry and then has a latte? She must have been delighted to hear Miriam pin it on me, and even more thrilled when I showed up at her father's house.

Things were working out for Stormy, weren't they?

Why, when she was alone in her father's house, had she not been afraid that the murderer might show up there?

Because it was her. It was her the whole time.

My only hope at this point was that my sleuthing hadn't made anything worse.

Waggery didn't get the memo. He took my brisk pace as a sign that we were out for fun, and he soared from tree branch to tree branch, squawking like he was laughing at me.

"Waggery. Come." I held out my arm. I needed him to be on his best behavior; I didn't have time to drop him off at home —I was absolutely determined to tell Officer Bucket everything I knew. And if that meant I met a fate like Miriam's, so be it.

Waggery flew to me and landed on my arm. "Mwah," he said, giving me a kiss. He flew into a tree a few feet in front of me. I kept moving.

Okay, I thought. He's playing, and there's nothing I can say or do to snap him out of it. Waggery is going to do what Waggery does whether I like it or not.

I decided to ignore him. Keep moving, I thought. He'll follow along.

I approached the tree where he was perched, determined not to make eye contact. He pelted me with walnuts.

"Hey," I said. "What are you doing?"

"What are you doing?" he repeated.

The game was afoot.

I felt a sharp pop on my skull from a perfectly aimed

walnut. I had to hand it to him. Waggery sure knew how to get my attention.

I picked the walnut up off the ground and put it in my pocket. Keep ignoring him, I thought, refusing to be outwitted by a bird.

"Quok." He was mocking me.

We were getting close to the plaza where there were fewer trees. Instead, I had the duck pond—and the irresistible charms of Ligeia—to contend with. I held the walnut in my palm and rubbed it like a talisman as I mentally re-routed around the plaza to keep Waggery away from Ligeia.

It was easy enough, I thought. I'd sweep right instead of left at the end of Prosperity Street and take the long way around toward the hospital.

I briefly considered going by to see how Grist was doing and quickly changed my mind. I had crimes to confess and a rogue raven to deal with. I made a mental note to ensure that Grist was on my visitor's list when I ended up behind bars.

I dropped the walnut on the ground, and that's when it hit me like, well, a walnut thrown at me by a raven from a tree on my murdered friend's street.

In high school, I hosted a mini dinner party where I'd made a big deal about the fancy summer meal I'd whipped up from Inez's garden. It was a homemade penne pasta with fresh pesto. I was beaming with pride as I set a steaming plateful of pasta in front of Grist and Inez, pleased that I could make something delicious and share it with the people I loved the most in the world. He effused praise on the presentation, the freshness of the flavors...

Until his tongue swelled up so much he couldn't speak.

"Bemmmanil," he kept saying over and over. "Bemmanil. Bemmanil."

"Get the Benadryl," Inez said, "Hurry."

I raced to the bathroom and grabbed a pink pill that Aunt Inez used when her seasonal allergies flared up. (*"They should call them 'sneezenal allergies,'"* she would say.) Grist washed it down with a healthy swig of Hoggarty Heaven Cabernet and within about ten minutes he could speak again.

"Allergic to walnuts," he said, happily, as though it had never happened. "One or two bites and my mouth swells—I'll be fine. But more than a few," he drew his finger across his neck. "It's lights out for Grist."

We eventually were able to laugh about it, chalking it up to yet another culinary disaster by Carrie. Cheap food, bad food, food that could kill you—you never knew what you were going to get when you dined at Chez Carrie. People who had never shared a meal with me mentioned how they'd heard I was bad at dinner because "someone" had mentioned it to Walker, Lister, or Daisy.

That "someone" was also a dinner guest at my house that night. That "someone" was Emma.

Chapter Thirty

I chastised myself for forgetting this. Inez got sick shortly after so the memory must have been buried somewhere under my trauma. Is it possible that someone slipped Grist some walnuts? How would anyone even do that while he was in the hospital? And were they trying to kill him—or shut him up?

I stopped dead in my tracks. How did these pieces fit together with what I was going to tell Officer Bucket? I had zero proof that someone had tried to poison Grist with walnuts. And I had no real motive other than it looked like he suspected that the items in his museum might be fake. But what did that have to do with anything? A few inauthentic wine presses hardly seemed worth murdering anyone over.

In the blink of time it took for me to attempt to connect the dots on all these unrelated things, Waggery took the opportunity to duck out. Literally. I found him at the duck pond, the exact thing I'd hoped to avoid.

I was living on repeat. Here I was, for the second time today, begging Waggery to get out of the pond. Here I was, for the second time today, watching tourists snap photos and laugh at my raven. Here I was, for the second time today, wondering how I'd gotten here.

I was so accustomed to seeing Grist here, showing off Prosperity's Prohibition-era oddities and other historical curiosities to throngs of amused tourists, that I found myself scanning the plaza for his top hat out of habit.

On his tours he shared the story of how Agustus Hoggarty made and stored wine at full winery capacity for thirteen years during Prohibition so that when it was lifted—as he predicted it would be—he would be one of the only winemakers with enough capacity to slake the thirst of every drinker in the Bay Area. Grist loved telling high school classes about the clandestine network of tunnels underneath Prosperity, and then refusing to tell them where to find the hidden trap doors. He grew positively incandescent when he talked of Prosperity's bright future, and how the mayor was leading the charge.

And when he wasn't on a tour, his favorite thing to do was sneak into the backgrounds of people's photos. I told him he was the world's first photo bomber, and he might have been. I smiled when I thought of the hundreds of people over the years who got their film developed or posted on social media, only to find a be-whiskered man in a silk curlicued vest, old-timey pants, and a top hat smirking in the distance, like he'd arrived by time machine.

He was a Magician, and his influence on me was nothing short of enchanting.

I was snapped out of my reverie by Waggery, who was diving head first into the duck pond.

"Waggery, stop," I yelled. He continued to dive into water that was too deep for him to stand in. It wasn't hard for me to imagine him injuring himself, or worse, and I couldn't bear it. Not ever. But especially not today.

"Waggery. Come here right this second or you're going to be in trouble. Get over here right *now*."

My outburst attracted the attention of the tourists, who started filming me instead of him, no doubt to have proof when they contacted animal control with reports of an abused corvid. I never spoke to Waggery this way. Not even the time he got into the dumpsters behind High on the Hoggarty and dragged trash down the entire block, which I alone had to pick up lest our fastidious mayor cite me for littering.

The tourists were shocked, but my raven got the message, and he perched on the guardrail in front of me. He dropped something into my hand. Was this a gift? Something new for his treasure pile? An apology?

I couldn't begin to sift through what Waggery's intentions were. That, along with an apology and lots of snuggles and snacks, would have to come later. That's because Waggery handed me a shiny object shaped like a cigar holder with a deadly corkscrew and a small, jagged knife inside.

Chapter Thirty-One

I was drying the item off and trying not to attract more attention when I was startled by my favorite Fool.

"You know what you should do—"

"Flynt. You've got to stop sneaking up on me like that," I said. "This is not the day for surprises."

"Sorry, Carrie. I noticed that you've got something that might be of interest to me. To the wine museum. You should bring it by."

"Oh, this?" I held up the corkscrew. "Yeah, Waggery fished it out of the pond." I put it in my pocket.

Now that I wasn't screaming at my raven, the tourists turned their attention back to enjoying the duck pond. Occasionally someone would glance over, probably charmed by how docile Waggery was behaving, perched like a pet parrot on the guardrail.

"Strange how something like that ended up in the pond," he said, gazing at me through his Dolce & Gabbana sunglasses.

"It's entirely possible that Waggery put it there himself," I said. "He's been on a bit of a crime spree lately."

"Why don't you give it to me? You've been having a tough

time and taking responsibility for a valuable item like this and finding its owner could be daunting." He put his hand on my shoulder. "I don't know for sure, but I think Grist might have made a spot for an item like this in the museum."

Flynt's kindness and the mention of Grist's name were too much for me. I started to cry.

I stuttered through my tears. "Thank you, F-Flynt. I'm on my way to the police station. Hopefully, I'll be able to give it to Grist myself. At some point."

"Carrie, why don't you sit down for a minute? Collect yourself."

He motioned to an empty bench under a weeping willow. Its long branches swept the ground lazily, blown by the cool afternoon breezes that whistled in from the coast every afternoon at this time.

"Take a deep breath," he said. "Tell me what's going on. Why are you going to the police?"

"Oh, Flynt," I said. "I've got some bad news. Awful."

"Worse than the news we got yesterday?"

"I think it's all connected. I don't know how yet, and I don't know how I even fit into any of it. I appreciate your concern. But I can't talk to anyone about this yet. I need to go to the police first."

"Are you sure? Do you think maybe you're overreacting?"

"Overreacting? Absolutely not." I stood up. "I am one hundred percent not overreacting, Flynt."

"You know what you should do?" He asked. "You should sit down, relax, and tell me everything. I'll go to the police with you. You look like you could use a friend. Let me help you, Carrie."

Exhaustion washed over me. How easy would it be to sit back down on this lovely park bench, in front of this picturesque duck pond, unburden myself to Flynt, and let him take the lead with Officer Bucket. Who knows? He might even have an attorney he can recommend who will work for me pro bono. I knew I wasn't going to get in trouble for murder, but the things I was doing—running around town trying to solve a series of crimes on my own—couldn't possibly be legal.

"Flynt, I—wish I could, I do. But I need to get to the police. Come on, Waggery."

"Wait," he said, grabbing my arm. "Are you sure you don't need a friend?"

"You have no idea, Flynt. That reminds me, have you ever heard of—"

My phone rang.

"Hold on, Flynt," I said. "Hello?"

"Hi. Is this the psychic?" A female voice mumbled this. I could barely understand her,

"Not a psychic. But I am the tarot card reader. Can I help you?" I held a finger up to Flynt to let him know I needed to take the call.

He nodded.

"Yeah, this is your client from this morning."

This morning was a lifetime ago. "Misty? With the umlaut?"

"What?"

"Misty, how can I help you?"

"Misty, right. So, I came by to talk to you again about something in my reading. But you're not here, so I called the number on your sign."

Meddling Misty. Hank had warned me.

"What can I help you with, Misty?"

"Are you moving?"

"What? Misty, look. Now is not the best time—"

"There's a moving van in front of your cottage."

"A moving van?"

"Yeah. There are these guys, and they are loading up a truck with all your stuff," she said. "I asked them what they were doing. They said they were from a collection agency, and they showed me some paper that says they can take your stuff. I signed it for you."

"What?"

"Yeah. You should come home right now," she said. "And you should probably get a doorknob."

Beep.

My phone died.

I shook it, like that would help.

"What's going on?" Flynt asked. "I've never seen that color on a human face before."

"It looks like the collections agencies finally found me," I said in disbelief. Why today, of all days?

"You know what you should do?" Flynt began. "You should come with me to the museum. Have some tea. Tell me everything that is happening. I want to help you. You and Grist."

"I can't, Flynt. There is literally a moving van in front of my house, loading up my stuff. Then I'm going to the police."

"I'll come with you," he said.

"No. Absolutely not," I said. "It's too embarrassing."

"What can I do to help?"

I didn't answer him. I called Waggery, and I was grateful that he flew to my arm with no fuss.

"Let's go, buddy," I said. "We're being robbed."

Chapter Thirty-Two

On the sprint toward my cottage, I had some decisions to make.

I had been on my way to the police for several reasons, one of them quite specific: Emma was dead in her bed with a bag over her head, and I was certain that keeping that information a secret from the authorities for longer than a reasonable time frame was also a crime.

I was also sickeningly sure that Stormy had something, if not everything, to do with both horrific deaths, and I needed to call the police right now, tell them what I knew, and make arrangements to come in and talk about it in person after I figured out what was going on at my house.

One problem: my phone was now dead.

Two problems: Grist's phone was also dead.

Apparently, my phone only had enough juice to receive the call from Misty. Who knew how long Grist's had been unusable?

I was trapped between a rock and a prison sentence. All my choices were terrible.

Waggery flew ahead of me, making this whole turn of events slightly easier. I could relax if he remained in my sight line.

As I rounded the corner, I fully expected to see workers in jumpsuits, scurrying like ants, filling a moving truck with Aunt Inez's burled walnut credenza, her mahogany reading table, and her well-loved sofa. I was steeling myself for the shock of discovering her antique mirrors and her beloved armoire stacked among her other items in the back of a dirty truck. The thought of her ceramics being mishandled or broken sent me into a panic.

What I saw instead was...nothing.

There were no movers; there was no truck. There was no notice on the door or any indication that anyone had been there at all.

I opened the door and turned on the lights. Waggery took his spot on his perch, fluffed his feathers, and made a few contented purring sounds. I took a mental inventory of everything in the room, and from what I could tell, nothing was out of place.

Was this a prank? Was Misty messing with me? Why would she do that? I didn't even know her before today. How was she involved in any of this? Is this what Hank meant—that Misty sowed chaos? If so, I could see why he didn't want to continue dating her.

Numb, confused, and losing my resolve, I thought about what Aunt Inez would say to me when I was upset or worried. She would ask me how I was doing right then. The answer was always that I was fine. And she would remind me that all we have is the present. And in the present moment, there's nothing to worry about.

She would say, *"Most of the things we worry about never happen."*

And I would respond, *"That's why I worry about everything. It's like magic."*

"I'm fine," I said to Waggery. "We're fine."

He blinked at me, content on his perch, and I marveled at his confident presence. He could be a handful and hard to wrangle, but if I'd had to choose a life unbothered and alone or a life with a mischievous creature who sometimes made life messy, I would choose the mischievous creature every time.

"And with that," I said, "I need to plug in my phone."

I went to the kitchen desk and saw the pile of collection notices and finally saw them for what they were: noise. People I don't know yelling at me about something I had nothing to do with. They were from people—or not even actual humans, but corporations—screaming for what they thought was theirs. These letters had no understanding that there was a person on the other end who'd had a tough turn of events and was doing her best. A person who had recently lost three people, and two of those in the last twenty-four hours. These notices meant nothing, not when people were dying and others were working to cover it up.

I would pay attention to them again when I was good and ready. I shoved the whole pile into the trash.

If nothing else, these past few hours had helped me get my priorities straight. Who had time to worry about debt when everyone around you harbored secrets and they were using them against you?

I watched my phone charge, as if that would make it go faster. I was even more rattled by what had been a confusing turn of events. Why would Misty lie to me about collection agency vans? What did she have to do with any of this?

My phone rang. It was a number I didn't recognize. I left it plugged into the wall and answered it.

It was Grist.

"Grist. What's happening? I've been so worried. I have your phone, but it's not charged. Do I need to come there?"

"Carrie, listen to me," he said, sounding weary but determined. "I'm a little beat up and the drugs are disorienting. But your old uncle is going to be fine."

Hearing his voice was all it took to throw wide the floodgates. I started sobbing uncontrollably. I couldn't speak; I could barely breathe.

"There, there," he said, over and over. I remember when Aunt Inez died, he stayed with me for hours and hours, letting me cry it all out. He never once told me to stop or that I needed to pull myself together. He allowed me the space to be in my sorrow for as long as I needed. I have to think now that he did that at the expense of expressing his own grief. But that's how he was. Always putting other people's needs before his own.

I needed to pull myself together. I could fall apart again—and properly mourn my friends—when I got to the bottom of how these violent, distressing events tied together.

"How are you calling me?" I asked when I had finally calmed down enough to speak. "I have your phone."

"It's called a landline," he said with a weak laugh. "Surely you've seen one in old movies."

Millennial jokes were a favorite of his. "I'm so glad to hear your voice."

"Have you had a chance to collect yourself?"

"Yes," I answered. "I have so much to tell you."

"I can't wait to hear it. But I need you to do something for me. Right now. It's important. And it might be dangerous."

"I'm listening. But there's some weird and terrible stuff going on that you might not know about yet. I need to tell you what's happening, but I have to go to the police first."

"Police?"

"Yes. Grist, Emma is dead, and I think I know who killed her. What I am not sure about is why."

"Emma Fort-Knightly? She's dead? Oh, no. What happened? I saw her this morning." His voice sounded small.

"You did? When?"

"She came in with the ladies from the Historical Society. She came by for a quick minute and left shortly after they brought in my breakfast. Then you came, and I had my episode."

"Grist, I think she might have poisoned you."

"Emma? Well—" and he went silent.

"Grist? Are you still there?"

He took a deep breath. "And now she's—dead?"

"Yes. I don't even know if the police know yet. I was on my way to tell them what I think happened, when I was stopped by Flynt Burns. While I was with him, Hank's girlfriend called and said that there were men here repossessing my furniture. I got here and there's no one. No van, no moving guys, nothing. I plugged in my phone, which had died, and then you called. Grist, what does all this mean?"

"I'm not sure," he said, carefully, slowly. "I'm going to need you to do something. Something drastic. Did you go to Finders Keepers?"

"That was you? You put the receipt in my pocket?"

"Yes," he said.

"Not Lillian?"

"Lillian?" he asked. "No. It was me."

"I went," I said. "And I know that the items in the museum are fakes. But Grist, I need to go to the police. Now. This can't wait another minute."

"I will call Officer Bucket anonymously from this phone and tell them to go to Emma's house. But you need to do something equally as important before you do anything else. If I could do it, Carrie, I would. But I am obviously out of commission for a while."

"What is it?"

"Do you know how to get into the tunnels?"

"Of course. Other than tarot cards, spelunking Prosperity's Prohibition tunnels is something for which I am impeccably trained."

"You need to get into the museum. Right now. And you need to steal the accounting books. And you need to bring them to me. With my phone."

"Your phone isn't charged," I said, stupidly, like that's what matters.

"Listen," he said, calmly. "Grab my charger before you head down into the tunnels. It's in my office."

"I should mention now that your house has been totally ransacked," I said, once again surprising myself with my inability to stay focused.

"Oh boy," he said. "That's bad, but it's not surprising given everything else that's happening. Not to worry. No one got hurt with that, so we'll deal with that later. The most important thing is that you get those books and come here."

"They still enter everything by hand? It's not on a computer?"

"You'll see. Get them and bring them straight to the hospital. Don't let anyone see you."

"Flynt's already seen me a few times today," I said. "You know, telling me what I should do."

"Don't let him catch you doing this," he said.

"But what if—"

"Carrie, stop. Listen. My neck is broken because Flynt Burns pushed me down the stairs."

§

"*How am I supposed to learn all of this?*" I had asked, dropping my head to the table. We'd been studying all afternoon. It was past my snack time, and the cards were blurry. "There are seventy-eight cards and infinite combinations. It's impossible."

"First off, let's get you something to nosh on."

Aunt Inez disappeared into the kitchen and returned with a plate with fresh basil, sliced beefsteak tomatoes from her garden, bread she baked that morning and her homemade buffalo mozzarella—and a plum for Waggery.

"Eat," she said. "And we'll talk about cues on the cards you can use to keep a reading going when you may not remember exactly what they mean."

"Sounds like a plan," I said, through a mouthful of food.

"As you know, each card has a picture that should, over time, signal you to remember what it means. Like flash cards. But when you're stuck, you can interpret a meaning from the colors."

"I can?"

"Many of the cards have yellow skies," she said. "Why? Is it an artistic choice? No. Yellow in tarot represents our higher consciousness. When you see yellow, mention to your client that something is trying to get their attention on a spiritual level. Now what other color is the sky in tarot?"

"Blue," I said, knowing that this was low-hanging fruit.

"True blue," she said, "is an expression of our subconscious. Do you know what that is?"

"It's the thoughts underneath your thoughts that you don't know you're thinking, but that make you think certain things at a certain time whether you want to or not."

Aunt Inez looked at me with a furrowed brow. "I'll allow that," she said, after some consideration. "Blue on a card represents an outcome driven by forces that they may not even be aware of."

"A warning?"

"Not exactly," she said. "More like something underneath the surface that you may not know about. Blue is typically found in cards with a more 'positive' spin, although there is no good or bad in tarot."

"Right," I said, licking my fingers. "This was delish."

"You're welcome," she said, with a nod of her head. "What other colors are there?"

"There's gray," I said. "A lot of the cards have gray skies."

"And what do you think of when you think of gray?"

"Gloomy," I said.

"Excellent," she said. "Cards like the Three of Swords have a gray background and that one is a darker card. And the Hanged Man, which means indecision."

She showed me the image of a heart run through by three swords and the one of a man in page's costume dangling by his foot from a cross. "But here's the Eight of Pentacles, which has a man working at his bench and the gray is pretty neutral—you can assign almost any mood to it."

"Interesting," I said. "What about this one?" I held up the Emperor card. It had an orange sky.

"What a detailed eye you have," she said. "That card is the only one with an orange sky."

"What does it mean?" I asked.

"It's volatility. Random chance. Power. Fire."

"It's beautiful," I said, tracing my finger along the shading on the card.

"It is," she said. "But it's unpredictable."

"I'll watch out for that," I said, getting up to take my plate to the kitchen.

But the years went by, and I didn't.

I didn't watch out for that at all.

§

Chapter Thirty-Three

It was getting dark out, and I was on a mission. I'd been bouncing all over town for two days trying to get to the bottom of a mystery so unfathomable that the best I could do to solve it was to keep putting one foot in front of the other.

The gas lamps of Hoggarty Heaven flickered in a light-hearted, festive welcome, no doubt designed to make party guests feel the enchantment of the place. Grist's door was still off its hinges, but there was police tape that read, *Police Line Do Not Cross.* I ignored it, of course, getting more and more accustomed to breaking the rules as the hours ticked by. What would they do? Arrest me? Fine. That seemed inevitable at this point. I would welcome the chance to unburden my conscience.

The place looked pretty much as it had before from what I could tell in the twilight and with the lights out. I'd luckily remembered to snag a flashlight before I left the house, causing a little flap with Waggery. He knew I used it to find him when he flew off on our night walks, so I think he was confused. Why would I need it if he was right there? I didn't want to let him out, but he screamed when I tried to leave, so I decided to risk setting him free again. I hoped I didn't come to regret it, but desperate times called for desperate measures.

And I couldn't remember feeling more desperate.

Fortunately, Grist's charger was plugged into the wall behind his desk. It would be better time management to plug the phone in here and have it charge while I was in the tunnels and grab it when I was done. I wanted to bring it to him fully charged in the hospital so he could answer the multitude of concerned texts and voice mails that were no doubt coming in from friends. And Lillian.

There were several entrances to the tunnels in Prosperity, but the one I was using was in Grist's drawing room. Growing up, this wasn't the entrance Hank and I preferred.

The one we liked best was situated behind the main manor house underneath a tangle of ivy that looked like nothing more interesting than a hiding place for rats. But if you could find the loop of rope that had somehow survived decades of weather and neglect, and you pulled up on it, you'd find a trapdoor that led to a stone staircase.

"No shoddy wooden stairs for the Hoggarty family," Hank used to say. "When my grandfather did something, he set it in stone."

I thought I'd remind him of that sentiment next time he got mad about the weakly written contract that resulted in Grist living in "his" carriage house.

There were some items strewn atop the rug that I needed to get under, so I moved them out of the way. I pulled the corner back to reveal the trapdoor in the floor. I wiggled my finger under the notch and gave a lift—well-oiled hinges made it easy for even the daintiest lady to use, you know, in case of a Prohibition-related emergency.

I was glad I'd worn sneakers today, rather than my usual Mary Janes. I took the stone stairs carefully—it had been a while since I had navigated a narrow descent into a pitch-black tunnel, and I wanted to be sure I didn't tank my mission with a twisted ankle or some other careless injury. Plus, I didn't have health insurance. One more un-payable debt would mean I'd have to sell the house.

I kept moving.

Despite the stress of this covert mission, I noticed a little spring in my step. I'd missed making mischief. I took in the dusty, musty scent, tinged with the pleasant decaying fruit smell that came from years and years of wine transport, storage, and spillage. It was the fragrance of my childhood, a childhood that had been filled with imaginative play, doting guardians, and a close friendship with someone with whom I thought I would be forever friends.

I didn't know how all of this was going to turn out. Anything could happen, and I wasn't sure that any of this would be good for me, or anyone else in Prosperity.

I trembled in the chill. Or was it the anxiety? I wasn't sure.

The flashlight was surprisingly effective at slicing through the blackness. I moved too cautiously through the tunnel, too slowly for the urgency of what I was tasked with doing. But this meant had the chance to notice that there were areas underneath Grist's house that appeared to have been dug out, damaged, or demolished. The foundational joists were exposed. In some parts, entire sections of the concrete underpinning that secured the house from falling into the tunnel had been removed, and the flooring appeared to sag. It didn't look safe.

I needed to warn Grist about this. Even with an uninjured neck, he could step on a weak spot in the floor and fall all the way through. My shoulders tightened at the thought, especially when I remembered how Stormy and I were stomping through there the day before.

Through cobwebs, puffs of dust that came from nowhere

and unsure footing, I soldiered on. I still had several hundred yards to navigate, and even though it was impossible to get lost on this route, time was running out. I didn't understand exactly why I was doing this, but I trusted Grist. I knew that this mission might provide the final piece that completes the puzzle I had been struggling to solve.

The path forked in three prongs, and I took the left one toward the Wine Museum. The one to the right would have taken me to High on the Hoggarty and the one in the center would have delivered me straight to the Visitors Center.

The deeper I went, the more it became clear this tunnel expedition wasn't a silly game with Hank.

I was in these tunnels because people were dying, and I needed to find out why. I would never forget how Emma looked in her bed, her eyes cold and lifeless, her aristocratic features obscured by a cheap plastic bag. Her elegant life was snuffed out by a cheap piece of trash.

Step after step, my brain told me everything was fine, but my body betrayed me.

Sweaty palms.

Heaviness in my chest.

Flutters in my stomach.

Who did I think I was?

I had no business doing any of this.

My flashlight blinked. The batteries were dying. The tunnels would flash into view and disappear, like a strobe light.

I put my hand on the wall. The cool rocks would have to be my guide—and my only guide—if my flashlight failed.

And then it did.

I groaned, and the sound collapsed. Nothing reverberated down here. There were no echoes.

I stood paralyzed in my spot. My feet refused to move.

I held my hand up in front of my face. Nothing but dark, black void.

But unlike the games Hank and I played in these hidden tunnels so many years ago, I couldn't quit when it stopped being fun.

"Your phone, dummy," I said to myself. I laughed, relieved. I fired up the phone and pointed it down the left tunnel.

"Technology saves the day."

My cheap phone didn't have the range of the flashlight, but it offered me enough visibility to shake me out of my paralysis.

"Pull it together, Dettwiler. This is the beginning."

I looked at the phone and realized I only had ten percent battery.

"I guess charging for fifteen minutes from a dead battery doesn't provide enough juice to your fake-ass iDroid."

I never enjoyed being poor, but I especially hated being poor when it affected my ability to do normal things successfully. My life was filled with annoyances like this: cheap appliances that broke down, fabrics that tore and pilled, knockoff technology that fell apart with reasonable use. People had no idea how inconvenient and expensive it was to be poor.

But my bitterness wasn't helping me now.

I decided not to use the phone. The tunnel was dark, but there were no surprises down here. If I used the walls as a guide, I would get to the trapdoor that led to the basement of the museum even without light.

"Time to be a big girl," I whispered. And I turned off the phone.

It was as if someone put a cloth bag over my head.

Blind.

Breathless.

I put one foot in front of the other, feigning confidence.

Faking it until I made it.

I kept moving, grappling the wall like it was the only thing saving me from imminent death, touching the ground gingerly with one toe before taking a step, in case the earth opened up underneath.

I could barely make out the faint, lighted outline of the trap-door that led to the basement of the Wine Museum, though it was impossible to determine the distance. My perspective was faulty in total darkness, and I knew I hadn't been down there long enough or moving fast enough to be within striking distance yet.

Nevertheless, I had the confidence to take a few full steps.

"Almost there," I said. "Almost there."

I hit something soft.

I reared back, and a lightning jolt of adrenaline shot through my limbs. I half expected to hear the squeak of a disoriented rat.

Instead, a kick landed on my shin.

I swung outward with the flashlight and didn't hit anything. I took a few more swings until, thud; I hit something that, if I had to guess, was a ribcage.

"Mmph."

Another kick landed below my knee. I fell to the ground, half from pain, half from sheer terror.

"Mmph."

Whatever it was that took me down was human.

And it was furious.

Chapter Thirty-Four

What came forth from my gut was a combination scream and groan. I frightened myself with the sound of my own raw emotion.

I was breathing heavily, inhaling dust from the floor of the tunnel.

I coughed, trying to empty my airway. I was unsure whether it was the dust or the panic that made it hard to breathe.

The sounds coming from this person were a combination of struggle and pain.

"Wha—Who—"

From what I could make out, they were grunting and writhing around. Were they injured? Were they dangerous?

"Mmmnn."

"What? I can't—Are you hurt?"

I could hear them shuffling and kicking.

"I can't see you," I cried. "Please don't hurt me."

I scrambled backward, hoping that their desperation would make them unable to move or find me.

"Mumph."

"Are you—are you gagged?"

"Mmm. Mmm."

"Oh my god. Oh my god. Please don't hurt me."

I reacted exactly like I did that time I left the backdoor open for Waggery to let himself in and a baby possum scooted into my kitchen: sheer, stultifying terror.

I smelled sandalwood.

"St-Stormy?"

"MMeh."

"Stormy Portwood?"

"MMEH."

"What the—"

I crawled on my hands and knees toward the sound. I reached out to find two feet clad in Chucks, the laces loose, almost untied. I felt my way up the leg—it was jeans like Stormy wore. I couldn't find her hands, and I respectfully did my best not to run my hands over her front.

I found her neck and face—those cheekbones.

Focus, Carrie.

There was something over her mouth. Duct tape.

"I'm going to pull this off. It's going to hurt. A lot. I'm going to count to three."

I felt her nod her head.

"One—Two—" I ripped off the tape in one aggressive stroke.

"What happened to three?" Stormy screamed. "God. Ouch." I could feel her kicking the air.

"That was a trick Aunt Inez used on me once when I had a particularly sticky Band-Aid situation."

"Aunt Inez sounds like a real bitch."

"Watch what you say about Inez," I said. "

"Sorry."

"I did say she only got away with it once. Never quite trusted her with Band-aids after that."

We sat in stunned silence, trying to catch our breaths. I couldn't see her at all. And I know she couldn't see me.

"I could use some water," she said, finally, breathless. "Do you have any?"

"I'm not on a hiking expedition," I said. "So, no."

"Can you untie me?"

"Why are you tied up in the first place? What are you doing down here?"

"Your buddy Hank," she said.

"Hank?"

"Yes. He's handy with tape and rope. Not a great listener. Seems to care about you, though."

"That's one of the most surprising things I've heard in a day filled with surprises," I said. "Tell me what happened."

"Untie me first." I heard her shift around.

"I guess you'll stay down here. I didn't come here for you. In fact, I still plan on going to the police about you. Murderer."

I stood up in a way that made sure she heard me.

"No. Wait. You win. I'll tell you everything."

I sat back down, but not without reservations. I believed Stormy was responsible for the deaths of two people already. Would she also be responsible for mine? I moved as far away from her as I could, or at least I thought I did. It was impossible to track her in the dark.

"After you left Emma's, I followed you."

"I thought you'd go on the run. If I had brazenly killed two people, I'd be halfway to Mexico by now. But not you. You like to see the damage you inflict, you psychopath."

"I didn't flee, and I hope you will take that as a sign that I am innocent of these crimes."

"I'm not sure you're innocent of anything," I said. "In fact, finding you in a tunnel, tied up by Hank, makes me more suspicious of you than ever."

I hoped Hank had done a good job securing the knots. I remembered the corkscrew and felt slightly better about defending myself. Slightly.

"I can explain," she continued. "I was right behind you the entire time after you left Emma's. I saw Waggery pelt you with walnuts. I saw you stop at the duck pond."

"So? Were you trying to find the right time to snuff me out, but there were too many people around? The duck pond is popular with both tourists and locals alike."

"Not at all," she said. "I was trying to keep you from going to the police before we sorted it all out. I was willing to go, eventually. I wanted to have all the information in case they locked me up on my warrant and I was pulled out of commission for the next few days."

"That's right," I said, thumping my forehead sarcastically before I realized she couldn't see me. "I forgot. You're a cold-blooded killer."

"I thought if anyone could understand, it would be you."

I sat up straight. "Why would you think that? I've never so much as gotten a parking ticket."

"You don't have a car," she said.

"Touché," I responded. "Way to rub my nose in it."

"My warrant, ironically, is for parking tickets," she said. "About eighty-six of them to be exact."

"How does that even happen?"

"How does a person accrue so much debt that a van pulling up in front of your house to load up all your stuff is a credible threat?" she asked.

"How did you—."

"Life happens," she said. "In this case, I renovated my tattoo shop myself and I would park right in front to unload items, tools, that sort of thing. There was a parking attendant who had it in for me. If you must know, we dated briefly, and it didn't end well. I couldn't leave my car out there for more than a few minutes without getting a ticket."

"That's terrible."

"It's a small problem, all things considered, but I knew if Officer Bucket ran my license rather than glancing at it quickly to confirm I was who I said I was, that he would be forced to lock me up. I wouldn't be any use to you at all."

"How thoughtful," I said.

Hearing all of this while not being able to look at or focus on anything else was a strange sensation. Sitting there in the dark, in a sort of sensory deprivation, made everything she said more dramatic. Her words seemed to come from inside my mind.

"Stay with me," she continued. "I saw Waggery pull something shiny out of the duck pond. I saw him give it to you. And I saw Flynt Burns react strangely. You didn't notice, probably because you were so focused on getting to the police station. But he didn't want you to take it, whatever it was, with you."

I wished I could see her. It was impossible to gauge someone's honesty when you couldn't see their face.

"I ran to your house because I needed to get you away from him, but I knew you wouldn't come with me because you suspected me of double homicide. I didn't have your phone number, but I knew it was on your sign."

"That was you that called? But you said you were Misty? How do you know Misty?"

"I don't," she said. "You said 'Misty.' I only knew that you had a client that morning. I was rolling the dice that you wouldn't recognize her number."

"You were criming again." She was equally terrifying and impressive.

"Sort of. I also knew that the only thing that would get you off your task is if you thought that the collection agencies found you. I made that up to get you to come home. Once you got there, I was going to try to convince you to let me help you. That I'm innocent. That I feel—"

"How did you end up down here?"

"I was getting to that," she said. "As soon as I hung up the phone, I turned around and Hank was there. He'd heard the whole thing. He didn't like my explanation."

"Oh."

"Right. He's feisty. And he grabbed me, Carrie. He physically grabbed me and took me to the back room of High on the Hoggarty. He's up to no good, Carrie."

"Hank's up to no good? That's interesting coming from the person he tied up and threw in a tunnel to protect me." I heard how that sounded when I said it, but I didn't retract it because I was still angry with her.

"Okay, whatever," she said. "That makes zero sense, but since you're having a hard time and this is a strange set up, I'll stick to the facts of this situation. Hank was suspicious of what I was doing in front of your house. He also heard me use the name *Misty*. He interrogated me, and I told him everything I knew. He was shocked. About Emma, all of it. And weirdly angry."

"That describes Hank most of the time these days," I conceded. "Why did he tie you up? Why did he throw you in a dark tunnel? Even if he planned to come get you, this is dangerous. He must have felt threatened. By you."

"He was worried about you," she said. "The last thing I said to him was that I was going to find you at all costs, and he misunderstood what I meant. I'm trying to help you. He thought I meant I was going to kill you."

"Are you going to kill me? Is 'parking tickets' a mob euphemism for 'murders?'"

"No. I'm not going to kill you, and they are actual parking

tickets. But Hank is out there looking for you right now, and I have no idea what his motivations are."

"I'm sure he's concerned about me," I said.

"Maybe? I thought so when he was tying me up. But he said something about my appearance monkeying up his plans and shoved me down here. I don't even know how long I've been down here."

"What plans?"

"I don't know what he meant, Carrie. But I don't think he was planning your surprise party."

Chapter Thirty-Five

I'd lost track of time and was in a quandary about what to do with Stormy. I didn't think it was safe for her to be down here alone, tied up. I also didn't think it was safe for me to spend time with her untied.

I didn't have ample time to weigh my options. Like plugging in Grist's cellphone before, I decided to take the most efficient route. I would leave Stormy here while I grabbed the books and fetch her on my way back. What I would do with her at that point was anyone's guess. I'd have to figure that out later.

"Be that as it may," I said. "Right now, I have a job to do."

"What are you doing down here anyway?" she asked, as if she just realized that a lone woman wandering around in tunnels was a weird thing.

"None of your business," I said. "But suffice it to say it has nothing to do with you."

I got up to leave and fumbled my way over and around her.

"Watch it," she said as I apparently stepped on her foot or came close. "Are you leaving?"

"I am, but I'll be back quickly," I said.

"You can't leave me down here alone."

"Watch me." Bad choice of words. I fumbled my way down the dark passage toward the light. "I found you down here alone. You'll be fine. If anything furry touches you, don't scream. They bite when they're scared."

"Carrie. You can't leave me here. I'm tied up."

"Sit tight, Stormy," I said, in a tone more callous than I had intended. "I'll be back to rescue you shortly, and we can figure out what happens next. You can have this flashlight." It fell to the dirt floor and made a barely perceptible thud.

"I thought you were a nice person," she said. "A sweet, cozy-cottage type."

"I am," I said. "That's exactly who I am. I don't know what you are, though."

"I'm coming with you," she said. "Because, unlike you, I still have faith in us."

"Us? No, you're not," I said.

"Help me up."

I knelt in front of her. "Your laces are untied," I said. "Let me fix this for you." She held still while I tied her laces together. That would keep her from following me, I thought.

"If you can get up, you can come with me."

I heard her struggle, grunting and swear words mixed together. She stood, but when she must have fallen as soon as she took one step.

"Carrie." she screamed. Or at least I think she screamed. Sound sure dies down there.

* * *

The light from the trapdoor to the lower floor of the museum building glimmered faintly. It wasn't enough light to illuminate the passage I was in, but it was enough to give me a much-needed focal point. I was so grateful for this small magic that it didn't occur to me to think what it meant.

As Aunt Inez used to say, "*Sometimes the light at the end of the tunnel is the train.*"

In this case, what I discovered after I crept up the stairs and slowly lifted the door was that the light at the end of this tunnel was a fire roaring in the furnace. In summer.

"This doesn't seem right," I whispered.

I'd been in this basement before, several times. Hank and I would wind up here in our tunnel travels, or I'd play by myself down here while Grist was upstairs working on some maintenance project for the Hoggarty family. It had only recently been transformed into a building that could be used, and the museum was set to open Friday night.

The basement seemed to be set up as a staging area for the grand opening event, with long banquet tables stacked with odds and ends like cloth napkins, a collection of wines from the Hoggarty Heaven Estate and Winery, and wine glasses, all emblazoned with the museum logo.

The tables formed something akin to a labyrinth. I snaked my way through it toward the staircase that led to the main floor, trying not to touch anything or leave any trace that I was here. My whole body warmed from the heat from the furnace—the hatch was wide open, and I was mesmerized by the flames licking the interior walls. I couldn't remember if I'd ever seen it lit in all these years.

I was hypnotized while staring into the flames and sifting through my memory to see if I could retrieve any instance when this old beast had been used, when the door at the top of the stairs creaked open.

I ducked under one of the banquet tables and watched a pair of leather driving moccasins trot down the stairs.

It was Flynt Burns.

He was carrying a cardboard box. I couldn't see what was inside of it. He placed it on the floor in front of the furnace. He put things into the fire. Papers, it appeared to be, mostly. Some small items that I couldn't discern. I remembered about the fake items from the museum, and I wondered if these were fakes, or things he didn't want anyone else to know he had.

I watched him throw a cell phone into the fire.

That's a terrible idea, I thought, and I was right. Total Fool move—impulsive, not realizing the consequences.

The phone exploded, sending debris flying out of the front of the furnace, barely missing Flynt as he dove out of the way.

A piece of burning plastic landed right in front of me. I had no choice but to scramble out from under the table and stomp on it to put it out.

Flynt stood unmoving, his expression flat, his usually sparkling eyes dead.

"Carrie Dettwiler," he said, kicking the box at his feet aside, as if that would make it disappear. "To what do I owe the pleasure of your surprise company?"

"I'm here doing some organizing for the, uh, for the grand opening."

The lie sounded like a lie. And he knew I was lying.

"Of course," he said. "You're organizing the things that have already been organized in perfect stacks, alphabetized and ready to be taken upstairs for a party. Did Grist send you? Or Lillian?"

I didn't respond.

"I thought you were at the police station," he said. "Reporting a murder."

"I went to the police station," I began, wondering, even as the words came out of my mouth, why I was continuing down this path when we both knew I was full of it. "I told them everything."

"Everything?" he said. "You told them everything."

He casually tossed what looked like a receipt into the flames.

"I did."

"What exactly is everything?"

"I told them how Grist found some fake items in the museum," I said. "And that someone had replaced them with fakes purchased at Finders Keepers."

"Oh, that's so interesting, Carrie," he said. "Who on earth would do such a terrible thing, and why?"

"I'm pretty sure it was Hank," I said, the lies coming easier now. Flynt's tone and his movements were dangerous, frenetic, desperate. "He hates Grist, but I can't seem to put my finger on why."

"No?" he said. "You can't put your finger on why Hank hates Grist. That's interesting."

He picked up a hat out of the box. It was a High on the Hoggarty cap. He threw it into the fire.

"Oh, no," I said, feeling like I'd been punched in the gut. "Oh, no, Flynt."

He wanted me to know. He was taunting me.

He kept pulling things from the box, glancing at them, and tossing them into the inferno.

"Flynt—?"

"Yes, Carrie?"

"How did you know I was going to report a murder to the police?"

"Huh? What?" He threw a clear plastic produce bag from the Prosperity Market into the fire. I winced at the memory of Emma. "How did I know what, Carrie?"

I couldn't answer. Not only could I not formulate words, but I cycled through the events as I knew them to be.

"How did you know about Emma?" I asked.

"Bad news travels fast, Carrie. Especially here in Prosperity."

"Yes. But no one knew."

"Have you ever worked hard for something, Carrie?" he asked. "Something you wanted more than anything?"

"Every day of my life, Flynt."

"But you. You're nobody. You grew up here and you'll die here alone except for that devil's parrot."

"But you're different, Flynt? You work harder?"

This was a common refrain I'd heard from Flynt and the mayor over the years. That the reason I was so poor was because I didn't apply myself properly. The reason I couldn't get out of debt is because I didn't follow his brilliant marketing ideas to the letter.

"I don't work harder, Carrie. I work smarter."

"So smart that you had to push Grist down the stairs? Such an intellectual that you had to murder Emma? Did your better-than-average brain come up with the brilliant idea to stab the mayor to death?"

His silence said it all. I half expected him to start slow clapping like a movie villain.

As we stared each other down, my mind reeled. How could I be here in this room, looking at someone who was once my friend, accusing him of murder and more?

It was as unfathomable to me as what happened next.

He leaned over and pulled a book out of the box. "Is this what you're here for, Carrie? This accounting log?" He absent-mindedly opened it and leafed through the pages. He tore out a few and threw them into the fire.

"This was the proof," he said. "Not of murder. The motive. Did Grist send you here for this?"

I didn't answer.

"It's the real accounting log," he said. "What we show the town council, the auditors, hell, the IRS... is a fiction. It lives on the computer, so official. But this is where we tracked the truth. You wouldn't believe how rich we were getting."

"Who is we?" My throat was dry, my voice nothing but a whisper.

"Me, Your darling mayor. Even untouchable Emma. Look at me now. Last one standing."

"I don't understand."

"Of course, you don't, you peon, you sad sack. You and I are nothing alike. I have ambitions. I helped transform Prosperity and brought it to the brink of international renown. I realized that Preston, I mean Mayor Brix, only wanted to use me as a cover to line his own pockets."

"That makes no sense," I said. "The mayor was wealthy."

Flynt let out a guffaw. "The mayor lost all his money at the craps table five years ago when I was working as a dealer at a casino in Vegas. I offered to help him. That's how I ended up here in Prosperity."

He threw a few more pages into the fire.

"What's in this book is a record of all the skimming your ethical friend the mayor and I were doing. Oh look, here's how he paid for his Tesla. He stole some donations from the Hoggarty Charitable Foundation for the Wine Museum. Clever. That's how he paid for a lot of things. Donations to his campaign, donations for the duck pond, donations for this museum your uncle is so proud of." He said that last bit about Grist like he had a bad taste in his mouth.

He put those pages in the fire. "Lookie here. Here's the real budget for the items in the Wine Museum. Gosh, if Emma hadn't freaked out about the swaps and confessed to Grist, he might not be in the hospital right now."

"They're all fakes," I said. "Every single thing in the museum. All of Grist's hard work undone."

"Not everything," Flynt said. "These Hoggarty Heaven wines are real." He gestured to the cases of wine on the table close to me. "They were donated. By Grist. From his own personal cellar. He's been collecting for decades. What a generous guy."

Hearing Flynt say Grist's name with such disdain stung me to my core.

"You pushed him. A bottle didn't fall on him."

"No," he said. "A bottle didn't fall on him. I didn't want to push him. I would have preferred that he hadn't spent the money in the first place. I had to replace all those expensive, authentic items. It was a real pain in the butt, but I got the money out of it. Money that the mayor was going to use to pay for his wedding. Then Grist wouldn't shut up about revealing the truth to the mayor. He thought the mayor didn't know. I told him I would handle it, but he wanted to tell the mayor everything himself. I got there first. I saved Grist from the mayor."

"How so?"

"By killing the mayor before Grist got there," he said. "The mayor fired me, told me to go back to Las Vegas, that he would handle Grist and everyone else. I was not going back to that desert hellhole. Not with everything I knew. I tried to reason with him, but he wouldn't listen. Shame. Please know that the mayor would have killed Grist if I hadn't killed the mayor. I did the old codger a favor."

"And Emma?"

"She was terrified," he said. "She knew everything but played along so that the mayor would marry her. After the incident, she came straight to me, and I confessed that I had killed the mayor. Grist was in the hospital, and we needed to shut him up. She offered to poison him with walnuts, some desperate idea she got from a party at your house or some nonsense. But it didn't work. I had no choice but to take her out. She knew too much. She threatened to go to the police. Shame."

I saw the cards in my mind. I saw how the Emperor had plucked the Fool from obscurity to have a minion to execute his corrupt plans. And whatever they were doing was working perfectly until the Emperor announced he was proposing to the Empress—who had stolen a card from the reading that showed a proposal was imminent and given it to him as a mischievous gesture of love. But trouble was on the horizon; the combination of their two empires made the Fool redundant. And that, in turn, made him desperate.

The cards shifted in and out my vision, revealing everything. I saw Stormy's strength—she was only here to get what was rightfully hers and was fearless in her pursuit. Miriam's Tower brought big drama, but not murder. I saw Grist's Magician conjuring questions and demanding answers. The cards revealed everything I needed to know about the secrets, sadness and sickness that stalked Prosperity.

Maybe I was a little psychic after all?

Flynt threw the rest of the book into the fire.

"Why are you telling me this?" I asked, hoping he would tell me more.

"Oh, well, Carrie. You're psychic. You tell me."

"I'm not psychic."

"That's too bad. Because if you were, you would have known that this is the night you were going to die."

I remembered the corkscrew. It was still in my pocket. I slowly pulled it out and held it up, its polished surface twinkled menacingly in the firelight. "You know what you should do?" I began. "You should probably throw this in the fire, too. It's what you murdered the mayor with, isn't it?"

He lunged toward me, the banquet table the only thing between us. I dropped my phone and fumbled with the top of the corkscrew, where the small knife for foil cutting was. How did Mr. Gonzales say to do it? Twist and flip. *Et voila*! I pulled the knife out before he got too close and wielded it like I knew what I was doing.

Flynt dispatched the table in one quick motion, and I backed into the wall, slamming my head. Flynt seized my wrist, his grip like a vise. My wrist felt like it might break from the pressure, and my fingers released involuntarily.

The corkscrew tumbled to the floor. I kicked it and it slid toward the furnace. It was a race to get to it, each one of us shoving each other and tearing at each other's clothes, like a couple of kids roughhousing, only with much darker intent.

I fell, hard, banging my knees on the concrete floor. Flynt was on me, holding me down with the full weight of his body. He reached out to the corkscrew and nearly grabbed it, but I heaved myself forward enough to repel it out of his reach.

I crawled like my life depended on it—it did—Flynt still on top of me, punching my back and pulling my hair. I screamed and struggled, but I kept going with the determination of a bill collector with a correct address, and I was able to grip the corkscrew. I held it like a knife and made repeated stabbing motions over my shoulder. I made contact a few times until he gave up and rolled off me.

I hit his shoulder, and I was relieved to see that I hadn't sliced his neck or face. Nevertheless, his grimace was evidence that he was in severe pain. There was already considerable blood on the floor, and I slipped a bit as I stood up. I ran to the furnace and threw the corkscrew in. I didn't want any more bloodshed, whether it was his or mine. I thought of Grist, who would have hated that I was destroying a piece of Prosperity's history.

I was horrified by my behavior. Had I stabbed my friend? Who was I?

"You should confess, Flynt," I said, hoping to put a stop to this chaos. "None of this is worth it. You're going to get caught. You're in over your head."

I panted like a cornered animal, my eyes tracking his every move. Adrenaline raced through my system, like jolts of low-level electricity.

He got up from the floor, gripping his shoulder. His knuckles were smeared with blood.

"Let me take you to the hospital," I said. "Let's get you help, and we'll decide what to do next."

He appeared to consider my suggestion. I relaxed a bit, blew my hair out of my face. I scanned my body for injuries and didn't find anything too serious. My knees throbbed; my neck was tweaked. I looked at my hands in disbelief that I had used them to stab somebody.

Flynt walked to the furnace and snatched up the box that had stored the items he was destroying.

He dipped it into the flames.

It caught fire.

He flung it into the corner farthest from me, onto a pile of freshly laundered cotton tablecloths, each one probably neatly ironed and starched by Lillian.

"Flynt, no."

I ran toward the trapdoor.

Flynt scooped my phone off the floor and threw it into the fire as well. I shielded my eyes as it exploded, shooting flames across the room.

I glanced up again, and the last thing I remember seeing was

Flynt's face, his eyes wild, his arm raised high above his head, right before he slammed a wine bottle into my temple.

§

"The answer is that you need to go on a long trip," I said, with a theatrical gesture. "And that is what I see for you today."

I put my hands in prayer position and bowed my head like I'd seen a yoga teacher do. I liked it so much I'd decided to make it part of my brand.

Aunt Inez sat across the table from me, her eyebrows raised in surprise—an expression one might see on a person when they've witnessed a dinner guest accidentally take a sip out of someone else's glass.

"That it?" She asked, finally.

"Oh, um," I searched my mind for what I'd forgotten. "Namaste?"

She collected herself. "That was a fine first reading, Carrie," she began. "But there are a couple of things that could help you refine."

"Like what?" I asked, with no effort to hide my hurt feelings. The criticism stung.

"You're a guide, not a boss," she said. "Never tell a client what to do."

"Is this the same thing as not predicting their future?"

"In a way," she said. "Future predicting would be something like 'you're going to marry a man with dark hair.' In the reading you gave me, you ended by telling me what to do."

"Not supposed to do that," I said. "What do I say if that's what the cards told me?"

"Frame it this way," she said. "Instead of telling me to take a trip, let me know that the cards 'suggest' that travel may provide a solution to my problem."

"*And let the client make their own conclusion,*" I said. "*But what if I feel it strongly? That the trip is necessary?*"

"*That's not for you to decide, Carrie. It's for you to suggest.*"

"*I'm trying to be helpful,*" I said, still confused about the nuances of a tarot card reading.

"*The best way to help people,*" she said, "*is to illuminate the path that allows them to help themselves.*"

§

Chapter Thirty-Six

"My bell is rung," I said to no one. "My bell. Is rung. Is my bell rung?"

My bell *was* rung. And the basement was filled with smoke and flames. The heat was furious; the fire only a few feet in front of me. I used my collar as a filter to protect me from the smoke that burned my lungs. I couldn't make it to the trapdoor; the flames and debris blocked my way.

Coughing and disoriented, my head throbbing with each panicked heartbeat, I crawled toward the staircase that led to the first floor of the museum.

I scrambled up as quickly as I could and reached for the doorknob.

It was locked.

I shook the doorknob. Nothing budged.

I was breathless and woozy, a combination of smoke inhalation and head trauma.

I pounded on the thick wooden door as hard as I could, which is to say, not hard at all.

"Help? Fire?" I did my best to muster some energy. I

knocked on the door a few more times and realized that it was hopeless.

No one was coming. Not for me. Not ever.

A strange calm washed over me. The pain in my head seemed to vanish in an instant; my breathing became shallow, as if my body naturally knew what to do to compensate for the toxic vapors that threatened my lungs.

I sat down on the top step and thought of my Aunt Inez, and her pretty face that would light up when she saw me come through the door for a holiday weekend from Stanford. I thought of Grist and his silly jokes. His jokes were fire, I thought, unable to help myself from punning in his honor. I thought of sweet, naughty Waggery and I imagined him safely ensconced in a corner of Grist's carriage house, gently quoking while Grist read to him from a book about Prosperity's history—one that he couldn't get anyone else to sit still for.

The crackling fire sounds gave way to enormous booms followed by gushing liquid and splashes. The wine bottles were exploding, becoming dangerous liquid cannons that fired glass shards in every direction.

"My bell is rung," I said again, and I nodded off. The flames were leaping up the walls.

"Carrie? Get your ass out here."

Someone grabbed me by the top of the arm and was dragging me out.

Hank pulled me to the center of the room, smoke billowing through the doorway behind us.

"Can you walk?"

"My bell got rung," I said.

"Get ready, ding dong, I'm going to pick you up."

Hank hoisted me over his shoulder and transported me down the stairs and into the center of the plaza, far away from where the fire trucks were now pulling in.

He put me on the ground.

My throat and lungs burned, and I drew in deep breaths of the cool night air to soothe myself.

Waggery hopped around my head. "Mwah," he said. "Quok."

"This bird," Hank said, his eyes wet, "saved your life."

"How so?" I asked. I'd never felt such relief, stretched out on the lush plaza grass, gazing into Prosperity's star-speckled sky. My throat relaxed; my lungs cooled.

"What did my good boy do?" I tickled him under his beak. Lifting my hand was a chore.

"I love you," he said, in Hank's voice.

"He does love you," Hank said. "I saw the flames from the building as I took the trash out behind the bar. I called 911 and came out to get a closer look. Waggery was on the top of the building, screeching like a gargoyle. I called him, and he came to me, landed on my arm, like he does with you. He flew ahead, leading me to the door. Against my better judgment, I followed him inside and he went straight to the basement door. He said your name, Carrie, like he was a human. This bird is spooky." He shivered.

Fire trucks had arrived, and police patrol cars motored in right behind. The Plaza was alight with flashing red and blue, and uniformed men and women were pushing stunned onlookers back toward the grass and away from the burning building and setting up barricades.

"It's so pretty," I whispered. Clearly my head injury was having an effect. "Ugh, is that Daisy?" I saw her hair bobbing around a few yards away, or was I hallucinating?

"Hey, Daisy," I said. "*Flynt Kills People. News at Eleven.*"

I slumped back into the grass.

"Carrie, focus," Hank continued, snapping his fingers in front of my face. He seemed unbothered by the organized chaos that was happening around us. "The door was locked, and I tried to get him out of there. I thought the smoke might kill him. I wasn't convinced you were in there. I thought he was messing around like he does, playing a game or something. He took the doorknob apart like it was his full-time job. It was crazy, Carrie, I—"

"Oh, no. Stormy."

"Oh, no." Waggery said.

I scrambled to my feet. I was so dizzy. My skull felt as if it were cracked in two.

"She's fine," he said, motioning for me to sit back down. "She's tied up in the tunnel right outside my office—long story—but we'll go get her now. We need to get some ice on that temple of yours. It's swelling up. I always knew you had a big head, but this is—"

"We have to go," I said.

"Carrie, it's done. It's over. Everyone is safe enough. Rest a minute."

"No, you don't understand," I said. "She left that part of the tunnel. I ran into her down there."

"Well, when she smelled the smoke, she moved, I'm sure." He stood up alongside me. "We'll go, but let's take it easy. You got your bell rung." He smiled.

"I tied her shoelaces together. She can't walk. She's in the tunnel that ends at the museum trapdoor."

"In the tunnel that leads to the carriage house?"

Now he was paying attention.

"Yes."

He walked toward the Visitors Center.

"We've got to go. That part of the tunnel might collapse."

"I thought the Hoggarty family made things to last."

I fell in line behind him and did my best to keep up. Waggery flew from tree to tree.

"They do," he said. "But I've been digging it out for months so it will collapse under the carriage house. To sabotage Grist."

Chapter Thirty-Seven

I was sure I had a concussion, but there wasn't much to be done about that. My head thrummed with every step and Hank was leading the way at an uncomfortably fast clip. I couldn't help but acknowledge that old feeling I'd get when Hank would suggest an adventure and I would gleefully, trustfully run along behind him to see what excitement he had waiting for us both.

In a way, running from imaginary monsters and dashing off to stow away on made-up pirate ships had prepped us for circumstances like these. Waggery followed along, forever delighted to be part of a game.

Since I'd last seen Stormy in the part of the tunnel closest to the edge of the Carriage House, we went through the trapdoor in the living room. That way we wouldn't have to traverse the length of tunnel from High on the Hoggarty or break into the Visitor's Center illegally. It was a bit of a hike, but it was the smartest option. I hoped she hadn't moved. Or maybe I hoped she had, depending on the situation.

Waggery flew into one of the live oaks and sang a bit of

Psycho Killer, a song by The Talking Heads that Hank taught him one autumn afternoon.

"I can't believe he still does that," Hank said.

"He loves you," I said. "And despite how you've been treating me lately, I do, too."

Hank wouldn't look me in the eye.

"Someone did a number on this place, didn't they?" Hank said, as we finally made it through the doorway of the Carriage House.

"It wasn't you?" I asked, as un-sarcastically as I could muster under the circumstances.

"No, Carrie, it wasn't me." He let out a deep sigh.

"Excuse me for thinking it might have been," I said. "You confessed to digging out the foundation underneath the house."

"That was so that the Historic Society would take it back from Grist. The contract clearly stated that if he was unable to do basic upkeep that the property would revert to the family—and that's me."

"There are so many things wrong with that sentence that I don't even know where to begin," I said.

"Wait, shh." Hank stopped and threw his arm out in front of me, like a mother does to a kid in the passenger seat during an unexpected stop.

"Hank, we must hurry. Stormy—"

"There's someone in here," he mouthed, silently. He put his finger up to his lips.

I looked around, on high alert. I put my hand on Hank's arm and pointed to the drops of blood on the floor.

I don't know if it was the head injury, the fact that I had been pulled, half alive, from a burning building, or my rage at the secrets and mayhem that lay beneath the surface of the town, but I wasn't going to be scared anymore. Not today. Not ever again.

Not by this Fool.

"Flynt Burns, come out here right now."

"Carrie," Hank said.

"No, Hank. Enough. I'm exhausted. And I know Flynt is here and I know exactly why."

Right on cue, Flynt emerged from Grist's office, doing that villainous slow clap I had anticipated less than an hour ago.

What a cliché.

"Well done, Miss Dettwiler," said Flynt. "Someone give a point to the psychic."

"Close your mouth, Hank," I said. "You're going to catch a fly. And for the last time. I am. Not. Psychic. But you, you are a classic Fool. You think the world is your oyster, but you're too impulsive to do anything the correct way. Legally. Ethically. Without conning people."

Flynt looked stunned.

"Now, Hank, go save Stormy," I said, pointing to the trapdoor in the floor. "Mr. Burns and I have some business to address."

"Can you do this right now?" Hank asked. "With your head?"

"You mean am I going to let him kill me like he did the mayor and Emma?" I asked. "I'll be fine, Hank."

"Whoa," Hank said. "I'll be right back. Holler if you need me."

In two quick strides, Hank made it to the corner of the room and lifted the trapdoor. He disappeared into the darkness below, out of sight and out of my range of hearing.

I could see Flynt sizing up the route to the open door behind me. There was no chance he could get by. I took a step toward him to show him I had nothing to be afraid of and angled him so that his back was facing the trapdoor. If he were to make a move I would lunge, and unless he somehow overpowered me while profusely bleeding, he'd tumble down the stone stairs.

"What are you doing here, Flynt?"

"I've told you everything," he said.

"You told me what you wanted me to know, and then you tried to burn a building down around me."

"You got into the building yourself, Carrie. I was going to burn it down no matter what. You would have been collateral damage. But you know all about collateral, I suppose."

"Debt jokes," I scoffed. "Even in your darkest hour."

He was seething. His eyes were rimmed with red, his face smeared with soot.

"I see," I said, piecing this together. "This was the plan all along. You were replacing the expensive museum items with fakes, and you were going to burn it to the ground. But why? Was this one of your schemes with the mayor? To steal more money from the people of Prosperity? The people who trusted you?"

Flynt's eyes darted around the room.

"Grist may not have known the exact plan, but he knew enough to want to go to the mayor about it. When I found the mayor's body, he probably thought you needed to know his suspicions, which hadn't yet been confirmed by the appraiser, LeMarcus, who called me when I had Grist's phone. He went to you to protect you, probably, but when you realized what he knew, you pushed him down the stairs. Like you lashed out at the mayor in his office."

"The mayor wasn't a good guy, Carrie," Flynt said. "He was embezzling hundreds of thousands of dollars. He stole a ring from his own daughter to propose to Emma with. He bribed a government official for you."

"Those things are bad, but not a death sentence, Flynt. You could have turned him in, and he would have gone to prison.

That would have been the right thing to do. And I believe that even though it means I would have gotten in trouble for my involvement with him, too."

He avoided my gaze.

"But you couldn't turn him in because you were in on it," I continued. "To implicate him would be to implicate yourself. You were cornered."

"I wanted my fair share," he said. "You know what it's like to be poor."

"Do I ever." I said, making myself laugh. "The mayor told you to kick rocks, that he didn't need you anymore to cover for his skimming. He was going to marry Emma. And he would rely on her accounting skills to find ways to launder the money he was embezzling."

Flynt didn't move or utter a sound. Like a divine breeze, the whole plot unfolded around me.

"You went to the mayor and told him that Grist was suspicious, that the jig was up on the embezzling he was doing, and that you might not be able to cover for him, so to speak. But that wasn't exactly true, was it? You were using that for leverage. You wanted help with an entirely different plan."

"Grist was onto you, but not the mayor," I said, on a roll. "You wanted the mayor to help you get rid of Grist. But he refused and fired you instead. And you killed him for it."

"Grist told you his suspicions. And you shoved him down the stairs. When he didn't die, you were afraid he was going to talk. Did you try to kill him that night in the hospital when you sent me home?"

"I didn't have a chance," he mumbled.

I put my hand up to my ear. "You know what you should do, Flynt? Speak up."

He continued to stare at the floor.

"How did you get Emma to poison him? Did you threaten

her, too? You threatened to implicate her in the mayor's misdeeds. She was grieving and feared for her reputation, which was already challenged, and she went along with it. When the walnuts didn't work, you killed her for failing you. Because she knew your secret."

My heart fluttered remembering Emma, my beautiful Empress card.

I could see Flynt looking for a way out. I positioned myself more securely between him and the door.

"Emma went in with the sweet ladies from the Historical Society so that no one would suspect her, right?"

Flynt remained silent.

"I'm surprised to see you at a loss for words, Flynt. Always telling other people how to do stuff, aren't you? The man with all the plans."

What was this feeling I was experiencing? Oh yeah, woozy. My temples pulsed.

"You rang my bell," I said. "Not nice, Flynt."

"Carrie." Hank emerged from the trapdoor.

"Hank. I totally solved the mystery, right Flynt?" I said, doing an awkward little dance move. "Who's your psychic now?"

"Yeah, that's great, Carrie," Hank said.

"Where's Stormy?" I asked.

"I don't know."

He held up a pair of Chucks, still tied together.

Chapter Thirty-Eight

Hank closed the trapdoor behind him. "Safety first," he said. "Wouldn't want anyone getting hurt, would we, Flynt?"

"Did you follow her footprints?" I asked.

"Yes," he said. "They were all over the tunnel, but I followed the barefoot ones here."

All three of us looked out of the front doorway, as if she'd breezed by and we hadn't noticed. I worried she was running through Prosperity barefoot with her hands taped together. I wondered if I would ever see her again, making my heart hurt as much as my head. I needed to apologize.

"What do you want me to do with this guy?" Hank asked.

"I have one more question before we call Officer Bucket and put this issue to bed," I said. "I get that your murders were revenge. But I don't get why you'd want to burn down the museum. What was in it for you?"

"I think I know," said a voice from the direction of Grist's office.

I nearly jumped out of my skin.

It was Stormy. She was holding a sheet of paper.

"I think it must be this," she said. "Is this why you ransacked the place, Flynt?"

He didn't say a word.

"I am so happy to see you," I said. I went in for a hug.

"Not yet," she said. "You left me in a tunnel with my shoes tied together. We are not friends again yet."

"Understood." I backed off.

Why were there two of her?

I was concussed.

"What is it, Stormy?" Hank asked.

"And you. After that stunt you pulled, we'll never be friends, so stand down, Hoggarty."

"I may have acted rashly—" he began.

"Nah-ah," she said, holding a hand up. "I have the floor now. Which is precisely why I found this. I think Grist knew about the plot to burn the museum, or something close to it. This is an insurance policy for the building. I found it in a secret compartment in Grist's desk. The owner is listed as Ravenous Partners. Insured for two million dollars. That's a tidy sum to get out of town with."

"That's not even true," I said. "The Historical Society owns that building. That's fraud."

"Oh, I'm sorry," Stormy said. "You're outraged about the fraud against the—" she held the paper out in front of her. "Double Indemnity Insurance Partners of Fresno? The man standing in front of you, panting like a trapped wolverine, committed two murders. That I got blamed for. This seems like the least of his crimes. And it looks like The Historical Society is a subsidiary of Ravenous Partners?" She shook her head in confusion.

"So Ravenous Partners 'owns' the Historical Society?" I didn't understand what I was hearing.

"Mayor Brix, my dear Daddums, is listed as the CEO, next

to Chief Marketing Officer Flynt Burns and Chief Financial Officer Emma Fort-Knightly. But it's registered in Las Vegas."

"This is all a scam," I said, as I was putting the pieces together. "Flynt killed the mayor because he was going to marry Emma and cut him out of all the lucrative embezzling schemes they had. But now that they are both out of the way, he could burn the building down and claim the insurance before anyone found him or found…"

Before I finished my sentence, Flynt had shoved me out of the way. I fell to the ground, and he ran toward the door. Hank, wasting no time, lunged toward him and wrapped him in a bear hug. Stormy helped me to my feet. We ran to Hank and tried to subdue Flynt, who was writhing around like a terrified beast and kicking violently into the air.

"Jump," Hank yelled. He had a good hold on Flynt, but I could tell he couldn't keep it up for much longer.

"What?" I cried.

"Jump," Hank said. "Hard as you can."

Stormy and I jumped up and pounded our feet on the floor as hard as we could.

"Keep going," Hank yelled. "Don't stop."

The floor wobbled, and I stopped when I understood what he was going for.

"This is a terrible idea, Hank."

As usual, he ignored me. He gained a physical advantage over Flynt, and was able to slam him to the floor, landing right at our feet.

That was all it took—the floor split open underneath us, and all four of us tumbled into the unforgiving, dusty ground of the tunnel below.

I was a cannonball shot into a wall. The pain that had infiltrated my skull was unutterable.

I was breathless as clouds of dust swirled around me. Bits of debris and particles of floorboard dinged my face. We lay in a dog pile, all four of us, peering up at the light streaming in from the hole our violence had created.

"Hello?"

I could see a form, but I couldn't make out a face. The light from the flashlights blinded me, and I hoped I might be going to heaven.

But it wasn't St. Peter. It was Officer Bucket.

"That you, Dettwiler? Hank? I've been wanting to talk to you guys."

"I got my bell rung," I said. And I let go into the blackness.

Chapter Thirty-Nine

"We've got to get you to the hospital, Ms. Dettwiler."

Officer Bucket somehow had time in the shuffle and bustle of the arrest of a suspected murderer to check on me. "We should call an ambulance." He pulled his radio out of its holster.

"Don't," I said. "I'll go to the hospital if you promise not to call the wee-woo wagon. It's only a few blocks away and I can walk."

"Let me get you the ambulance," he said. "I insist."

"No," I stood up. "Stormy can walk with me."

"She probably needs one, too," he said. "You all do. You fell through a floor."

"I don't have insurance."

I wanted to launch into my explanation of how taking on thousands of dollars for a five-block ambulance ride would tip me into bankruptcy, but the objects in the room were swimming, and my stomach roiled.

"I can go," Stormy said. "We'll walk together."

"What is wrong with you two?" Officer Bucket demanded. "This is nuts."

"It will cost thousands of dollars I don't have," I said. "Come on, Stormy. Let's see if Hank wants to go."

"You kids are crazy," said Officer Bucket. "I'll allow it. But make sure you go. I'm going to come by shortly and get your statements. I don't care how late it is."

"Aye, aye Captain," I said.

"And Carrie?"

"Yes, Officer Bucket?"

"I don't want to hold you up from getting medical attention, but why did you run out of the station earlier?"

"Oh, sorry about that," I said. "I got a clue I needed to follow up on. And I thought you were going to arrest me for murder."

"Arrest you? For murder? No. I was going to ask you if you wanted to read cards for my daughter's surprise birthday party. She's turning thirteen on Friday the 13th. I thought it would be a little spooky fun." He waggled his fingers in the air.

"Huh. I wish I'd known," I said. "I thought I was a suspect."

"You? Nah."

"But you said—"

"Cop humor," he said. "Next time I'll remember I have the right to remain silent."

"Good one, Officer Bucket," I said, weakly.

"You could have looked at your cards, maybe?" He laughed lightly. "Maybe I'll come in for a reading, you know, after you feel better."

"Why didn't you ask me to come to the party on the phone?"

"My daughter walked in."

Everything was much simpler than I imagined it to be. I had to learn to get out of my own way.

"That'd be great," I said. "I'll need the cash. Oh, but how did you know to come here?"

He pointed at Stormy. "That one."

She held up Grist's phone. "It was smart of you to charge this," she said. "Mine's been dead for hours. Otherwise, I would have called for help in the tunnels."

"So many mysteries we've solved today," I said. "Hey Hank, we're going to the Emergency Room. Want to join us?"

"I'll make sure you get there," he said. "But I'm fine."

"You sure?"

"Yeah. I mean, it didn't feel great to fall fifteen feet through a floor, but I sort of deserved it."

"You did," I said. "On second thought, Stormy and I will go alone. You've got some confessing of your own to do."

* * *

At the entrance to Emergency, I told Stormy I wasn't coming in.

"You've got to get checked," she said. "I don't mean to freak you out, but that looks bad. Your whole eye is... Ugh. Like an alien burrowed under your eye. And laid eggs."

"You should see the other guy," I joked.

She didn't laugh. "You look like you got in a bar fight."

"It's fine," I said. "I'm going to go see Grist first. I'll probably have to make plans to sell my house to pay for whatever treatment they're going to give me."

"I hope you're kidding," she said.

I wasn't.

* * *

Grist was sleeping when I got to his room. I couldn't help but smile. I knew he must have been concerned about me. It had been hours since we'd spoken, but I liked the idea that I was out having dangerous adventures while he was peacefully unaware of how bad it almost got. How he almost lost me, too.

I stood at the foot of his bed for a few minutes, grateful that I had him at all.

His eyes fluttered lightly. "What's that smell?" he said, weakly. "Is someone barbecuing?"

"Oh, wow, no." I smelled my jacket. "I was in a fire."

"What?" He tried to sit up a little straighter, seeming to forget that he was in a neck brace. "What in the name of Agustus Persimmon Hoggarty happened to your eye?"

"Did you know Flynt murdered the mayor?" I cut right to the chase.

"I had my suspicions, Carrie. I knew he pushed me. And I knew he tried to have me poisoned to keep me from talking to the police."

"You knew. About the poisoning."

"Emma told me what she was about to do, and I allowed it. She was afraid for her life. Flynt had threatened to attach her name to the mayor's crimes. She told me to keep quiet about Flynt and the mayor until after she could get more evidence. I couldn't lie to the police if I couldn't talk."

I saw a tear track down his cheek. I walked over and wiped it off.

"And I am so sad that I didn't say something sooner," he said. "She might still be alive."

"You couldn't have known," I said. "You let her poison you. That's huge. She knew you cared."

We sat in silence, regarding everything we'd lost.

"You smell, Carrie," he said, breaking the silence. "Like Hank's ribs at High on the Hoggarty."

"Wait till you hear what's been going on with Hank," I said. "It's not a very funny story. I don't know why I'm laughing. But the reason I smell like a basket of baby back ribs is because Flynt tried to burn a building down around me. I'm sorry, but your beautiful museum is gone."

"It's a building, Carrie," he said. "It's nothing to me if I don't have you."

"Well, it looks like our patient is...Holy cannoli. What in Zeus's great ghost happened to your eye?" It was Brian on his nightly rounds. "You don't look human."

"I got my bell rung."

"Kevin. I need a wheelchair in here stat," Brian called into the hallway. "You need to have that looked at. Right this minute. It's upsetting me."

"I guess my chariot has arrived," I said to Grist. I gave him a kiss on the cheek. "Wish me luck. People are saying my face looks bad."

"Does your face hurt?" he asked. "Cuz it's killing me."

I could hear him chortling at his own joke as Kevin wheeled me down the hallway.

Epilogue

nd with a flourish of Daisy's purple prose, I was exonerated.

Girl on Fire: Card Charmer Survives Blaze, Reveals Tourism Boss's Wicked Ways

Like most of her stories, the facts weren't reported exactly as they happened, and Stormy was erased from the narrative, other than being described as the *"Mayor's smokin' hot daughter"* and my *"eternal flame."*

But since it let me off the hook, I had little room to complain—and Stormy didn't care how she was portrayed in the *Prosperity Post* so long as Daisy kept her distance now. I'd taught Stormy the "puh" curse. It was surprisingly effective.

Stormy and I caused quite a stir walking around town, hand in hand, with Waggery either on my shoulder or wafting from tree-to-tree. I like to think our joy radiated around us, offering people a reason to smile, and we basked in it, along with the continual barrage of good-hearted raven jokes.

"This is exactly the kind of wholesomeness I needed in my

life," Stormy often said. "Being here, with you, in this magical setting? I can hardly believe my good fortune."

"Is that a pun?"

"It is," she said. "And that's the other thing I'm glad I have more of. A woman who gets my bad jokes."

"I get them," I said. "But I can't promise I'll always find them funny."

Accomplishing this serene togetherness didn't come easily, though. After Flynt was detained and convicted, the rumors quashed, and the wounds (mostly) healed, we were left with not much more than each other. We were each equally determined to make this relationship work, no matter how much sobbing, hair-tearing and apologies were required.

She had accused me of stealing and paying off a debt with her father in unthinkable ways. That was tough to let go.

But I had accused her of double murder and left her tied up in a dark, scary tunnel, so... Weren't we even?

Not by a long shot. But lucky for me. Stormy is as forgiving as she is beautiful, and we were able to find ways to move forward. I even let her give me a tattoo. We have matching ravens on the insides of our wrists now.

And Waggery loves her, of course. And so does Grist.

Our favorite hangout was the newly renovated duck pond complex. Despite Miriam's meddling and mischief, the duck pond was completed and was as spectacular as promised. The funds recovered from the mayor's estate after the sale of his Hoggarty Heights mansion resulted in enough equity to replace what he stole along with a small sum that was enough for Stormy to pay off the mortgage on her shop—like her first reading showed.

And to remove any suspicion that I may have benefitted from my friend's death, I donated the amount I owed him for the bribe, despite vehement protests from Stormy and Grist.

They looked after me, and I appreciated that. But it's important to do the right thing, even when it's hard, inconvenient, or painful.

The rest of the donations for the duck pond came from a surprising source: Miriam herself.

"I was deeply ashamed," she told me. "I didn't know how I was going to live with myself after what I had done."

"Do you remember that morning, when I pulled the Death card for you?"

"How could I forget? The mayor, dead, and I stepped over his—Oh, Carrie, I am so, so sorry."

"You could have shown better judgment," I agreed. "But sometimes even the best of us makes a wrong turn when under great pressure. I left my girlfriend tied up in a tunnel. It was an extraordinary couple of days."

"I am so, so sorry." Miriam teared up, a common occurrence now.

"Miriam, before all this happened, you said to me, quite plainly, that you never thought you had to apologize for anything you did."

"I was wrong. I've changed." She dabbed at her eyes with a tissue she pulled from her bag. A bag, I should mention, that no longer had a hammer in it.

"That's what I'm trying to tell you about the Death card. It wasn't trying to tell you that you were going to encounter death. It was illuminating the possibility that your life would transform. And it did. Look at you. You're a new woman."

"Brand new," she said.

And she was. Not reporting a murder, while it's unethical, is only a misdemeanor in California. Since she turned herself in, her punishment, while not exactly light, wasn't unbearable. She was asked to pay a fine, and she did so without complaint. She was required to do community service at the duck pond.

She used the remainder of her husband's pension to fund the final phase of building it. It's now the Harold Cringe Memorial Duck Pond, Botanical Garden, and Petting Zoo, and one of the few things in Prosperity that isn't named for a Hoggarty.

On one of Prosperity's endlessly sunny Saturdays, the kind *Whereabouts* magazine described as *"bright and fresh, with gentle, fragrant breezes that make you believe that all good things are possible,"* Ligeia emerged from the shady coolness of a hydrangea, followed by six impossibly fluffy, butter-yellow ducklings. Stormy and I watched, charmed, as Miriam cleared the path of visitors so the new mama and her little charges could make it safely to the deep water of the expanded pond.

"That's not something you see every day," Stormy said. "But wait, what's she doing?"

Miriam was rustling around in the shrubbery. She reached in and pulled something out.

"What is that?" I asked. "No—"

Miriam was holding a tiny, lone duckling, speckled black and white as newsprint.

Waggery flew over to get a better look.

Waggery was hopping around the duckling shouting, "I love you." in Aunt Inez's voice.

"I mean, that happens a lot," Stormy said. "Waggery hops around and yells things. It's his gift."

"Sure—" I agreed. "But he seems sort of—excited. You don't think?"

"Is it even possible?"

"I can't imagine—"

"No—It can't be."

"But maybe it could?"

"No. Stop. This is ridiculous," Stormy said.

I took a closer look. "I think we'll have to resign ourselves to the idea that this is one Prosperity mystery we may never solve. But it sure is cute."

Miriam put the duckling down and tried to shoo it into the pond with its siblings. But the die was cast. That baby imprinted on Miriam and, from that day forward, they were inseparable.

Miriam called her "Poe."

* * *

Grist stayed with me for a few weeks after he was released from the hospital because he needed assistance during his convalescence, but also because there was a giant hole in the floor of the carriage house.

My concussion was serious, but Stormy stuck around to help, and I eventually healed, although the doctor strongly recommended that I avoid head injuries in the future. I tend to agree. I secured a payment plan with the hospital for the rest of the bills—Grist gave a little to help, and Stormy kept trying to talk me into letting her pay it off. But it was my burden to carry.

Lillian came by frequently to help, always laden with pies or snacks and a toy or two for Waggery. It was obvious that she had feelings for Grist, and I warmed to the idea, slowly. Seeing her sweet face every day and being in her cheery presence lifted everyone's mood. I can't believe I suspected her—even for a second—of any kind of foul play.

Hank, deeply contrite over his terrible behavior toward Grist, made quick work of repairing the damage he'd intentionally done to the carriage house. (And the ladies of the Historical Society polished every surface and swept every corner with the good-natured efficiency of Cinderella's woodland helpers). To pay for the repairs, he'd had to sell High on the Hoggarty, which summarily erased his financial interest in any remaining Hoggarty properties in Prosperity.

Misty was thrilled with her purchase and had transformed the formerly seedy watering hole into a hip bistro called Moërning Star, exactly like her cards predicted.

Hank's cards looked good, too. Before all of this happened, I would try to read him, but he would shoo me away. "I was afraid of what you might find," he said. "I was so angry all the time."

But now, when I pulled a card for him before a walnut-free Saturday night dinner Lillian and I made from fresh-picked veggies, I saw Temperance.

"There's peace in your future," I explained, my finger tracing the wings of the angel, standing in water, pouring wine from one chalice into another. "You're letting go of your frantic drives and unrealistic expectations and seeking balance. You're taking all those bad vibes and putting them into this good-vibe vessel. Also, Temperance could have a more literal interpretation that you let go of the bar. See the sun coming up over the mountain? Sunnier days await. The universe has your back on this one. I'm proud of you."

"I am too, Hank," Lillian chimed in. "In fact, you get an extra helping of my famous panzanella for being so much nicer to Grist."

She handed him a plate. I noticed how she beamed at all of us, completely at home. I loved Lillian and I appreciated her help, but I had an unsettled feeling about how comfortable she had made herself in my cottage. And with Grist.

"Everything changed after I pulled you out of that burning building," Hank said, oblivious to what I was thinking. "I've lost a lot of things in this life, as you know. But to come so close to losing you—"

"I know, Hank," I said. "Let's put the past behind us. I accused you of murder, in case you forgot."

"Do mine," Stormy said. She arranged some roses, Black-

Eyed Susans, echinacea, and herbs in a jar for a table centerpiece. "What's happening with me?"

"I read your cards every day," I said. "Let someone else have a turn. Besides, tarot is not a parlor game. It's serious."

"If you're going to be like that—"

"Okay, fine." I shuffled and pulled a card off the top. "Wheel of Fortune."

"I love that show," she said. "I'm going to buy a vowel in my future?"

"I would like to buy an IOU," Hank chimed in.

He constantly apologized to Stormy in the hopes that she would warm to him, but I'd had yet to see her respond with more than chilly detachment. Hank could come around for dinner, help with small house projects, and hang out with us occasionally, but she wasn't going to make it easy for him. I didn't blame her. She didn't press charges, but she was determined to make him pay for tying her up, taping her mouth, and throwing her into a tunnel.

"It means your luck is about to change," I said. "Probably for the better."

"I've had enough change for a while, thank you," she said, an indication that she was done with the reading. Stormy liked tarot and enjoyed my readings, but she had a knack for ignoring the cards that didn't say exactly what she wanted them to.

"More wine, Grist?" she asked, moving on. Grist was contentedly sitting at the head of the table, ignoring Waggery, who was sitting on his perch and gently pecking at Grist's head.

"Don't mind if I do," he said. He pushed his glass toward Stormy, and she poured an amount that would only be appropriate for an at-home Saturday night party when you're not driving.

Grist sat up and grabbed Stormy's wrist.

"Hey. That hurts, Grist." She struggled to get her hand back.

"What is this?" he demanded in a tone I had not heard Grist use before.

"What is what?" Stormy drew back her wrist and rubbed it.

"That ring. Where did you get it?"

"You haven't seen it before?" I asked him. Stormy didn't wear it every day, but the stone was so big that it was impossible to ignore. "It's the reason she came to Prosperity in the first place. How'd you miss that? Oh, right. You were in the hospital."

"What do you mean?" he asked.

"My father stole it from me the week before he was murdered," Stormy explained. "I came to get it back, was suspected of murder and fell in love. It was a big week."

She tried to make light of it, but the look in Grist's eye made it clear that he meant business.

"I'm so sorry I tied you up and kidnapped you," Hank chimed in.

"Shut up, Hank," Stormy said.

"That ring—," Grist stopped himself. "Carrie. I'm going to ask you to do something, and I need you to do it without asking any questions."

"You're freaking me out, Grist."

"I want you to go to the fireplace."

I did so.

"I want you to count three bricks from the upper left."

"This one?" I asked.

"Now push it."

I pressed it and a brick on the corresponding space on the right opened. It was a little drawer.

"There's a box in here."

"Open it, Carrie," he said, quietly.

The box was a standard velvet ring box. I pulled it apart like a clamshell. There was a ring inside. It was an exact twin to Stormy's emerald one. Same stone, same filigree.

"Whoa," said Stormy.

"That's incredible," said Hank. "Hidden compartments never get old, right Stormy?"

"Damn straight," said Stormy. It's the first thing I had ever heard the two of them agree on.

"I need you all to sit down," Grist said. "We need to talk."

"Grist, what does this mean?" I asked, turning over the ring in my hand, looking at it from every angle. From what I could tell, it was an exact replica.

Lillian sat at the table, a strange look on her face, hands folded in front of her.

Unable to resist anything shiny, Waggery hopped over to get a closer look.

"Carrie, the time has come."

"For what, Grist?"

"It's about 'Ravenous Partners.'"

Stormy and I exchanged surprised glances.

"Hey, wasn't that the name on the insurance—?" Hank asked.

Grist let out a long sigh, as if he was preparing himself for something unpleasant.

"Get comfortable, Carrie," he said. "There are some things you need to know about your Aunt Inez."

—End—

Acknowledgments

I've had so much help along the way with the House of Cards Mystery Series. Thank you to Northern California Writers' Retreat, run by Heather Lazare, for offering a supportive space for new writers to learn, grow, and network. Leah Eichler and Meg Coogan, my dear friends and critique partners—I've come to rely on your excellent edits and patience. Thank you for reading and reading and reading again. Eve Porinchak, your edits were invaluable. Briana Labuskes, you were so generous with your time, and I will forever appreciate your encouragement. George Webber, my inspiration for Grist, thank you for allowing me to riff on your popular characters. Thank you to Tim Zahner and the Sonoma Valley Visitors Bureau for your support and inspiration. My mom, romance novelist Pamela Browning, whose writing career is one we could all aspire to, has always supported me in every oddball thing I've tried. Thank you to Linda Shaw, who is always enthusiastic about my work. And Dante and Tazio, who quietly listen to me read out loud and never check their phones once. Little Bumblebee, you're the "heartbeat at my feet." And, George. Thank you will never be enough. None of this happens without you.

Bonus Content

COME TO DINNER

By Bethany Browning

When they finally called off the search party, my shriveled crone's heart swelled with joy. I'd grown weary of the performance. "My babies disappeared," their mother wailed. "Where could they be?" their father wondered in that disconnected, befuddled tone that's universal to fathers.

"There, there," I said, the model helpmate in a crisis.

They had no idea I'd witnessed what they'd done. And what would have been a run-of-the-mill abduction, fattening, and feast transformed into something completely unexpected. Can you believe it? These parents ditched their children in the middle of the dark forest because they couldn't afford to feed them. He spent his nights wobbling atop a barstool. When she had pocket money, she ducked into alleyways to roll bones with the local derelicts. These "grieving" parents had the gall to solicit sympathy and donations all over town.

What kind of dirtbags dump two able-bodied kids in the middle of the dark forest? *There are witches in there.*

Naturally, I did what I always do: I snatched their little darlings. Witches gonna witch. Don't want to be in our ovens? Don't wander near our covens.

And the breadcrumbs! Those kids deserved their fate for thoughtlessly ruining the digestive tracts of our native bird population.

My captives securely imprisoned, I felt free to have a little fun. I introduced myself to the parents, Wheresmeine and Wotsyürz, and joined in the search. No one ever knew I was plumping their petite *schnuckiputzi* for my own purposes.

I poured the parents tea in their kitchen, held their hands, and tut-tutted over their faux woes. I hung posters around town. I tromped through the dark forest with do-gooders calling out the children's names, knowing full well they were locked away where no one could hear.

"Danke," Wotsyürz said to me one day, looking deep into my eyes. I had to force myself to not ensorcell her with an embarrassing malady. Do you know how rare it is for a human to look into my eyes? I'm ugly, and my breath can whither a house-plant. Most people can sense danger, but not this *dummkopf.* "You're a true friend."

"Bitte," I replied, my eyes filling with tears from biting my tongue.

The frenzy around these missing children was nothing short of enraging. Townsfolk made casseroles and held candlelight vigils. Money was collected. New safety protocols were enacted. I wanted to shriek with ravenous rage. Witches like me have been getting a bad rap for centuries for doing our thing. Your kids try to eat our candy house? We're going to deal with that like we do.

But when parents do something unthinkable like this, it

makes you wonder which neighbors we should really worry about. A word of advice from an ancient sorceress who's seen some stuff? If you live inside a walled community, take a minute to assess whether you're keeping the bad guys out or trapping them inside with you.

After a few weeks of this shameful charade, the cobbler continued cobbling, and the *braumeister* resumed *brauen.* Mothers kept their children close; fathers forgot all about it. The *Oberbürgermeister* declared Hansel and Gretel dead (huzzah!), and I whisked to Wheresmeine and Wotsyürz's side.

"It's God's plan," Wheresmeine said, his forehead notably less craggy. "They're in a better place," Wotsyürz agreed, her lips twitching. "Have some casserole," I said, piling their plates high. "You'll feel better if you eat."

In other excellent news, Hansel had packed on the pounds like it was his job and Gretel was naïve enough to think that if she was a good girl, she'd escape my well-seasoned cauldron. You couldn't find a speck of dust or smudge of dirt if you tried— and I did. If I didn't absolutely *need* to slurp down her kidneys and gnaw on her neck bone, I might have retained her as a maid.

Unfortunately, Gretel's goodly nature and willingness to scrub floors until her knuckles bled couldn't erase my witchy need to feed.

I yearned to be satiated again, for my powers to vibrate deep in my marrow like a rung bell. But like a farmer planning for winter, I also knew that I'd need to fuel up again eventually. Children were best, but why work so hard to lure, cajole, and trick, when I'd already cultivated some low-hanging fruit?

"So nice to get out of that house," Wotsyürz said, draping her cloak over my sofa like she owned the place. "Your home is enchanting."

You have no idea, I thought.

"You're out here all alone?" Wheresmeine asked, and we

both silently acknowledged that he'd never once asked a question about me. "Doesn't seem safe."

"Keen observation," I said. "Please, won't you have a seat at the table?"

"Smells scrumptious," Wotsyürz said.

"My signature dish," I said. I placed two plates of savory pie in front of them. I drizzled some fat squeezings over each slice.

Wotsyürz took a bite. Her eyes widened. "Delicious," she said. "What's that savory flavor?"

"I believe it's called *gerechtigkeit*," I said, after licking my fork clean.

"*Geshundeit*," Wheresmeine said. He chuckled lightly at his own joke.

I rolled my eyes so hard I saw my brain stem.

"I'm not leaving without the recipe," Wotsyürz said.

"Promise?" I said, and the sound of my cackle bounced off my walls, reverberated through the dark forest, and swirled 'round the town square like an alarm.

END

This story first appeared in Flash Fiction Magazine.

About the Author

Bethany Browning is an author of cozy mysteries, horror novellas, strange short stories, and any other genre that strikes her fancy. She lives in a redwood forest with her partner George and their dog Bumblebee.

You can find more of her published work and sign up to receive updates (not spam) at bethanybrowning.com. She's also on Threads @bethanybrowningbooks.

Help an indie author! If you like this book, kindly leave a review on Goodreads or Amazon.

Praise for Sasquatch, Baby!

SASQUATCH, BY GOSH!

The vivid setting in the northern California redwood forest becomes a character in the story. When setting illuminates plot, that's storytelling at its best. This author has mastered the technique. Read it! I read it twice. WHERE'S THE SASQUATCH SEQUEL?

BIG TROUBLE WITH A BIGFOOT

What a thrill ride from start to finish. Part creature feature, part redeeming story of hope and transformation, and part found family, Sasquatch, Baby! Is a unique and creative story! I have to admit, I got this book on a whim, because the concept was intriguing and I wasn't sure exactly where Browning was going to take me. However, I was pleasantly surprised and still found myself looking for the squatch over my shoulder.

4 STARS

Honestly, the only thing holding this book back is how short it is. I'd happily read a 300-page version of this story.